UNTIL THE STARS GROW COLD

Terence West

UNTIL THE STARS GROW COLD

GRAVESTONE PRESS

Dedication

To Shannon, Rich, and Donna
They made sure I was still around to finish this novel.
Thank you. I owe you three my life.

PART ONE

The darkness is patient.

Its time would come again.

The darkness is all consuming.

A drop in a pond, the darkness spreads out, quickly diffusing. Unseen currents of emotion carry the globule deeper into the clear water as it undulates and transforms. Reaching out with tendrils of anger, regret, and desire, the darkness begins to vanish.

Hiding in plain sight.

The darkness is patient.

It will be until the stars grow cold.

Chapter One

Hell found him.

Skittering across the floorboards with bare feet, Thomas hit his knees and rolled toward his bed. He pushed his diminutive frame into the space almost too tiny for him and quickly pulled down the covers to hide his location. Kicking old toys, books, and discarded hobbies out of the way, he pressed up against the wall and pulled his knees up to his chest. This was it. He had fled into a literal corner with no means of escape. If they came now, there would be nowhere to go. This was his punishment. He knew why. Silent tears rolled down his cheeks while he did his best to stifle the sobs that so desperately wanted free. He had watched them die and did nothing.

After all, Thomas was only twelve years old.

Taking a long, deep breath, he held it and became very quiet. The house was silent. It had transformed from a loving home to a tomb. He couldn't hear them, but that didn't mean they weren't close. Peering between two clear Tupperware containers that held his multicolored Legos and Tinker Toys, he stared intently at the open door across from his bed. It was dark in the house, except for the nightlight his mother had installed in the hallway for him. The tiny light cast long shadows across his doorway from the grandfather clock that stood outside his room. It had never worked in his lifetime, but his mom always referred to it as an heirloom—she would have it repaired someday. It seemed like a moot point now. He heard the scuffle of shoes on the stairs outside. His heart thumped and jumped in his chest. He feared it was loud enough for them to hear it. Crossing his hands over his chest, he tried to muffle the sound pounding in his ears. He watched the door intently.

"Where are you, little one?"

The voice was light and playful as if this were some horrible game. And Thomas knew it was, to them.

"Why don't you come out? It wasn't nice to run away like that."

He pushed himself further into the corner, the darkness enveloping him. He had seen his mother, father, and sisters die tonight at the monsters' hands. He would not willingly suffer the same fate. He had been assured—many times—that monsters didn't exist and yet here he was, hiding from his nightmares become reality. Anger began to well up deep within his heart. Those who had hurt his family would be made to suffer...he would see to it. His tiny, innocent heart was suddenly engulfed in flame as it became a furnace of hatred. Holding his hand in front of his face, he balled his fingers and squeezed until the fragile, still developing tendons and muscles popped and cracked in protest. His tears, no longer salty and distressed, were now drops of raw venom rolling down his face.

You can kill them all.

In his anger, he heard a voice whispering to him from the blackness that surrounded him. It was as familiar as an old friend. It was deep and gravely, as if a normal, human voice had been dropped several octaves and scarred with the coarsest sandpaper. He shut his eyes tightly and gritted his teeth. He had heard this voice many, many times in his life, and only through an act of sheer willpower was he able to ignore it. Each time it reappeared, it somehow became more persuasive.

Use your gifts. You can make them pay.

Yet this time, he didn't want to ignore it. The voice was right. He could seek his revenge on those horrible creatures, and every act of evil they wrought on his family would be returned in kind. He lowered his hand to the floor and started to pull himself toward the edge—

Yes…the fire that burns in you now, use it to make them suffer for what they have done to you. Unleash your true potential!

He stopped. Biting his lower lip, he withdrew his hand and scooted back into the corner. His heart grew cold once again as the flames were snuffed by guilt and promises made—promises now growing cold in the family room below. He would not betray the memory of his mother and father this way. He had long ago assured

9

them that he would not unleash his gifts in anger. He owed that much to them. There was another way.

The sound of scuffing against the hard wood silenced his internal struggle. Glancing out between the semi-clear containers that surrounded him, he saw a pair of dirty, black boots appear outside his bedroom door. The nearest one had a dark discoloration on the toe. He knew instantly what it was. Several streaks ran down from the blotch to the thick rubber sole. It was his family's blood. The sight both sickened and infuriated him. He felt nausea hit his stomach like a clenched fist and a spark ignite in his heart again.

They should be made to pay. You have the power. Use it!

He watched the boots turn to face his position. Closing his eyes for a moment, he took a slow breath to calm his nerves. This wasn't the way, he reminded himself. Only his self-restraint could save him now. This was, after all, his fault. He had tempted the fates after his parents warned him not to and called down the very wrath of Hell to his doorstep. He was to blame. He would not attain salvation this way. But without his parent's guidance…he frowned.

Perhaps there was no salvation at all.

The boots took a step into his room and paused. Another step. Then another. They were practically on top of him now. He could feel his heart pounding in his chest again. His eyes were wide and unblinking staring at the silver eyelets on the shoes before him. The thick, black laces fell down over the sides and pooled around the soles. Just above the tongue, he could see the hem of the black leather pants stuffed messily inside. His eyes wandered to the glistening spot on the toe of the boot. He tried to avert his eyes but couldn't. It was all he could see.

That is your family's life spilled so recklessly on that shoe.

He clapped his hands over his ears. He would not listen to the voice. It was the voice's fault he was here—that they were here. He should not have listened. Not ever.

They enjoyed killing your mother, hearing her scream. And your sisters...

He clenched his eyes closed and doubled over into a fetal position.

They will kill you, too, if you don't act... You can make them suffer!

The voice was overwhelming in his head as if it were screaming at him. His stomach was in knots as he tried to ignore it, bile crept up his esophagus and washed like waves burning the back of his throat. His fists were balls of rage digging into his temples as his body shuddered. It was too much. He couldn't—

KILL THEM! NOW!

Throwing his hands forward, a burst of unseen energy grabbed everything around him and flung it immediately toward his attacker. Before he could comprehend the first motion, he was already on his feet and moving forward. The small flame in his heart blossomed into a full-blown nuclear furnace. The heat shot out from his heart along the pathways of his veins and arteries to every centimeter of his body. The creature that had killed his family was digging itself out from beneath the rubble he had just created. He stared at the monster's golden eyes and took a step forward. Lifting his right hand palm up, energy stretched out from his body and lifted the vampire into the air. It shrieked in protest and struggled to break free of the invisible grip, but to no avail. Anger and hatred smoldered in the eyes of the young boy. Lifting his free hand, he sent out another wave of energy that started to choke the vampire. As he slowly closed his hand, he could see the creature's pale flesh compressing and collapsing in.

The twelve year old boy was gone, leaving only raw rage in its place. Releasing his invisible grip on the vampire's throat, he stared into the monster's golden eyes. "Why?" he hissed.

Not expecting an answer, the boy lowered his hand and dug an invisible tendril into the vampire's chest. Clenching his hand into a fist, he concentrated the tendril into a solid ball around the vampire's heart. With a smirk on his face, he stared at his family's killer.

Do it.

Opening his hand in one fluid motion, the ball of energy he had created instantly expanded inside the vampire's chest cavity. The creature's eyes widened, but only for a moment. His chest exploded open, completely eviscerating him. Arms, legs, and body parts were thrown haphazardly around the room. A red haze of blood began to slowly settle around him as it fell.

The second vampire appeared in the room, drawn by his companion's screams of agony. He charged inside faster than the human eye could follow. But the boy snapped his head around and stared right at the vampire as if he were running in slow motion. Lifting his hands again, he snatched the creature and flung him hard into

12

the ceiling. The vampire careened into the drywall with a crunch of bone and wood. Before he could recover, Thomas pulled the creature back and began to jackhammer him into the wall. As the studs gave beneath the repeated assaults, he slung the vampire against the floor instead.

Pinning him down, Thomas spotted the implement of the creature's destruction. The boy ripped a six inch piece of wood from the wall and floated it in midair above the shrieking vampire. Rolling the creature onto its back, he brought the makeshift stake up to eye level so the vampire could see it.

"We were just doing what we were told," the vampire pleaded. "We weren't supposed to hurt you—"

Kill him now!

There was no mercy to be found here tonight, only swift retribution. Moving the stake down the vampire's chest, he sent it straight into the creature's heart. Releasing his grip, he watched as blue flames erupted from the newly created wound. As the fire quickly spread across the vampire's body, he shrieked and screamed in agony as he was reduced to ash.

Good, very good. You are powerful.

Amidst the red mist and glowing embers, Thomas fell back to the hard floorboards; his body completely exhausted. Every ounce of energy he had in his young frame had been expelled in that one moment. He had nothing left. His eyes slowly rolled back into his head as he lost consciousness.

A dark figure stood in his doorway. This wasn't one of the killers, but another who had arrived moments too late. Snapping his scythe shut, he slid it into the pocket of his faded brown trench coat. Moving tentatively into the small room, he knelt down next to the boy and cautiously pressed his fingertips to the child's throat. Detecting a pulse, he slid his hands under the twelve year old and lifted the boy from the floor. Turning, he headed toward the stairs at the end of the hall, but didn't stop. There was nothing left here but death. He didn't know what this boy's future held, but it wasn't to be found here.

He folded the boy into his coat, left the house behind and vanished into the night.

**

She was in Heaven.

She leaned back in her office chair and rested her head against it. Her blonde hair spilled around her shoulders as she felt a smile grow wide across her slender face. Taking a deep breath into her lungs, she felt like screaming. Her first instinct was to jump up from her desk and charge through the halls yelling to anyone and everyone, but she was more restrained than that. She was a professional now. To do so would be unbefitting her stature. Lifting her hands from the armrests, she balled up her fists and held her arms up like an Olympian finishing a flawless routine.

Grabbing her mouse, she quickly hit the print command on her browser to capture the moment. Carefully watching the screen to make sure it didn't change—and to make sure she wasn't imagining it—she heard her printer sputter and whir to life behind her. She spun in her seat and watched the white sheet of paper slowly being churned out by the old ink jet. Inch by inch, it completed the image captured from her screen. She snatched the page and held it in her hands, careful not to bend or crinkle it. This was for framing. She wanted to remember this moment forever.

She was no longer an executive assistant—she was now a best-selling author.

Carefully tracing her finger around the rectangular cover image of her book on the page, she looked at the blue emblazoned number next to it: one. This was the New York Times Best Seller's List, the most prestigious list in all of noveldom, and her book was sitting at the very top. She had no doubt the Today Show or Oprah's people would be knocking on her door for an interview in no time. Leno and Letterman would certainly not be too far behind. Why stop there? she thought with a smile, a book tour, the talk show circuit…they were all in her grasp now.

She wanted to rush into her boss' office and shove the paper in his face. He told her that she had been wasting her time. He felt she should focus on a more realistic goal. How she had enjoyed showing him the large advance check that Penguin Putnam had given her for the novel. How she had loved taking time off to travel to New York with her agent to meet with her new publisher. How she had relished telling him stories of five-star restaurants, limousines, and nights spent in the Jacuzzi in her private hotel suite sipping champagne. This would be the icing on the cake—one final nail in his coffin.

She had come back to the company out of some misguided sense of loyalty. In a time when she should have been thinking about her next project—both her agent and publisher were pressuring her for a sequel—she still came into work every morning, made coffee, answered the phone and took messages. She had been here for nearly ten years after all. Maybe it was more a sense of fear that kept her here than loyalty. This was only the second job in her life, and now on the verge of twenty-nine years old, she was becoming complacent, comfortable.

A smirk appeared on her face. That was all about to change.

She was quitting today.

Her new profession as an author stretched out in front of her. Her first novel—her first attempt to even write a full-length book—had been sold to a major publishing house and was now sitting at the top of the best seller's list. The future was bright for her. Her mind spun with possibilities.

Carefully minimizing the browser window, she opened up her word processor. Clicking the "file" button at the top of the screen, she scrolled down to the open command and clicked once. This day had been a long time coming. She had spent many hours thinking about it...dreaming about it. It wasn't that she was unhappy here—it just wasn't what she wanted to do with her life. Bringing a man who claimed to be her "superior" coffee every morning wasn't her idea of a life—she merely existed. She would not just exist. She had too much to offer, too much to experience. Scrolling through the files in her documents folder, she came to the one she was looking for. Highlighting the file, she clicked the open button beneath it.

As she waited for the file to load, she lifted the paper

16

from her desk and stared at her cover again. She already knew every detail of it, yet she couldn't take her eyes away. The cover, designed by one of the publisher's top artists, had been sent to her as a gift. It hung in a beautiful frame on the wall of her home office, just above her computer. It was less of a display piece and more of a reminder to her that she had done it. She had set goals and worked hard to achieve them. It was better than any trophy or medal. It was hers.

Her requested document appeared on the screen. She scanned over it one more time but she knew exactly what it said. She had spent almost as much time crafting this two paragraph letter than she did the entire first draft of her novel. She had poured over every sentence, every word, to ensure it was exactly what she wanted to convey. She wanted her feelings to be abundantly clear and her thoughts concise. She wanted to turn in this letter so often, but the time hadn't been right. Her conditions hadn't yet been met. She looked at the printed page one final time and took a slow breath. Everything was in order.

She had made a promise to herself almost four years ago: she would quit her day job and become a full-time writer if a) her novel was purchased by a major publisher (check), b) it was released in both hard cover and paperback formats (check), and c) she made the New York Times Best Seller's List (check). Of course, when she made this promise, she had been setting partially unrealistic goals. She was afraid to throw away this steady paycheck that paid for her apartment and food in favor of a much more unreliable career. But here she was.

She printed the letter.

Grabbing a small box from beneath her desk, she started to place her meager possessions inside. She didn't need to answer phones anymore, or tolerate the smell of burnt coffee at two in the afternoon. She had her next novel to work on. Pulling the letter free of the printer, she placed it on her desk and retrieved a pen from her drawer. Holding the tip just above the page, she hesitated. Her hand was shaking. Lowering the tip of the pen to the paper, she took another quick breath to steady herself. Her hand started to move and suddenly, her flowery signature was finished. There was no turning back now.

Lifting the resignation from her desk, along with her personal belongings, she walked out from behind it and headed toward the hallway that connected the rest of the office to the lobby. A lone light was on in the back of the building. It was her employer working late—a rare occurrence. Usually he already had in a full round of golf by now and was drinking with his friends in the clubhouse. Many times, she had picked him up and driven him home while he was three-sheets-to-the-wind. And more than a few times, she had brushed off his awkward, clumsy, inebriated advances.

She knocked gently on his open office door. "Mr. Sullivan? George?"

George Sullivan looked up from his desk through tired eyes. His dark suit jacket was slung over the back of his chair while his tie was hanging undone from his collar. He was a middle-aged man with a well-trimmed beard and blue eyes that burned with the intensity of someone who had gone from the bottom and clawed his way to the top. He wasn't necessarily a bad man, she just wanted more than this. "What is it, Katherine?" he asked softly.

Katherine Sharp wasn't sure what to say. Her first instinct was to laugh out loud, stuff the best seller's list in his face, then climb on his fancy black desk and dance gleefully. She assumed that wouldn't be proper. She took a step into his office. "I'm resigning." She handed him her letter.

Accepting the letter, he leaned back in his chair and started to read it. He motioned for her to sit down in one of the two chairs in front of his massive desk.

She remained standing.

He looked up from the letter. "You're not even going to give me two weeks' notice to find a replacement?"

"I'm sorry," she stammered, "no."

He placed the letter on his desk and rubbed his chin. "Okay. Can I ask what brought this on?"

The urge to show him the list reappeared. She stuffed it down into her chest. "A new opportunity has arisen."

Sullivan nodded. "I understand." He stood and walked around his desk. "You've been a valuable employee for the past nine years and you'll be missed. I'm sad to see you go, Kat."

"Thank you," she said slowly—a twinge of guilt in her voice. She took a step back and started to turn toward the door.

"Wait," Sullivan said quickly and turned back to his desk. Opening the top drawer, he produced a copy of her novel and a pen. "Can you sign my copy?"

Kat's eyes grew wide. "You read it?"

Sullivan nodded. "It's good."

She accepted the paperback and pen and stood looking at the man before her. This was the same person who scoffed at her dream of becoming a novelist—the same man who told her that she had no chance of getting published. She understood in that moment. He knew she was talented...he just didn't want to lose her. He had come to depend on her not only in business, but in life as well. She was probably as close to being a wife as Sullivan would ever get.

Opening the cover, she looked at the crease lines along the spine and the ragged, dog-eared corners. He had indeed read the book, and it looked as if he had spent some time pouring over it. Flipping to the title page, she signed her name below the byline. Closing the book, she passed it back to its owner. "Thank you."

Sullivan smiled as he accepted the book. "I think that's my line."

Kat laughed out loud. Setting her box on the mammoth desk, she rushed forward and wrapped her arms around Sullivan's chest and hugged him tightly. "I'll miss you, boss." It was a term of affection more than of submissiveness.

As he returned the embrace, Sullivan smiled. "Me, too. I wish you the best of luck in your new career."

"Thank you," she said into his shoulder.

Pulling free, Kat brushed her blonde hair over her shoulders, lifted her cardboard box, and turned away. Walking back into the darkened office, she felt a weight lifted from her shoulders. She was no longer a receptionist and executive assistant, she was now a professional author. It felt good to say it. She was free to live her dreams now. Stopping in the lobby, she looked at her desk one final time. With a smirk, she snatched a stack of post it notes and deposited them in her box.

Sullivan could afford more.

Pushing through the double glass doors, she felt the cool night air touch her alabaster skin. She looked up at the full moon in the sky above her and the stars glittering around it. They were shining for her tonight. The fog was starting to roll in, but she wouldn't let that get her down. Everything in the world was perfect.

Turning, she headed down the empty sidewalk. She almost felt like skipping. Her apartment was only three blocks from here. She liked to walk in the mornings and at night. It gave her time to clear her head and imagine all the wonderful and gruesome things she would do to her characters when she arrived home and sat down in front of her computer. She wondered for a moment if the book truly warranted a sequel, or if she should start a completely new manuscript. She smiled. Didn't matter right now.

She was in Heaven, but the feeling was fleeting.

A flash of intense pain knocked Kat to the ground. Her box and personal items spilled to the concrete around her as a gasp escaped her lungs. Grabbing the back of her head, she tried to stop the throbbing pain. She winced in pain as her fingers slid through a wet, sticky patch of hair.

She was bleeding.

A pair of vicelike hands wrapped around her upper arms and ripped her from the ground. She was spun in midair and slammed against the side of a nearby building. She wanted to scream out, cry for help, but everything was moving too fast. Before her eyes could focus on her attacker—or attackers, she couldn't tell—she felt another shock of intense, searing pain radiate out from the left side of her neck. She tried to struggle and fight, but it felt like a truck was holding her in place.

Quickly, the pain receded leaving only the pressure on her body. She began to feel very tired as her vision blurred. Turning her eyes skyward, she watched the stars and moon slowly fade away leaving only darkness. She could feel her heartbeat and breathing slowing as well, yet she wasn't concerned about it—she was just so tired. Closing her powder blue eyes, she felt the pressure on her arms and chest release and her body become limp. As her knees buckled, she slid down the wall. Hitting the concrete, Kat fell over and crumbled into a heap. She felt her heart struggle to beat and then fail.

It stopped.

Exhaling her final breath, she died.

***

Four figures stood around an exposed pit of churning, bubbling lava. The molten rock cast an evil red glow over the three as they went about their Machiavellian plans. Heat waves from the lava distorted the air around them as they worked. None were in danger of burning as the ancientness of their bodies could withstand the extreme temperatures.

This place, this exact time, was everything they needed. The center figure stepped forward and glared into the lava, its red hue casting an evil glare across his mental projection. His golden eyes burned intently behind two slender eye slits as a smile crept across his hidden lips.

It begins.

Chapter Two

Darkness scratched and tore at him as he tried to fight through it. Lifting his hands, he swung wildly, while at the same time, trying to shield his face. It was suffocating as it folded in around him. Spotting a clearing ahead, Thomas charged forward with a speed and fortitude he wasn't aware he possessed. He gritted his teeth as he neared the edge. The darkness was determined to keep him. His feet felt as if they were encased in quicksand as his pace slowed. He was so near the edge. His heart pounded in his chest as he focused and pumped his legs harder.

Breaking into the clearing, he skidded to a stop and took a deep breath into his lungs. Taking a tentative step forward, he saw a small cabin sitting on the edge of a large lake. There was something familiar about this place…like it was out of a dream. He felt at ease here, as if the weight of the world just melted from his shoulders. Taking another breath of the clean air, he walked toward the cabin confidently. He belonged here.

Moving up a well-worn path that led to the front door, he could hear no sounds of the destruction he had left behind. The woods surrounding him were full of animals, chirping crickets, and the soft rustling of foliage. Gone was the darkness that threatened to consume him. This place was warm and inviting.

Stopping just short of the door, he caught his reflection in a nearby window and was startled for a moment. His face was older and more mature, while his blond hair had darkened somewhat and hung in waves to his shoulders. His once brown eyes were now steely blue. Toned and athletic, his body was clad in dark fabrics. A sleek, midnight-black leather trench coat hung smoothly off his wide shoulders and terminated just above his chunky black boots. He wore a pair of black leather gloves on his hands, a black sweater, and baggy trousers. An odd silver cylinder nearly concealed by his coat hung off his belt. Reaching for it, his hand paused. He could feel the vibration of power emanating off it in waves. This was a weapon—and it was his. It reverberated with his unique personality and energy.

Reaching for the door handle, he saw a flash of bright blue light in the window. His heart leapt up into his throat. Rage gripped him as the darkness descended again...

Thomas' eyes snapped open. A moment of confusion washed over him as he tried to remember where he was. Slowly, his mind became cognizant. He lifted his arms and stared at his tiny twelve year old hands. It was just a dream...

His head was throbbing and his mouth felt as if wads of cotton had been stuffed inside. Working up as much saliva as he could, he wet his mouth and licked his lips. Sitting up slowly, the vague recollection of what had happened hit him. The loss of his family hit him like a dull ache deep within his chest. His heart, once a furnace of anger and hatred, was now frozen solid. A single tear rolled down his cheek, but it had no company. He was alone, and surely that was part of his punishment for unleashing the monster he held within.

He glanced around his surroundings through tired

eyes. No spark of familiarity grabbed him. It was empty and spartan with very little hint of personality—merely a room with a single cot that he currently occupied. Nothing more. Outside the lone window, he could see the moon shining brightly amidst a blanket of stars. It was steadily sinking toward the western horizon in its perpetual escape from the light. At least it would be daylight soon. The sun would rise and wash away the stain of sin on his soul. At least he hoped so.

Sliding to the back of the cot, he rested his head against the wall. He drew his knees tightly up to his chest and pushed a lock of wavy blond hair out of his eyes. He had been letting it grow, despite the complaints of his father. "A boy should always have short hair," his father argued, "high and tight." A former marine, the man had worn the same buzz cut for practically his entire life. But it really didn't matter now.

A pang of guilt hit him. Why hadn't he acted when the monsters first presented themselves?

He knew the reason: Roy Rasmussen.

Roy had become the bane of Thomas' life in the third grade. He was bigger than most of the other kids his age. It was no quirk of fate that made him a bully. Amidst a sea of scrawny kids, Roy could take what and when he wanted. His target of choice: Thomas. He was the little, quiet, towheaded boy who was always more interested in schoolwork than anything else. He often found that he caught on much quicker than the other students, and this made Roy secretly hate Thomas—even though Roy would never admit it.

It was during the spring semester that Thomas' unique power first manifested itself. During the tenth

25

consecutive lunch period that Roy had stolen his lunch money and bloodied his nose, Thomas decided he'd had enough. In his rage, he had taken matters into his own hands. Roy suffered a broken spine after being pushed through the school's lunchroom wall. Roy then spent the next three years learning to walk again.

Of course, no charges were pressed against Thomas. The school's surveillance video clearly showed that no one was touching Roy at the time of the "incident." Thomas knew the truth though. He had admitted it to his parents a few weeks after he was cleared of all charges. His mother—extremely religious by nature—was sure she had given birth to the very spawn of Satan. His father, more rationally minded, never believed the story, although a marked change in his treatment of his only son became readily apparent. Where once the two had spent hours on the back lawn tossing a baseball around, he now hid away in his private study with more than a few bottles of his favorite alcohol.

Thomas was transferred to a private school a short time later, only to have a similar incident occur. In the end, his parents decided it was best to home school the boy. His mother had set him on a decidedly Catholic lesson plan. While never coming right out and saying it, her lesson plans were wracked with guilt and anger because of him. It was because of him that she was no longer welcome at her church, and whispers of "devil spawn" circulated through her congregation.

In a moment of rage, he had changed his family's entire life. He saw the hurt and pain he had caused them and decided then and there never to unleash his inner demon again. He would bottle it up and try to live a normal life so his family would be accepted again. He would not be responsible for them being social outcasts, but he didn't realize he would be the reason for their deaths. He hadn't acted tonight because of that solemn promise he made to himself and his family. When his power could have saved them, he had been too afraid to use it.

His mother told him once that the devil worked in strange ways. Thomas finally understood. He had been gifted with the power to save his family, yet through a quirk of fate, had been unable to use them. He watched his mother, father, and two sisters die when he could have easily stopped it. This was his punishment. The room's only door cracked open slightly allowing light from the adjacent room to spill inside. Thomas snapped his head toward the light fully expecting to see the horned one walk in on cloven feet bellowing laughter from the black pit of his heart. Instead, the head of a man appeared. His look was of genuine concern.

"Hello?" the man asked with a soft British accent.

Thomas didn't reply.

"Can I come in?"

Still there was no response.

"I'm going to open the door and step inside," the man said slowly, "I don't want to hurt you. I just want to make sure you're all right."

He slowly pushed the door open and took a single step inside. He was a man in his late twenties with short brown hair and a soft goatee clinging to his chin. His face showed a hint of his age as cracks and wrinkles were beginning to spider out from his eyes. His face was gentle, yet stern, while his hazel eyes were pools of knowledge and discipline. He was tall, but not outrageously so. He was dressed in a simple white t-shirt and khakis. A faded and worn brown leather trench coat hung just past his knees.

He stood with his hands clasped together, the light from the open door spilling over him. "My name is Conrad," he spoke evenly with little inflection in his voice, "Conrad Verge. What's yours?"

Thomas shifted slightly in his cot, but remained silent.

"Okay," Conrad said with a breath, "if you don't want to talk, it's okay. I just wanted to let you know that there's food in the icebox for you. Just in case you get hungry."

He took a step back toward the door but paused a moment longer hoping the boy would speak. Lowering his head, Conrad placed his hand on the knob and stepped outside. He understood what the boy had been through was extraordinarily traumatic and it would probably take some time to recover and heal. As he looked at the boy's face, his heart broke. He was an orphan now. There was no amount of time in the world which could heal that wound. He started to pull the door closed.

"Thomas Cross."

Conrad poked his head back into the room, unsure he had actually heard something. He looked inquisitively at the boy. "Your name is Thomas?"

The boy nodded meekly.

A soft smile crossed Conrad's face. "Are you hungry, Thomas?"

The boy nodded again.

Conrad pushed open the door and stepped through.

28

"Let's see if we can't find you something to eat." He stopped and looked over his shoulder. "Are you coming?"

Thomas slid to the edge of the cot and gripped his hands around the wooden frame. He felt as if he would fall into darkness if he stood up. This cot was his sole life preserver. He felt his palms get sweaty against the canvas. He looked up at Conrad again and scanned the man's face. He could detect no hint of deception, only kindness and genuine concern. Swallowing, he placed his foot hesitantly on the floor, followed by the other. Letting go of the cot, he stood up and tested his balance. Exhausted to the point of muscle failure, he felt shaky. The overwhelming urge to fall back onto the cot gripped him, but the emptiness in his stomach was overriding. He took a step, then another. Before he knew it, he was standing next to Conrad.

Conrad looked down at the boy with a smile. Reaching down, he placed his hand on the boy's shoulder as reassurance. Sliding his hand to the center of Thomas' back, he paternally guided him into a chair around the kitchen table.

***

After a long and restless night, Thomas watched Conrad preparing a duffel bag on the kitchen table. Rubbing his eyes with the heels of his hands, the twelve year old walked slowly in and headed for the refrigerator. He knew there was a jug of orange juice inside that was exactly what his body was craving. Still dressed in his pajama bottoms and stained white t-shirt, he listened to his bare feet plop against the wooden floor.

Pulling open the tall, white fridge door, he snatched the half-full plastic jug off the top shelf and quickly began to unscrew the top. The two had discovered a lack of plates and glasses in the house last night—and to call it a house was being generous; it would be better classified as a three-room shack. Conrad admitted that he rarely stayed here, but he kept coming back for sentimental reasons. What those were exactly, he didn't specify. Either way, it was a rundown shack in Northern England no one else would want. Tipping the orange juice back to his lips, Thomas took four healthy swallows before taking a breath. Hitting the jug again, he took two more gulps and screwed the lid back on. Setting it back in the refrigerator, he turned to see Conrad staring at him.

"What?" Thomas asked, almost startled.

"Are you okay this morning?" Conrad asked. "It sounded like you had a bit of a rough time last night."

"I had a dream." He paused, embarrassed he had been heard. "It was just a dream."

"Dreams can often be much more than that," Conrad advised. "Don't take them for granted."

During dinner the night before, the two had talked sparsely. Neither knew exactly what to say, as each was uncomfortable in their own way. The morning light didn't show any signs of easing the situation. Conrad wanted so desperately to reach out to the boy to console him. He wanted to let Thomas know that time would ease his wounds, but to this child, Conrad was a complete stranger. Thomas would no sooner take advice from Conrad than the bum who begs for spare change on the corner. Thomas, on the other hand, just wanted to be left alone. His grief was all-consuming at this point, and

Conrad knew it. It was a dangerous place to be for a boy his age. There was a fine line between grieving and losing one's self. He knew Thomas was teetering dangerously at that point.

"Listen, Thomas," Conrad said as he dug into his olive green duffel, "you have a choice this morning. Come over here and sit down," he said, motioning to the empty chair opposite his.

Thomas hesitantly complied.

Conrad produced a pair of white sneakers from his bag and handed them to Thomas. "I went back to your house last night and picked up a few of your things," he admitted. He leaned his elbows on the circular kitchen table and looked at the boy. "This choice will affect the rest of your life," he warned.

"Okay," Thomas breathed as he pulled on the shoes. He stopped for a moment and looked at them. His mother had purchased them for him only a week ago. They were supposed to be for his back-to-school wardrobe. He felt his heart sink a little deeper into his chest.

Conrad stared into Thomas' brown eyes. There was so much intelligence there, he paused—so much pain. "I can either take you to the authorities this morning, or—"

"Or?"

"Or," Conrad said again, "you can come with me."

Thomas finished tying his shoelaces and leaned back in the chair. "What happens if you take me to the cops?"

"Foster home," Conrad guessed, "probably."

Thomas weighed the option for a moment. "And if I go with you?"

"I could offer you a new life. This life won't be easy," he warned.

Thomas bit his lip. "What would I do?"

"You could come with me and become a Wraith," Conrad said with a smile. "A vampire hunter."

"Vampires," Thomas felt the word ooze with hatred from his mouth. "What do I have to do?"

"Meet with the Esgobaeth," Conrad replied. "They will determine if you can be trained."

"The Esgo-what?" Thomas asked quickly.

"The Esgobaeth," Conrad said with a smile, understanding that the Celtic names within his order could get confusing, and difficult to pronounce. "They are also known as the Council of Seven—the ruling body of the Wraith. They are very old and very wise."

Thomas nodded and paused. He turned his thoughts inward for a moment. "I want to come with you. If I can stop people from dying…" He let his own words trail off. He would stop people from dying.

Conrad stood and looked down at Thomas. The shadow of a smile formed on his lips, but he quickly quelled it. His mission was a success. "Grab your things. We have a long journey ahead of us."

Chapter Three

Nothing.

Blackness. Darkness. It neither began, nor ended. It simply was.

Then something changed...

A spark—

Life.

***

Pulling his rain slicker tightly up around his neck, George Sullivan stepped out of his oversized sport utility vehicle. Huge drops of rain fell around him making a deafening clatter against the metal and glass shell of his SUV. Standing still, he stared up at the monstrous gothic building before him. Amidst the dark clouds and sporadic bursts of lightning, it seemed almost ominous and foreboding. Yet he knew it was a place of safety and worship. The high, arched roof culminated in a huge cross that looked down over its flock, telling them all everything would be okay if they just believed.

Sullivan couldn't remember the last time he was in a church. He was concerned less with the teachings of God and more with the holy church of capitalism. Sundays were the one day a week when he could truly take a day off and rest—although most of the time, he ended up back at the office tying up loose ends before Monday arrived. He'd be damned if he was going to sit in some uncomfortable pew for hours listening to some boring priest droll on about how he was going to Hell. He had better things to do. Yet today was important. This place was more than God's house right now. It was the final resting place of his dear friend—probably his best friend.

Katherine's funeral was here.

Digging his hands into his pockets, he started across the parking lot toward the front doors. He wasn't in a rush to escape the rain or to get inside. He learned just this morning it was an open casket ceremony. He didn't know if he was going to be able to look at her face—the pale imitation of life the mortician designed with makeup and chemicals. He stopped just below the concrete steps, unable to continue. He couldn't do it.

Yet he had to. He had to see her one more time.

One more time…

It sounded so final, probably because it was. After the ceremony today, she would be lowered into a six foot pit of dirt and mud, given back to the Earth which had spawned them all. She was dead. He wasn't sure if he had truly accepted that yet. He expected any moment to get a call on his fashionably small cell phone from Kat reminding him that the reports were due tomorrow or one of his employees' birthdays was coming up so he should pick up the obligatory greeting card. But it wasn't coming. Not now or ever again.

She was gone.

Lifting his foot, he placed it on the first step. Summoning all his strength and composure, the second foot followed. He slowly made his way up the stairs toward the heavy wooden doors. A small sign outside the door read, "No services today—Sharp funeral." Running his fingers over the silver frame, he felt a single tear well up in his left eye. Grabbing his already wet tie, he dabbed his eyes and reached for the door handle.

Stepping inside, it seemed smaller than the outside portrayed. The rectangular lobby gave way to two doors on the far end that led into the church proper. A long hallway spread off in both directions from the tiled lobby toward the private areas that were reserved for church functions, office space, and public viewing areas. Large portraits of Christ and his mother, done to emulate stained glass, adorned the walls along with inspirational messages and the church bulletin board. A single, circular table sat in the center of the room. An open book, a bouquet of pink and white flowers, and a small, silver stereo occupied it. Sullivan moved to the table and lifted the slender black pen into his hand. Hovering over the book, he looked at the names inscribed there. There was easily room for hundreds of names, yet only a smattering was on the first page. Signing his name conservatively at the bottom, he hoped there was more to come. This couldn't be everyone who wanted to pay their final respects to Katherine. There had to be more.

He paused and listened to the music emanating from the stereo's small speakers; soft piano that evoked deep emotions of melancholy. This wasn't the type of music Kat listened to. Many times, he had walked into the lobby of his business and seen her singing along to the songs on her favorite radio station, a hot adult contemporary format that played many of the songs from her high school days. She preferred The Police, Evanescence, Gin Blossoms, Better Than Ezra, and Maroon 5. He knew the songs almost as well as she did listening to them waft through the building every day. He wondered for a

35

moment who picked the music—or if anyone did at all. Perhaps this was a service the church provided.

Ignoring the music, he turned and peered down the hallway to his left. A single door was open. Shuffling his feet, he walked along the wet tile floors toward the door. Stopping just outside, he peered in. In the front of the room, he could see her coffin, the lid open revealing the white satin within. Large arrangements of flowers stood around her like guards expressing their sadness and fondest memories. At least fifty metal folding chairs had been arranged in two sections in the center of the room. A single aisle had been left open down the center to allow mourners to walk freely to Kat's side and say goodbye. A smattering of people dressed in black occupied the chairs—no more than twelve people. He hoped she wasn't looking down from wherever she was.

Stepping inside the room, he met the upturned gazes of a few mourners. One he instantly recognized as Kat's mother in the front row. A heavyset woman in her fifties, her nose and eyes were red from crying so much over the past few days. She nodded once in thanks to Sullivan for attending, then returned her gaze to her daughter. Moving down the aisle, he walked slowly trying not to make a sound. His feet were fighting his progress, threatening not to let him continue. He didn't want to see her face; he didn't want to look at her. Summoning every shred of his courage, he moved to the coffin.

Kat's slender face was expressionless. Her skin—crudely portraying the ruse of life—seemed oddly waxy as if the morticians had used too much makeup. Or perhaps it was the new chemicals in her body, Sullivan wasn't sure. She was in a white dress with her favorite blue sweater covering her arms and shoulders. A thick white silk scarf was wrapped around her throat and knotted carefully just to the left of her windpipe. Her hands were folded neatly on her stomach while two arrangements of flowers sat beside her head on the silk pillow. Her long blond hair framed her face and lay neatly behind her shoulders.

He wanted to reach out for her, to touch her hand and face, but his body wouldn't allow it. He stood, staring at her face, unmoving. He fell into a daze. His senses overloaded. The truth lying in the coffin before him was too much to take. Stumbling back, he spun and headed for the door. He could no longer see as tunnel vision set in. He was hyperventilating. Grabbing his chest with his clawed hand, he tried to steady his breathing and racing heart as he made it to the lobby. Reaching out for the small table with the book and stereo, his hand slipped off the edge sending him tumbling to the ground. The glass vase teetered and finally fell crashing to the floor, sending shards of glass and flowers in all directions.

Sitting up slowly, he felt his bottom lip starting to swell. Sullivan felt ashamed and embarrassed. He was not only disrespecting the memory of his friend, but making an ass of himself as well.

"Let me help you, son," a kind old voice offered.

Sullivan glanced up to see an elderly priest standing over him. "I'm so sorry, Father."

The priest extended his hand. "Don't worry about it," the old man said softly. "It wasn't the first time and I'm certain it won't be the last." His voice had a very calming sound to it.

Sullivan took the man's offered hand and stood.

37

Taking a slow breath, he steadied himself. He rubbed his palm down his face to try and wipe away the pain he was feeling.

"Some people just have a hard time dealing with death but it's all a part of God's plan," the priest consoled. "Was she family, or friend?"

"Friend," Sullivan replied. His own voice sounded strange, as if it were far away. "My best friend," he admitted for the first time.

The priest nodded. "Is there anything I can do?"

Sullivan shook his head. "No, but thank you." He looked down at the mess again. "Are you sure I can't help you clean this up?"

The priest lifted his hands and patted the air. "Don't worry. You just go home and get some rest. Everything will be fine," he promised. "The Lord took her for a reason. We just have to believe."

Sullivan took a slow breath and finally nodded again. He reached up and placed a hand on the man's black-clad shoulder. He was slightly more at ease now. "Thank you again."

"You're welcome," the priest said with a smile.

Turning, Sullivan walked back to the front doors. Flipping up the collar on his slicker, he pulled the doors wide and stepped out into the pouring rain.

She was gone.

***

It had been raining most of the day and well into the night. Huge drops plummeted from the sky and crashed into the already oversaturated ground. Tree limbs drooped from the added weight of the water as they swayed in the storm's winds. Massive banks of black clouds had settled in over the city and showed no intention of moving on. A crackle of blue energy lit up the night for a tenth of a second as lightning arced down to the Earth. The following roar of thunder rattled off the numerous headstones. No living soul would dare brave the storm tonight.

But two figures stood silently in the darkness behind the freshly created grave. Their expressions were blank and drawn. They didn't fear the storm, the lightning, or the bone-chilling cold.

They weren't living souls.

They waited patiently. It would happen soon, or not at all. Time wasn't an issue for them. They were governed by the cycles of the sun and moon, not the arbitrary system of hours, minutes, and seconds that man had created to suit his needs. Theirs were lives on the fringe of society: enjoying what man had created, yet eschewing those things men did to attain them. Hedonists in every sense of the word, they were beyond the laws of the land. They simply were.

They sank back into the darkness. A flash of their golden eyes and they vanished into the storm.

Deep below the ground—six feet, to be exact—she slumbered. Her metamorphosis was nearly complete. A biological clock was ticking down the final seconds until she was ready to face the world again. She was changed. No longer could she be classified as Homo sapien, she was something more, something beyond merely human. Yet to attain this change, sacrifices had to be made. She could pass for a human being, but only on first glance.

Hiding beneath the sheep's skin was a barely concealed wolf.

She felt her consciousness rise and slowly, her eyes opened. At first, she saw only darkness, but her eyes quickly adjusted. She saw as if the light of noon were upon her. Pure white satin enveloped her. She felt comfortable and rested, as if waking up from a full night's sleep. Her senses were immediately fully aware of her surroundings. She could feel the worms working their way through the earth around her; the small pack of rats that lived in the maintenance shed a short distance away, and the two shadowy figures waiting just beyond. In her mind, she completely understood.

She was a vampire.

She felt alive as her body tingled and reverberated with energy and power. She found it slightly amusing that it took her death to feel alive. Memories of all the vampires who came before flooded through her synapses. Every event, every secret that a vampire witnessed or knew was now hers to keep and pass on. She understood what she was in intimate detail…and it frightened her. More than words were capable of expressing, she felt a sense of dread cradled somewhere within her rib cage. Slowly, it began to spread out over her body. Unlacing her fingers, she brought her hands up next to her head and placed her palms on the white satin above her. Her last thought was of the searing pain in her head and throat as the moon and stars faded around her.

She wondered how much time had passed. Hours? Days? She drew a quick breath.

Years?

This wasn't what she wanted. It wasn't supposed to

be like this. She should be sitting in her small apartment typing her latest novel on her computer. Instead, she was dead—or at least the world thought so.

Pushing up with all her strength, she felt the lid above her crack and start to give way. Wrapping her fingers around the satin, she easily tore it away and felt a trickle of dirt fall down on her face. She pushed up with her hands again until the wood snapped under the pressure. Not concerned about the avalanche of mud and dirt about to fall on her face, she dug her fingers into the newly created cracks and started to break away large sections. As the dirt started to cave in on her, she sank her hands in and began to push it down toward the foot of the coffin. Instinct took over. Generations of vampires had been forced to do this exact thing. In the early days, it had been a rite of passage for the fledgling. Now, it was little more than a matter of inconvenience.

Pulling her body up into the newly created hole, she continued to claw at the dirt above. Now vertical, she could feel the ground's wetness growing. Mud oozed and flowed around her as she worked her way toward the surface. She felt as if she were suddenly losing ground as the mud filled in the hole with her still inside. Kicking and clawing forward, she felt her hand break through the surface. Freedom was almost in her grasp. Surging up, she pushed her opposite hand out and dug her fingers into the wet ground. Pulling with all her strength, she lifted her head and shoulders above ground. Raising her face skyward, she paused as the cold drops of rain fell against her skin. It felt refreshing and oddly exhilarating.

Throwing her arms forward, she pushed against the side of the hole with her legs and erupted from the Earth.

Falling forward into a mud puddle, she rolled onto her back and let the rain wash over her body. Her blue sweater was torn from catching on the jagged edges of the coffin. Lifting up, she pulled it off and tossed it back into the rapidly filling hole she had just created. Dropping back into the muddy water, she ran her hands over her face and then let her arms fall wide.

Closing her eyes, she savored the moment. This wasn't what she wanted, but she was alive.

She sensed them before they even made a move. Materializing out of the inky blackness, two shadows moved like lightning bolts and were upon her. Grabbing her arms, they hoisted Kat into the air and immobilized her with their preternaturally powerful limbs. Kat didn't even try to struggle against them. She knew what they were and what they wanted.

One of the shadows leaned close to her face and sneered. His yellow eyes and ivory fangs glistened in the low light. "You are a mistake."

She knew it to be true. Deep inside her mind, she knew what was about to happen and what she faced. The genetic memory told her everything. She knew the culture inside and out. Her new life was not without repercussions, but she wasn't finished yet. She would not quietly go back to death's wanting arms.

She was reborn.

Chapter Four

"How did you find me?"

The silvery light from the moon spilled over the two. Conrad was leaning his elbow against the sill of the train's large windows with his chin on his knuckles. Turning his attention away from the darkened landscape that blurred past, his eyes settled firmly on Thomas. He took a moment to compose and collect his thoughts as he looked at his young traveling companion. The two had boarded a train in London bound for Wales—more specifically, near Pembroke. The Wraith Academy was on the Western English coast near the Irish Sea. Amidst the rolling moorlands and glaciated mountains was the home of the Wraith, an ancient place originally settled by the Celts.

"The council sent me," he answered honestly.

Thomas shifted uncomfortably in his seat. He hated taking trains. The ride was so long and boring. "The people we're going to see?"

"That's right," Conrad said with a slight nod. He wasn't sure what he should be telling Thomas, but honesty to a boy of his age was everything. "They had a vision of you."

"What kind of vision?" Thomas asked, slightly startled by the answer.

Conrad sat forward in his seat and rested his elbows on his knees. He studied the boy for a moment. "They saw you using your," he paused, "gifts." Guilt passed over his face like a shadow. "Unfortunately, the thing about visions is they're not always specific about time." Conrad bit his tongue quickly.

Thomas cocked his head slightly and looked quizzically at the Wraith. "What do you mean?"

Conrad wanted to tell Thomas everything. He would have liked to inform the boy that he knew his family would be killed—the Esgobaeth had seen it. He wanted to confess waiting outside of his London home until the exact moment transpired and the council's vision was fulfilled. Conrad wanted to tell the boy everything, but he couldn't. Conrad knew it would irrevocably damage Thomas' view of the council and the Wraith. He couldn't do that.

"It's not important," he said, waving Thomas' question away. "What is important is that you're okay."

Thomas nodded, slightly uncomfortable with Conrad's avoidance of his question. Even at his age, he could sense a lie. He pushed away the thought. It was late and he needed some rest. He wasn't going to get any answers tonight anyway. Scooting down in the seat, he propped his head against the backrest.

A thump echoed through the mostly empty passenger car.

Conrad sat straight up in his seat. His hand was automatically on the hilt of his scythe. He slowly scanned the car and looked toward the roof. Thomas started to sit up, but a quick hand gesture from Conrad stopped him. The Wraith's eyes seemed spooky to the boy—far away and focused on something only Conrad could see or sense. Rising to his feet, the man stepped out into the center aisle. A scraping sound against the metal hull of the train caused him to perk his head up slightly. Drawing his scythe from his belt, he placed his thumb gently on the activation button. The small hairs on the back of his neck stood up.

They were here.

The blade of a chainsaw dug into the ceiling from outside. A shower of golden sparks rained down into the car as the saw chewed a vaguely circular hole. As the metal began to bend inward, Conrad reached over and grabbed Thomas by his shirt collar. Lifting the boy with ease, he placed Thomas abruptly on the floor next to him.

Conrad pointed to the door at the rear of the car. "Go now, and don't look back."

Fear gripped Thomas' tiny heart. He took a step back from Conrad but stopped. "But, Conrad—"

A chunk of metal fell free of the roof and smashed down against the seats and floor.

"I said go!" Conrad shouted without looking back.

Thomas took another step back. Several pairs of golden eyes appeared in the darkness above them. Swallowing hard, he turned and charged toward the back of the car. Grabbing the door's handle, he yanked it open and stepped inside. Slamming it shut, he pressed his hands to the rectangular window and stared inside.

Three vampires dropped down into the passenger car clad in black leather. The leader, a hulking man with long, raven-colored hair, still held the chainsaw he used to gain access. He wore a dark pair of sunglasses with dark blue lenses on the bridge of his nose. Lifting the chainsaw, he revved the throttle and smiled. Conrad leapt toward the vampires before he had even pulled his scythe. Drawing the weapon in midair, he activated it—instantly quadrupling it's length and turning it into a staff. Hitting

45

the button a second time activated a long, curved blade at the top. Coming down, he caught the blade of the chainsaw with his scythe. The saw was unable to slice through the metal of the weapon. Smirking back at the vampire, Conrad flipped his scythe clockwise and ripped the saw from the vampire's hands. The vampire wasted no time to retaliate. Before the chainsaw had even completely left his hands, he was on the attack. Leaning into Conrad, he head butted the Wraith solidly on the bridge of his nose. As Conrad's head snapped back, a trickle of blood fell from his nostril. The three vampires surged forward and grabbed the Wraith while he was off balance and forced him to the floor of the car. Knocking the Wraith's weapon away, the vampires piled on top of him.

Pinning Conrad's arms, the raven-haired vampire grinned. "We don't want you," Raven hissed. "We came for the boy."

All three looked up in unison at Thomas through the car's window. "And you can't stop us," Raven warned.

The three vampires bolted up and charged toward the door. Rolling onto his stomach, Conrad lashed out with his hand and caught the foot of one of the vampires knocking him to the ground. Rolling up onto the balls of his feet, Conrad sprang onto the vampire's back and quickly drew a wooden stake from his coat. Jabbing it into the monster's back, he jumped back as the creature shrieked and writhed in pain as it died.

Glancing back over his shoulder, Conrad saw his scythe on the floor about ten steps away. He knew he didn't have that much time. Turning back toward the vampires, he saw another option.

Thomas hit the adjoining car's door with a thump as the two remaining vampires started to open the first. Grabbing the latch, he worked his hands around it snapping it open. Sliding the door open just wide enough to squeeze through, he slammed it closed and locked it just as the vampires made it inside. Taking a step back, his mind was screaming for him to turn and run, but he couldn't take his eyes away from the horror of the vampires. Raven smirked at the boy. Rearing back, he balled his fists and jumped at the glass. Shards exploded out as the vampire's strength carried him through. Hitting the floor amidst the rain of razor-sharp glass, he somersaulted forward and was back on his feet before Thomas had a chance to turn and run. Reaching down, Raven scooped the boy up into his arms and hit a dead run toward the opposite end of the train.

The second vampire, a punk with more metal piercings on his face than most cars had in their entire bodies, reached through the broken window and tried to reach the latch. He was neither as agile or powerful as Raven and wasn't sure he could accomplish the same feat he had just seen. As his fingers snapped open the lock, he heard a rumble behind him. Pulling his arm free, he turned slowly to find the Wraith standing directly behind him with Raven's chainsaw. He closed his eyes and sighed.

Conrad gunned the throttle and rammed the spinning blade deep into the vampire's chest. The punk howled at the top of his lungs as the chain chewed through flesh and bone. Blood splattered in all directions as Conrad turned the vampire into hamburger. Lifting the blade slowly, he cleaved the vampire's skull in two. Splattering blood turned into flitting embers and flames as the monster's heart was destroyed.

Pulling the chainsaw free, Conrad lifted his finger off the throttle and looked at the burning ashes before him. Wiping the blood off his face, he slung the chainsaw over his shoulder and pushed the door open, only to see Raven disappear through the doors on the opposite side. Charging forward, Conrad pushed himself hard through the doors. As he moved from car to car, he could see Raven staying well ahead of him. He cursed under his breath. They had to run out of train soon. Conrad gritted his teeth. Dropping the chainsaw, he charged after the vampire. He didn't need the weight slowing him down. He would have to find another way.

Thomas felt his left shoulder slowly separating as Raven held him awkwardly. The vampire's arms felt like steel bars crossing over his chest. Ahead, he could see the blanket of night through the final door on the train. He struggled, but it was to no avail. There was nowhere for him to escape to, even if he did manage to get free. The vampire would be on top of him again faster than he could take a breath. He didn't have a choice.

"Put me down," Thomas said calmly.

Raven skidded to a stop and looked down at Thomas confused. His grip loosened ever so slightly.

"I said," Thomas put the weight of his gift into his voice, "put me down and step away."

Raven slowly complied and took a step back. His face was a mixture of pain and confusion as the boy's commands overrode everything in his own mind. His eyes turned to gold and his mental projection melted away as he lost control of his own thoughts.

No longer was a powerful, sleek vampire standing in front of Thomas, it was a frail, rotting corpse. Thomas looked at Raven in awe. Beneath all the fangs and leather, they were truly fragile beings. He stepped closer to the monster that had killed his family. He was the prey now. Focusing his mind, Thomas lifted the vampire into the air and began to apply pressure to his hands and feet. Using the invisible tendrils from his mind, Thomas increased the pressure. He could hear the vampire's flesh, muscles, and tendons popping and crackling as they started to give way. Raven's face was twisted into a horrible grimace of pain, but Thomas wouldn't let him cry out. Lifting his hands, he placed them palm-to-palm and shot out another tendril. Digging it into Raven's chest, he stopped and focused all his energy.

Conrad burst through the doors on the opposite side of the car. Skidding to a stop, he looked in awe at the vampire floating in midair before him. Lowering his gaze, he saw Thomas staring unblinking at Raven, his brow furrowed in intense concentration. Confusion quickly set in. "Thomas!"

Thomas slowly shifted his focus to Conrad. His expression remained unchanged.

"You don't have to do this," Conrad offered. "There's another way." He wasn't sure if he should just let the boy destroy the vampire or intervene. He wasn't sure if he could.

You don't have to listen to him.

Thomas tried to block out the voice in the back of his mind. Thomas looked at the Wraith's blood-soaked clothes and immediately understood what the other way meant. He wouldn't let the Wraith take this away. This was his kill. "They killed my family," he said softly.

"This isn't about revenge," Conrad countered quickly. "We are protectors. We fight when we must. We're not killers!"

Kill them all.

A dark shadow passed over the boy's face. "They killed my family!"

Conrad sensed the end long before it came. "Thomas, no—"

Yes, Thomas…

Snapping his head back to Raven, Thomas ripped the vampire limb from limb and tore the monster in half. Raven's pieces crumbled to the floor.

Stepping over the remains, Thomas headed silently back to Conrad.

The Wraith looked at the mess of blood and flesh on the floor of the passenger car, then turned his attention to Thomas. He reached out to place his hand on the boy's shoulder but couldn't bring himself to actually touch Thomas. He let his hand fall away. There was no comfort to be had. For Thomas or himself.

***

Claws bit into her scalp as the vampire pulled her dirty, matted hair. She scratched and tore at his hand and forearm with her fingernails trying to loosen his grip as he yanked her inside. Throwing her forward with his immense strength, Kat collided with the far wall and crumpled to the floor. Her head and body throbbed with pain as she lay in a dirty heap. Mud still caked her face and body, her white dress was torn and ripped from repeated attacks by the two vampires. It barely hung off her curvy frame. Finally, the two had enough—or were just bored with beating her—and brought her here. Lifting herself slowly, she rested on her elbow and stared at one of her attackers. The other had left moments before arriving here claiming he had other "business" to attend to. Kat had no idea what that meant, but she was glad he was gone.

The vampire could barely pass for eighteen with dark, messy hair that seemed to stick out in every direction. His eyes were a light chocolate brown that seemed hard and haunting at the same time. He was wrapped in the cliché fabrics of the vampire: silk and leather. A tight pair of leather pants covered his legs and were tucked into a pair of thick black boots that were only laced halfway up. A midnight blue silk button-up shirt—the top three buttons stylishly undone—draped off his shoulders. Kat felt a spark of recognition when she looked at him.

He killed her.

Hatred bubbled inside her. His memories had been passed to her through genetic memory. She could see herself through his eyes as he stalked her, watched her, and waited for her in that alley. He attacked, pinned her to the wall and bit her throat. He drank her blood. She felt revulsion at the memory of the warm substance pouring down his throat. Stepping back from his meal, he licked his lips and tossed her aside like a discarded fast food wrapper. He had what he wanted.

Stepping back into the shadows, he sat in the alley quietly smoking cigarettes like an after dinner treat, waiting for someone to find her body. This, for him, was half the fun. He wanted to witness the aftermath of the destruction he wrought, wanted to see the pain he caused in those left behind. It was his little game, and oh, how he loved it. To see a loved one find the bodies was his favorite. He had watched entire families break down under wails of pain and agony, but he had also seen the darker side of humanity. He once watched a body for three nights—retreating to his trendily unnecessary coffin each morning—decay in the middle of a well-traveled sidewalk. No one would stop to see what happened, but would instead step over it on the way to wherever. It was a testament to the innate evil of mankind.

He loved it.

He had watched George Sullivan stumble upon Kat's body and fall to his knees. Frantically checking her for signs of life, he drew away, his hands covered with blood. Shaking, his hands dove into his jacket pockets searching for his cell phone. Dialing 911, he gave the information the best he could in his state of shock, then crumpled over her. Holding her and placing his head on her forehead, he wept uncontrollably. All the while, the vampire watched from the shadows with a deep sense of satisfaction.

He took another drag from his cigarette. He was an artist, and humanity was his canvas.

"You're no artist, Dorian," Kat spat. "You're sick."

Dorian cocked his head slightly to the left and stared at the woman unblinking. He still wasn't used to the genetic memory of fledgling vampires. It never ceased to amaze, or unnerve him. "I think you have no right to judge," he said in a thick Italian accent. "You are an abomination. You aren't even supposed to be."

She knew it to be true, but couldn't understand why.

Perhaps once vampires were nothing more than an accident, but now they had to be made.

"You have no right to be alive," the vampire spat, as if reading her thoughts—he probably was. "Only the chosen are allowed the gift."

Kat looked at the disgusting creature before her with angry eyes. "And you were chosen?"

"I was," the vampire said proudly, "forty years ago. But you already knew that. You have my memories." He walked slowly across the carpeted floor and stopped in front of a large window. Through the darkness, the lights of the city twinkled on and off and stretched out in seemingly endless directions. "I love San Francisco. So many," he breathed, "possibilities."

San Francisco.

At least she knew she was still in her city, but there was the lingering question of time. How long had passed since her death and resurrection? Dorian's memories were no help. Bits and fragments floated around her mind, but with no timed event to anchor them to, they were useless. Kat glanced across the room at the door. She slowly let her eyes fall away. She could easily make a break for it, but it wouldn't do her any good. He would be on her in seconds. She wouldn't make it more than a few steps before being stopped. Lifting off the floor, Kat leaned back against the wall and studied the vampire. He was right. She had all of his memories. He was seventeen when turned, nearly forty years ago. He was an odd dichotomy. He looked much younger, but was nearly ten years her elder. Of course, she knew, he—and she—could look like anything they wanted. Fooling a human's senses was simple.

"What are you going to do with me?"

Dorian looked at Kat, then turned away from the window. Walking across his lavishly decorated apartment's living room, he sank into a leather chair. "That really isn't up to me," he confessed. "And be thankful it's not. If it were, I would have driven a stake into your heart as soon as you came out of the ground." He stopped and stared at Kat. She wasn't unattractive by any means...but she had to be dealt with. "You will meet the Coven Tribunal tomorrow night," he said ominously. "They will decide what to do with you."

Kat let her head fall back against the wall. She should be at home writing right now, not covered in mud from her grave and sitting in some deranged lunatic's living room. She wondered for a moment if news of her death had reached her agent and publisher yet. It didn't really matter anymore. She wasn't going to be collecting any royalties or attending any book signings. And that invitation to Oprah's show would now go unanswered.

At least she was alive. For now...

She knew what tomorrow night held. Memories of other vampires who faced the Coven Leaders swam through her mind. Running her hand over her face, she felt a grumble in her stomach. She noticed it for the first time. She was starving. She felt hollow inside as if her body were only a shell, a repository for the blood she needed to survive. She ached as the hunger spread into her mind. Wrapping her arms over her midsection, she leaned forward slightly to try and quell the pain. Kat quickly glanced up at the vampire. "You have anything to eat in this place?"

The vampire laughed. "Not what you need."

Kat ran her fingers through her messy, knotted hair and sighed. She had to focus on something besides the hunger. "Anyway I can get cleaned up?"

Dorian laughed again. "What do you think this is? A full-service hotel?" He stood up from his chair and marched toward Kat. "You're here to die, little one. I don't care what you look like."

Chapter Five

It was nearing dawn as Conrad and Thomas arrived at the Wraith Academy. The eastern sky was starting to show the first signs of morning as the blues and blacks of night faded into the soft reds, oranges, and pinks of daytime. The town of Pembroke stretched off to the coast of the British Channel. Growing from a medieval outpost to hold off invaders to a prospering fishing and shipping port, the town was a beautiful mixture of old world and new. Castles sat on the edge of coastlines amidst cobblestone streets, while state-of-the-art fishing boats trolled the harbors.

Described as one of the oldest countries in the world, Wales harbored evidence of human habitation stretching back nearly two hundred thousand years. The European Celts, who arrived just after 600 B.C., brought with them the well-known Welsh attributes of eloquence, warmth, and imagination. It was also the source of the much of the Gwyliad Wriaeth. An influx of Roman culture and beliefs altered the country before Christianity arrived in the fifth century from neighboring Ireland. Long the home of vampire hunters, it was the source of their worldwide fight. Every decision was relayed through the council's chambers. This was the heart of the order.

The walk from the train station had been uncomfortably quiet. Neither was talking. Conrad couldn't help wondering if the council had made a mistake in choosing this boy. A Wraith could be described as many things that humanity looked upon as

56

unsavory, but beneath the weapons and training, they were true of heart. A Wraith was mankind's unseen protector. Sworn to fight for those who could not battle for themselves. This was the very core of their beliefs, yet this boy had shown a streak of darkness that could not be ignored. Conrad couldn't bring himself to question the judgment of the council, but this didn't seem right. If the boy were to be trained, he would have access to even more power than he already possessed.

Conrad stopped himself as he saw the high gates of the compound ahead. This was not for him to decide. Plus, he may be jumping to conclusions. He had no idea what destiny held for this boy. The council had made no mention of training him as a Wraith. His task was to merely collect the boy and bring him before the Esgobaeth. He might simply be there to be studied or…

Conrad stopped.

A ball of guilt and anguish began to churn in his guts. He hadn't even considered that possibility before. His mood quickly turned morose as the idea ran rampant through his brain. The council certainly wasn't above it. He had seen it before, even experienced it himself once. After all, they were merely tools of the council. But those others had been hardened warriors, killers, or mortals with such extreme gifts, that they posed a threat. He felt a wave of sorrow grip him. This wasn't right. Thomas was only twelve years old. He could not willingly bring this child to his death.

But he had to obey his mandate. Again, Conrad knew he was grasping at possibilities that may or may not come to fruition. He had to stop his mind from wandering.

Standing in front of the large metal gates that

surrounded the entire compound, Conrad reached out and wrapped his fingers around the wrought iron. Pulling gently, he listened for the telltale squeak he had come to know so well over the years but instead, heard nothing. In his latest absence, the gates had been oiled and rehung. It was a good sign, yet why did it fill him with such dread? Something as simple as fixing the gate squeaking should have gone unnoticed, but things had changed. Whether this was a good or bad thing, he couldn't be certain.

Placing his hand on Thomas' back, Conrad guided the young boy into the compound. The two-story building in front of them loomed in the low light of the morning. Its façade had been redone many times over the years to reflect the changing architectural tastes of the times. The compound had evolved over the decades into its current incarnation, a very scholarly looking building. High arches, steeples, and a faded brick veneer denoted a place of learning. The grounds surrounding the main building were intricately landscaped with thick, lush grass, ancient trees, and hedges. Long cobblestone walkways led up to the entrance and off into unseen areas. As a light rain began to fall, the majesty of the compound was almost overwhelming.

Stopping in front of the huge double doors, Conrad placed his hand on the gilded handles. His gaze fell on his young companion. "Are you ready?"

Thomas sucked down a quick breath and nodded. "As I'll ever be."

Conrad smiled for the first time since the incident on the train. He remembered his first time through the doors and how nerve-wracking it could be facing one's own destiny. He had heard that opportunity always knocked and you had only to answer the door to accept it. In this case, Thomas had only to step inside. Conrad snapped the handle to the right and pushed the doors open. He stood patiently at the threshold, waiting for Thomas to make the first move.

Thomas looked up at Conrad with trepidation painted on his face in thick strokes. Turning back to the entrance, he stared inside. A golden hue permeated the main lobby of the academy. Slick marble floors stretched off in all directions and met with deep wood walls. A grand staircase on the left side swept majestically up to the second floor, while portraits of ancient and admired Wraiths adorned the walls. A huge, opulent chandelier ornamented with crystal and gold dangled from the ceiling. Tall, potted plants lived in every nook and corner of the room offsetting the golden hue, making it feel lush and alive. Thomas couldn't help but feel a sense of foreboding beneath the warm and welcoming veneer of the academy. Having the feeling that if he would step inside and move one of the plants, he would find blood and bones, a knot began to develop in his throat. He looked back at Conrad for guidance but found nothing but patience. Conrad was waiting for Thomas to make a move. This was his to accept or deny. He understood.

Swallowing the lump back down, Thomas lifted his foot and slid it forward. Holding it across the threshold just above the marble, he hesitated again. The feeling of dread increased. He saw the cultured surface melt away revealing charred ruins. Studs reached into an open sky like the exposed ribs of a decaying animal. The chandelier, once magnificent and beautiful, lay in a heap of twisted and broken metal under a pile of burned debris that used to be the roof. A gaping hole in the center of the floor opened like a toothy mouth threatening to swallow the boy whole. It reeked of death as the bodies of men and women lay scattered on the floor around him. From out of the ruins, a dark-cloaked figure strode admiring his handiwork. His golden eyes burned behind his metal faceplate and his voice cackled with glee. Turning, he caught sight of Thomas. His gaze burned like a laser into the boy's chest. Lifting his arm from beneath his billowing cloak, he snapped open a curved blade attached to his forearm.

Thomas gasped and stumbled back.

"What?" Conrad reached down and placed his hand on the boy's shoulder. "Are you—"

Thomas tore away from the touch, shocked by it. Blinking his eyes, he snapped his face around to see Conrad's concerned visage. He felt disoriented for a moment, dizzy, as if he were being spun around too many times. A final shiver ran down his neck and over his spine as he slowly straightened. Pausing, he drew a slow breath into his chest and nodded at the Wraith. "I'm okay. I just…"

"What?"

"I…" Thomas didn't know how to articulate what he had just seen. Glancing into the lobby, he saw that everything had returned to its previous immaculate state. It felt as if he had just awakened from a bad dream.

Conrad's face grew long. Kneeling down, he looked the twelve year old straight in the eyes. "What is it, Thomas?"

"I saw death." Thomas pointed into the lobby. "In this place."

60

Conrad's eyes grew wide in surprise, but quickly, he regained control of his emotions. Standing slowly, he again placed his hand on Thomas' shoulder. He was more certain than ever of his duty. "You need to speak to the council."

Thomas nodded slightly shaken by the images he had seen. Turning, he again faced the lobby. Steadying his nerves, he took a step inside and to his amazement, the world didn't come crashing down around his ears. It was just a hallucination, he scolded himself.

Once inside, the two moved quickly through the academy. Passing through the living quarters, they tried their best to stay out of the way of Student Wraiths trying to make it to class. Weaving through the bustle of the school, Conrad led Thomas down a well-worn path to the council chambers. The white marble floors faded into predominantly black. Stepping into the chamber's foyer, Thomas noticed two red satin banners hanging on the wall opposite the doors from floor to ceiling. Letters were stitched vertically down them in a language he didn't understand. The double doors, large, decorative and arched, stood silently on the opposite side of the room with two powerful looking Wraiths in long black coats guarding them. Each wore a maroon vest and had their hands clasped behind their backs. Standing at what could best be described as parade rest, their steely gazes fell on Conrad and Thomas.

Conrad marched confidently toward the doors but stopped well out of reach of the two men. It was a sign of respect and proved he had no hostile intent. Any Wraith, no matter who they were, would have to face the fury of the High Guard if they tried to enter the council's chambers without permission. Conrad had no intention of dying today. He nodded to both men.

"Conrad Verge," the High Wraith on the left spoke softly with a deep voice, "you and your guest are expected."

"Thank you, Master Xavier," Conrad replied. He knew this Wraith well and had served in battle with him on more than one occasion.

Xavier stepped to the center of the massive doors and drew them open. He had to use all of his preternatural strength to even budge them, but appeared as if he were barely pulling. Standing aside, he returned to parade rest with his feet spread shoulder width apart and his hands clasped behind his back. He had no other contact with Conrad and Thomas and his gaze seemed to be fixed on some distant point in the room that only he saw.

Conrad looked down to Thomas and motioned for him to move toward the doors. "They're waiting."

Thomas nodded.

The two walked through the entrance into the pitch black Council Chambers. The sound of the soles of their shoes echoed off into the vastness of the room. No details were visible from the light spilling in through the open doors. Slowly, the light behind them vanished as the mighty doors were closed. Conrad placed his hand on Thomas' back to comfort the child. He couldn't imagine what the boy was going through. Over the past two days, Thomas had lost his entire family, been forced to travel with a total stranger, and been thrust into a completely alien situation. He was proud of the boy.

"Welcome, Conrad," a voice echoed from the darkness. It sounded deep and inhuman as it rolled the syllables out. "Welcome, Thomas."

A row of candles on the far side of the room sprang to life illuminating a long stairway composed of black, decorative iron. The candles continued to light up the stairway exposing more of the raised platform on the far side of the room. Seven figures standing in a row became visible in the gloom. Each was wrapped in a light gray cloak that masked their features and faces. The council member directly behind the stairs slowly lifted its head allowing the candlelight to flicker off its golden eyes.

A wave of revulsion and anger instantly gripped Thomas at the sight. He felt betrayed. Conrad had brought him to the very creatures that destroyed his family and his life. They were vampires. The word dripped with venom in his mind. He started to focus his energy for an assault.

"That won't be necessary," the council member said. With a wave of its hand, it drew Thomas' energy away and drowned it within the boy. "We are not the enemy, young Thomas. We're here to help you."

Thomas suddenly felt at peace as the council member's words hit his ears. He relaxed his muscles slowly and felt the remainder of his focused energy drain back into his body. He took a step forward. "Who are you?"

"We are the Esgobaeth, the Council of Seven," it replied. "I am known as 'One'." One started slowly forward. Looking as if it were hovering instead of walking, it made his way down the steps. As One moved toward Thomas, more candles magically sprang to life along its path. "I am the head of the Council," One said, stopping short of the boy, "and I am the one who

63

summoned you here."

Thomas stared at One's shadowed features trying to catch a glimpse of the face within the hood. "Why?"

"You possess an amazing," it paused, "and somewhat frightening gift, young Thomas. We wish to see it put to its best potential."

"Killing vampires?" Thomas asked ambitiously.

One was a bit startled at the boy's bloodlust, but quickly pushed it from its mind. This could be trained out of the boy. "Yes," it said slowly, sounding out each consonant and vowel, "you are to be trained as a Wraith. If you wish it."

"That's why I'm here," Thomas admitted.

"Beware," One cautioned, "this is more than blind rage and revenge, this will be a life-long commitment you make to us. It is not to be taken lightly."

Thomas nodded.

"Perhaps we can give Thomas a while to think about it," Conrad interjected.

"That won't be necessary." One's gaze didn't shift from Thomas. "I think the choice has already been made."

"I have," Thomas confirmed. He looked into the deep golden eyes of One. "I want to be a Wraith."

One extended a bony hand from its robe and placed it gently on Thomas' shoulder. "Good. Very good." Turning away, it started back toward the other members of the council. "We shall watch your career with great interest. You are excused. Conrad," One paused, "will you see to it that Thomas gets a room and proper attire?"

"I will," Conrad said with a bow. "Thank you." Turning, he guided Thomas back toward the heavy doors.

Pulling them open, he strode quickly outside.

One stopped at the top of the stairs and looked at the remaining six members of the council. One could sense discontent but could not pinpoint it. "The decision has already been made. To question it now is pointless. Speak now," he commanded.

Two—the second oldest member of the Council—stepped forward. "This does not feel right. We have seen the destructive capability of this boy. Should we not eliminate him before he can bring more harm to others?"

"We can harness that power," One replied, "to our cause. He could be a great Wraith."

"Could be," Two echoed. "We do not know what the future holds for this child."

One nodded. "His future is uncertain. I cannot see it, as if it is shrouded," it admitted, "as if there is something or someone keeping me from it." He closed his golden eyes for a moment and tried to fight his way through the haze but could make no headway. "That does indeed trouble me…" One's words trailed off. "But the decision has been made. By a vote of four to three, we chose to admit Thomas to the Academy."

"We will have to wait and see what his future holds."

***

Opening her eyes slowly, Kat saw sunlight creeping across the floor toward her. Some deep, primal instinct, hardwired into her new vampiric subconscious, compelled her away from the light just before it touched her. Skittering back like a cockroach startled by a kitchen light, she pushed herself into the far corner of the room.

Why a vampire would have huge picture windows was a mystery to her. Pulling her knees up to her chest, she watched the light slowly move toward her. Soon, there would be no place to hide. It was only a matter of time.

She had no idea when she dozed off, but she knew her intense hunger was a factor. Her body was shutting down to conserve energy. She needed to eat, yet the very idea sickened her. Her vampire side rationalized it as survival of the fittest, but it was more than that. She murdered to live, taking the lives of others into herself. It was no way to exist. But she knew she was guilty of the same thing as a human—though not directly. She had consumed more than her fair share of steak and hamburgers in life, and each represented a dead cow. Though she was not personally killing the animal, she was taking its life to survive. How could this be any different?

She suddenly realized that her condition had not only affected her body, but had altered her mind as well. She was a soft, sensitive, caring person who wouldn't dare bring harm to another living soul, but she found herself contemplating nothing less than murder. This wasn't who she was…yet now it was. Some key component of her personality, her very humanity, was missing. She felt empty inside, like a vase with no flowers. She was fundamentally changed. Yet the chemical change within her body had surely tapped into some deep, buried recess of her mind. A human being was an animal after all, there must still be some vestigial trace of the wildness that so many claimed we had evolved beyond. She was now an elite predator at the top of the food chain.

It frightened her.

Lifting her mud-caked hands, she looked at them carefully. It was an illusion. She knew it, but she refused to let it fall away. The mud on her body was actually there, but she could easily project an image of a perfectly clean, and well-kept woman. For most vampires, control was nothing more complex than the functions used to regulate the heart beating or breath. It simply happened, no higher brain function involved, but to others, it became an art form. Vampires could change their appearance at will looking completely different from one moment to the next, or it could be as simple as a change of clothes. Others used it for more insidious ploys like a chameleon. Those truly gifted could vanish into thin air, or appear to burst into a hundred bats and fly away, or simply become mist and melt away. Of course, it was only a trick, a bit of misdirection.

Some remaining shred of her humanity refused to let her true vampire form appear, but she was curious. She needed to know. Focusing her mind, she took control of the mental projection and let it melt away. Her skin was whitish-gray and already appeared to be rotting away. The skin around her nails was peeling back and falling away. Bloodless gashes caused by her ascent from the ground ran up the back of her hand onto her forearm, while her fingernails—obviously painted by the mortician because she never wore this color in life—were broken, chipped and flaking. She seemed emaciated, the bones, muscles, and veins easy visible beneath her stretched skin. She was grotesque. Quickly regenerating her mental projection, she watched the dead flesh melt into healthy, clean, pink skin.

She became aware of a presence in the room.

Looking up, she saw Dorian hovering in the corner just beyond the light. His form was partially obscured in the shadows but his golden eyes shone like glowing coals. Lifting his arm, he tapped a switch on the wall. Unseen motors began to whir as heavy, metal shutters emerged and closed over the windows. As the sunlight disappeared, Dorian stepped forward. His face was a mixture of anger and disdain. From an open door just behind him, a second vampire emerged with a shock of ruby red hair falling around his head. Kat immediately recognized him from the cemetery the night before. Pulling off his dark sunglasses and coat, he dropped them in a heap on the floor. Opening the top drawer of a table that sat against the wall behind them, the second vampire—he called himself "Screamer"—lifted a roll of duct tape and a wound length of rope. The two vampires bared their fangs and advanced on Kat.

The thick rope around her hands and ankles bit into her flesh immobilizing her. Blindfolded and gagged using the thick gray tape, Kat struggled vainly against the mighty hands of the two vampires who had bound her. Dorian held her feet while the second lifted her by her shoulders. Blinded, her other senses were magnified to fill the void. She could sense other vampires in the building as they moved and she understood: they controlled the entire building. That explained how a piss-on like Dorian could acquire such extravagant surroundings. He and Screamer were merely enforcers for the Coven. They were awarded the apartment as a reward for their service. They were nothing more than goons with fangs—paid muscle.

She felt herself ascending higher into the building.

The two had obviously loaded her up in an elevator. Dropping her to the floor, the two goons stepped away from her. Neither spoke as they waited for the elevator to reach its destination. After what seemed like an eternity heading up, Kat heard a bell chime as the elevator lurched to a stop. Hands once again clamped around her arms and ankles like vice grips. She could actually feel her bones compressing under the pressure. She wanted to cry out in pain, but wouldn't give them the satisfaction. Biting her lip, she buried the pain deep in her chest.

Stepping out of the elevator, the vamp goons moved swiftly into the large, posh penthouse. Decorated in lush Earth tones, leather sofas and glass top tables dominated the floor space. The back wall was covered with high bookshelves stuffed with dusty volumes on every subject and genre. Original paintings from many of the masters occupied prominent locations on the walls as soft piano music filtered out of a small, tasteful bookshelf stereo near the back. Lush green plants rose high out of beautiful pots while handwoven rungs sat perfectly on the hardwood floors. It was warm and inviting, the exact opposite of what a vampire's lair was thought to be. Dorian and Screamer tossed Kat hard to the floor and stepped back just as three men entered the room.

"What do you think you're doing?" One of the men's voice boomed at the goons. "May I remind you that she is our guest?"

Dorian turned and looked oddly at Screamer, then back with a confused look painted on his face. "I—"

"Release her now," he commanded.

Dorian and Screamer quickly dropped down next to Kat and quickly pulled the tape and rope free. Grabbing her arms, they lifted her off the floor and righted her on her feet. Kat looked nervously at the two vampires and then to the three men who stood watching. Each looked to be in their early forties and was clad in designer suits that fit their bodies perfectly. All wore black with white shirts beneath. Only the color of their ties distinguished them. They could be triplets for all intents and purposes. Meticulously groomed, they moved with poise and confidence and an air of regality only money could buy. This was the Troika, the highest law of the coven. The three moved across the spacious living room and seated themselves on the cushy leather couch. They motioned for Kat to do the same. Looking up at Dorian and Screamer, they dismissed the two with a wave of their hands.

Kat watched the goon vampires exit back into the elevator, then turned her attention to the well-manicured men before her. Walking cautiously across the room, she chose a seat opposite them. She quickly and nervously scanned the room. There seemed to be no other exit than the elevator, but she had no idea what the other rooms held. She was trapped here. She searched her inherited memories and found random images of the Troika alternating from patience and generosity to extreme violence. The memories seemed incomplete, however. She knew nothing about them, except what Dorian had seen with his own eyes. No history, only legends and myths surrounded the men, and from the look of the three, it was the way they liked it.

"I'm sorry you were treated so roughly," one of the men apologized in a cultured and educated voice. Sitting forward, he clasped his hands in his lap. "I'm Mr. Black," he said, obviously referring to the color of his tie. "This is Mr. Blue and Mr. Yellow," he said, gesturing to his two companions.

Kat nodded nervously. "You've got a lovely mafia vibe working here. It suits you."

"The mafia," Mr. Yellow laughed, "they stole everything they know from us."

"Would you care for a beverage?" Mr. Blue asked. "You seem parched."

Kat perked up. "Blood," she said slowly, almost ashamed of the word.

"Of course," Mr. Black replied. "We're not big on other drinks," he added with a sly smile. Turning back toward the kitchen, he snapped his fingers. "Adolpho?"

A Hispanic man in a similar black suit emerged from the kitchen with a silver tray in his hands. He wasn't a vampire, merely a servant. Kat could immediately smell his natural musk and could hear the blood rushing through his veins. She felt her muscles tense as the urge to jump him grabbed her. Balling her fists, she waited for the feeling to subside. It would probably be in bad taste to kill the help. He moved quickly and gracefully to the glass coffee table in front of the Troika and gently set the silver platter down. It contained four elegant porcelain cups and saucers and a silver antique teapot that was easily older than Kat. Lifting the teapot, Adolpho began to pour the hot contents into each cup.

Kat's eyes widened as she watched the thick, red substance arc from the spout and fill the cups. She could already taste the blood from smell alone. Her senses became drunk with anticipation. Handing a cup to each of the Troika, the servant finally passed one to Kat. Lifting it to her nose, she took a deep whiff of the aroma and closed her eyes. Savoring the moment, she slowly tipped the cup to her lips and took her first taste of human blood. Her mouth felt alive as the viscous substance rolled down her throat. Barbs of pleasure shot out through her body as the liquid traveled toward her stomach. Tilting her head back, she swallowed the entire cup with an audible slurp. Breathing out with satisfaction, she slowly opened her eyes to find the tribunal staring at her with a mixture of bemusement on their faces. She looked apologetically at the three for her bad manners, but motioned for Adolpho to refill the cup.

"Sometimes, we forget what it was like to be a new vampire," Mr. Black said with a chuckle. "That first taste of blood stays with you for a long time. I'm sorry it came from a cup instead of a warm body."

Kat shrugged off the apology. This was better. She was getting the blood she craved without having to commit the act of murder. She accepted her refilled cup back from Adolpho and took another sip of the deep red liquid.

"I read your novel," Mr. Yellow said conversationally, taking a delicate sip of his beverage. "I enjoyed it, but I did find several flaws."

Kat looked at the vampire with amusement. Her work as an author seemed like an entirely different lifetime. So much of her own memories were drowning beneath the weight of the genetic ones she had inherited. She wondered if she was the first author in history to have an audience with a vampire that knew her work. She shrugged off the ego and immediately doubted it. "Really? What flaws?"

72

"Your main character," Mr. Yellow replied, "wasn't very consistent. In one scene, she spoke of her youth in Texas, and then she and another character reminisce about chasing fireflies as children in Upstate New York."

"Ah," Kat said with a nod. "That's a common mistake. I actually blame my editor for that one. I had a passage in the original manuscript describing the exact scene in New York, but it was cut. In retrospect, I wish it had been left in." She took another sip of the blood. "The two were on summer vacation there," she stopped, "from Texas."

Mr. Yellow nodded with satisfaction. "That explains it. Thank you. I can't comment on why the scene was excised from the book, but it certainly would have answered my questions. Perhaps you could sign my copy before you die."

Kat felt his statement hit her like a punch across the face. Her heart dropped into her stomach.

"Do you understand why you're here?" Mr. Blue asked, setting his cup on the table.

"I believe so," Kat answered bravely. She slowly set her cup on the glass table, her appetite suddenly gone.

"The vampire virus, Necolamia Morbus, acts in strange ways sometimes," Mr. Black commented. "It does not always behave itself."

"Our best minds have yet to fully understand it," Mr. Blue added. "But understand, there are laws against vampires of your kind. We don't want your kind mucking the gene pool, so to speak."

"I don't fully understand," Kat said slowly. It was a half-truth, but she was also trying to buy herself some time. The three men looked like tightly wound springs ready to uncoil at any time. They could as easily set their cups on the table and rip her throat out as explain anything to her. She hoped they were feeling generous.

Mr. Black leaned forward and placed his cup down. "When you first became conscious again," he asked slowly, "you were probably overcome with a flood of alien memories. Right?"

"I wouldn't exactly say 'overcome,'" Kat breathed, "but I'm still trying to make sense of the mess in my head."

"Laws are in place to stop that exact thing," Black said quickly. "When a human is chosen to become a vampire, they must be made by the leader of a coven, who was, in turn, made by the leader of their coven, and so on and so forth," he said, gesturing elegantly with his hand. "That way, the genetic memory—which is both a blessing and a curse—remains fairly streamlined and is useful knowledge."

"It helps quell the garbage, in a manner of speaking," Blue added.

"This is why you cannot be allowed to exist," Yellow said after a brief pause in the conversation. "We must try and eliminate the messiness. You cannot be allowed to pass on your virus."

"So this isn't about me at all," Kat said, "it's about future generations of vampires."

"Exactly," Mr. Black said excitedly with a clap of his hands. "We must think of our children."

Kat felt a shiver roll down her spine as the words left his mouth. She knew then and there that she was dead. Their cool, manicured exteriors hid a deeply psychotic core. These were, after all, monsters. "How am I to die?"

"Now let's not get too hasty." Mr. Black smiled devilishly, exposing his glistening fangs for the first time. "We have other plans for you."

Chapter Six

Thomas sat quietly in the atrium just beyond the living quarters. His hands folded neatly in his lap, he stared at the numerous kinds of foliage inside. Tall trees stood like silent guardians, observing and protecting, but never judging. Their branches lifted toward the heavens reaching for divinity that would never be theirs to have. The bright morning sun—which was uncommon in this rainy coastal city—filtered down through the tall glass ceiling and tree leaves creating a beautiful patchwork of shadows and light on the concrete floor. Turning his head skyward, Thomas closed his eyes and let his mind wander.

Did he do the right thing?

Was this where he was supposed to be?

Is there something more than this?

He knew it was much too early to answer any of those questions. Conrad told him the meeting with the council went well, but Thomas wasn't so sure. Something about that place, those people, unsettled him. Perhaps it was their vampiric eyes, or their hidden faces, Thomas didn't know. He felt a deep sense of dread in this place, but he couldn't pinpoint where it was stemming from. He remembered the vision this morning of the academy in ruins and couldn't help feel responsible in some way. "The future is what you make it," his mother always told him. "Nothing is ever written in stone," but he couldn't help feeling like he was on a path he couldn't escape.

Conrad had left him here almost forty minutes ago.

He had to see to Thomas' new living situation and thought it would move faster if he were alone. Thomas had no idea it could take so long. He watched several students in dark brown robes with books tucked under their arms make their way through the atrium. Laughing and talking, they cast a quick glance at Thomas but continued along.

"Who are you?"

Thomas looked up to see a boy and girl standing on a cobblestone path in front of him. The girl looked inquisitively at him, while the boy gave the impression he would rather be somewhere else. "I'm Thomas," he said cautiously. "Thomas Cross."

"Nice to meet you, Thomas," the girl said innocently. She brushed a bit of her raven black hair over her shoulder and extended her hand, "I'm Emily St. Louise, and this is Miller Barnes."

"Hey," Miller said gruffly.

Thomas cocked his head slightly and smiled. It was the first time he had heard an American accent in person. Thomas was a long way from home, but he knew Miller was even further. Emily seemed roughly a year younger than Thomas but about the same size, while Miller was a little older and a bit taller. Both were dressed in white t-shirts, dark blue jogging pants, and seemed a bit disshelved. A light gray robe hung off Emily's shoulders down to her ankles with long sleeves that hid her hands. Miller had his slung over his arm.

Miller looked apologetically to Emily. "I have to go, Saint." He was the only person who called her that, but she liked it. "Master Lee said I had to report directly to him after this morning's training session. He's still mad at me."

"I told you those cigarettes would get you into trouble." Emily smirked. She punched him on the shoulder with a giggle, obviously flirting. "You shouldn't smoke anyway."

Miller brushed off Emily's advice and continued to play the tough-but-misunderstood kid. "Catch ya later," he offered. Turning away from Emily, he walked toward the atrium's doors and disappeared.

Emily bounced toward Thomas and sat down on the bench next to him. "So, are you a new student here?"

Thomas nodded. "You?"

"I've been here a few months," she replied. "I like it so far. Who's your Master?"

Thomas paused, unsure of how to answer. "What do you mean?"

"Every student is paired with a Master Wraith," Emily explained. "Usually it's the one who brought you here. Master Quinn knew my mother and father and handpicked me. He brought me here to the academy, and is now my Master. When I'm ready for field work, he will instruct me."

Thomas understood. "I don't think I have a Master yet. I came with Conrad—"

"Conrad Verge?" Saint interrupted.

Thomas nodded. "Yeah. Why?"

"I've met Master Verge. Master Quinn speaks very highly of him," she answered. "He's a very nice guy."

"I guess so," Thomas shrugged. "I don't really know him all that well."

"Well," Emily said slyly, "you could do a lot worse for a Master."

78

"What do you mean?"

"One of the other students, a kid named Toby, told me that a few years ago one of the Masters went insane and killed his student," Emily said. "Toby said it took seven High Wraiths to bring down the Master. He killed at least seven students before he was stopped."

"Really?" Thomas' eyes were wide. "How could that happen?"

"Don't know," Emily said quickly. "Not everyone's cut out for this kind of life."

Thomas let her words sink in for a moment. He hadn't even considered if he was "cut out" to be a Wraith. Perhaps he was destined to be a great painter, or star athlete, but now his life path was changed. He was a vampire hunter now. He wasn't sure how he felt about that.

Emily stood up. "Hey, listen, I have to go. Master Quinn is expecting me for tea. It was nice meeting you though."

Thomas forced a smile. "Yeah."

"If you need someone to talk to," Emily offered as she moved toward the exit, "I'm always around." She paused just long enough to look at Thomas one last time, then walked out of the atrium.

"Thomas?"

He looked up to see Conrad standing on the opposite side of the atrium. Standing, he waved the Wraith down. "Over here, Conrad."

Conrad spotted the boy and nodded. Walking across the pathways, he smiled. "You're all squared away." He lifted a gray cotton robe from a pile of clothes he had slung over his arm and handed it to Thomas. "Put this on."

Thomas looked at the robe that was identical to the ones Emily and Miller had. Flipping it around, he slipped his arms in and adjusted the hood so it layed neatly on his back. His hands disappeared into the sleeves and the hem nearly touched the floor, but it was a very comfortable. "I like it. Why do I have to wear it?"

"Every student has to wear one of these robes while at the Academy," Conrad answered with a smile. "The color identifies your year. All first year students wear gray."

"Brilliant," Thomas said, looking down at the robe. He felt slightly different in it, not quite himself.

"You also have a room now," Conrad continued. "Luckily for you, there's a surplus of living quarters so you don't have a roommate."

"Conrad," Thomas said slowly, "am I doing the right thing?"

The Wraith watched the boy's expression melt to concern. Kneeling down, he looked Thomas straight in the eyes. "I can't answer that," Conrad answered honestly. "That's for you to decide."

Thomas sank back onto the wooden bench. "But I don't know if this is for me."

"It's always hard at first," Conrad admitted. "It takes a while to adjust." The Wraith rubbed his goatee thoughtfully. "When I first came to the academy, I was so homesick, that I made myself physically ill," he admitted. "I didn't eat, I couldn't sleep, I would only come out of my room to attend class, even then, I would sit in the back and not participate. I wanted to go home so badly, I couldn't stand it."

"What changed?"

"I did," Conrad laughed. "I started to make friends and enjoy myself. This is a rare opportunity, Thomas, but how you use it is entirely up to you."

The two sat in silence for a long while.

Thomas felt his lower lip quiver. "I miss my mom."

The Wraith reached over and placed his powerful hand on Thomas' shoulder as tears started to well up in the boy's eyes. "I know."

A sob erupted from Thomas' mouth. Falling forward, he wrapped his arms around Conrad's neck and buried his head. He felt the fear, anger, grief, and pain from the past two days begin to pour out of him. Conrad placed his hand on the boy's back and just let him cry. He hadn't mourned yet. He needed to heal.

Conrad smiled softly. Thomas would be okay.

***

Kat listened to the motors whir above her as the elevator slowly descended. The constant thrum of the air conditioning in this building was beginning to give her a headache. As the elevator began to slow, she heard two chimes from some unseen speaker. The noise startled her as she stared at her missing reflection in the polished silver surface of the elevator. Slowly lifting her hand, she held it just in front of the doors looking for any sign of change. Cocking her head slightly to the left, she spotted a small dent and blemish on the wall directly behind her that shouldn't be visible through her body. She felt a firm hand on her shoulder as the elevator finally stopped.

"You never do get used to that."

She turned and looked at the stoic face of Mr. Black, the only member of the Troika to accompany her. "Why don't we have a reflection?"

"There is no concrete answer." Black looked at his own missing reflection for a moment. "Some believe the virus affects our skin cells, altering the way they absorb and reflect light. Others claim that a reflection is merely a representation of the soul and not the physical body, and since most literature and films claim that vampires have no soul, we thereby cast no reflection."

Kat shook her head. "That defies the laws of physics and nature. We're still solid after all. This shouldn't be possible...soul or not."

"What we are defies the laws of nature," Black answered as the door slid open. "Please, step outside."

Kat looked through the open doors. The exposed hallway was something out of a horror movie. Dark walls with exposed wood and shredded wallpaper seemed to stretch off into eternity. Small hanging lamps with a single, dirty bulb swayed gently from the ceiling, moved by some unseen current of air. Trash and debris littered the corners of the hall and floor. Kat expected to see the boogeyman appear and float toward her, but she realized he was already standing behind her. Glancing back over her shoulder, she stared at Black's gaunt face. It seemed barely human in the low, flickering light. She thought for a moment—only the briefest moment—that she saw through his mental projection to the monster within. But as quickly as it appeared, it was gone again. Returning her attention ahead, she took a tentative step forward.

"Welcome to the Farm," Black said cryptically as he followed. "Please move to the door at the end of the hall and step inside."

Dropping her head, Kat shuffled slowly down the hall. She stared at her feet as she moved, unable to bring herself to look at her destination. She wasn't sure now she would rather be here, or back in the grave. Her life— or undead life—had become one colossal mistake. She had been nothing more than a late night snack for an apex predator. Now she felt like a chunk of popcorn kernel stuck in his teeth that he couldn't quite seem to get rid of.

Stopping short of the door, she slowly lifted her eyes to stare at the rusty handle. Kat opened her hand and slipped her fingers around the knob. It felt cool in her hand, which surprised her. She was sure that Hell was beyond this door with its eternal flames licking the interior. Tightening her grip, she tried to steady her shaking body. If she were going to die, she would do it with some dignity. Straightening her back, she stood tall and lifted her chin. Kat twisted the handle and pushed open the door.

Her dignity drowned as she immediately shrank away from the sight.

Bumping into the solid frame of Mr. Black as she tried to backpedal, she stared back at his stern face. There was no change in his expression, only the cool and collected appearance that had been there from the start. Kat turned back and nervously peered inside.

The roughly square room was filled with beds that radiated out from a central, tubelike device. Stark comparison to the hallway outside, the room was primarily mint green tile with white and chrome accents. Huge banks of lights were recessed into the ceiling and walls. Men and women lay silently on the beds connected by numerous tubes and wires to the central tube. Lifting her eyes up, she saw dozens more suspended from the ceiling connected to the central tube, via the same system of wires and cylinders.

They were all vampires.

She could hear the buzz of high voltage electricity like a swarm of angry bees poised to attack. Banks of monitors and control devices sat next to each patient studying whatever results they were trying to achieve. Each man and woman appeared comatose, except for an occasional twitch or shiver. A group of four vampires attended to the subjects. Clad in maroon scrubs and black coats, they buzzed between the beds checking and rechecking readings on the monitors. As they finished with a subject, the whine of electrical motors filled the room. The patient was lifted from the table by pulleys and returned to the ceiling. As soon as they were locked back into place, the system would rotate and a new subject was lowered onto the table.

"What is this place?" Kat whispered, almost unable to get the words past her throat.

"Your new home," Mr. Black replied. "This is the Farm."

Fear gripped Kat's mind. She was teetering on the verge of flight. "What are you doing to those vampires?"

"They are like you," Black answered, "all mistakes. Their lives were forfeit as soon as they came out of the grave. But instead of killing you, the Troika decided that you could serve a higher purpose."

Kat stared at a woman being lowered onto one of the tables. Her body was thin, emaciated, and decaying. None of the vampires hooked to the center tube were using mental projections, leaving their horrible true forms visible. She felt repulsed at the sight, more so when she realized she looked like that herself. "And that is?"

Mr. Black laughed. "Bettering our species of course." He pushed Kat into the Farm and shut the door behind them. "Vampires haven't evolved in over two thousand years, but to survive, we must. You are basically donating your body to science," he said quickly. "It just so happens, you're still using it." Black took a step back and leaned against the wall. Lifting his hand, he snapped his fingers to catch the lab tech's attention. "We appreciate your sacrifice."

Two quickly rushed across the room and snatched Kat's arms. Smiling and nodding to each other, they quickly went to work. Kat started to struggle against the vampires, but the first tech pulled a syringe from his pocket, jabbed it into her neck and emptied it.

Kat turned and shrieked at Black. "You can't do this!"

As her body began to feel weak and heavy, the techs tore off what remained of her white burial dress. Blinking twice, she felt her eyelids become too heavy to keep open. Closing her eyes, Kat drifted into unconsciousness. Her projection flickered and melted away as the anesthesia began to work. Falling back into the tech's arms, they quickly began to drag her toward an open table being prepped by the other two technicians.

"I already did," Mr. Black said smugly. Turning, he walked back to the door and left Kat to her fate.

PART TWO

The darkness is patient.

The darkness is all consuming.

A chemical reaction occurs. Molecules are broken down, reformed, and violently taken over by the new matrix as the darkness winds ever deeper into the mixture. The once clear water slowly becomes murky and opaque, visually signifying the revolution.

The darkness is moving.

No amount of filtering or distillation can reverse the process. It is forever changed. The darkness looks at the brightness of the stars and scoffs. It always has been and ever shall be.

But the darkness is patient.

Even stars grow cold.

Chapter Seven

It is a time of war...

Thomas Cross has grown into a young man of twenty-two. Partnered with his mentor and Master, Conrad Verge, the two fight back the darkness heroically and with startling precision. Wraiths speak their names with pride on the battlefield, exchanging tales of fighting side-by-side with the two heroes. Verge and Cross seem unstoppable together. No mission, no situation, was beyond their capability but in this time of darkness, their skills have been pushed further than ever before.

The Wraith turned Vampire Lord known only as

Bane struck the first devastating blow in the war. Decimating the original Wraith Academy in England, he almost single-handedly killed the entire Council of Seven—the ruling body of the Gwyliad Wriaeth—and brought the ancient vampire hunting order to its knees. The order was left in darkness. Everything they held sacred was gone. Nothing remained but ashes. Every Wraith was alone. They clung to the one thing they understood: battle.

Yet Bane's campaign against his mortal enemies continued undaunted. This was only the first step. Every Wraith and potential Wraith was targeted. None were spared. His vampires marched across the face of Europe, Asia, and the Americas almost unchallenged as they brought a new age of death and destruction. This was the end of the Wraith…and the beginning of a new era.

The Great Wraith Purge had begun.

And humanity was caught in the middle. This ancient war which had raged for countless centuries away from prying eyes was now spilling onto the streets, their businesses, their homes, and their lives. No one was safe. The Wraith were too few and scattered to hold back the encroaching evil. As the vampires claimed innumerable victims, their armies grew en mass. Humanity was losing a war it didn't even know it was fighting.

Pockets of Wraith and human resistance formed in the depths. These freedom fighters were a ragged band of warriors whose numbers were being decimated by the sheer number of vampires. Wraiths had been elevated from myths and legends to the fighting commanders of the resistance. Even the eldest of the order was not above charging into battle with their scythe raised. These were desperate times. The Gwyliad Wriaeth—which had stood in the face of evil for nearly two thousand years—was on the brink of extinction. Desperate times called for desperate measures. The Wraith sought out every potential in every corner of the world. They had to find them before Bane did. They had to survive the purge.

Yet there is hope.

Emily St. Louise—Saint—could hold the key to the salvation of the Wraith encoded into her very blood. Believing she is the Chosen One foretold of in a prophecy dating back nearly five thousand years, her destiny, along with that of the Wraith, is layed out before her. She must choose to walk the path. But there is more to the prophecy than once revealed. Major players weave in and out of the Gwyliad Wriaeth's tapestry fulfilling roles foretold countless generations ago. All has begun to fall into place, but does this prophecy lead to salvation…or damnation?

Amidst the chaos, Thomas felt alive.

The blade of his glistening scythe dug deep into a vampire's chest. Ripping it free with one motion, the Wraith stepped back just as the blue flames exploded from the wound. The unnatural fire overwhelmed the vampire. Screaming in agony, it reached toward the Wraith with its burning hands. The attack fell short as its fingers crumbled to ashes. Knocking the charred remains of the revenant to the ground with the butt of his scythe, the Wraith charged forward. There was no time to rejoice, or savor the victory. He was fighting for his life.

Glancing up at the high walls of the alley they were trapped in, he saw more golden eyes materialize out of the gloom. A full moon loomed over the concrete casting its silver light upon the stoic buildings. Blades clinked in the cool spring air as blows were blocked, parried, and returned. The unnatural sounds of shrieks echoed relentlessly off the brick walls finally dying somewhere in the stratosphere.

Thomas snapped his head to the right as a man's scream drowned in a gurgle of his own blood. He watched one of the three true Wraiths in his squad fall to the ground with a vampire wrapped around him. Gritting his teeth, he cut to the right and charged ahead. He knew the Wraith was already dead, but at least he could honor his memory with swift retribution. Leaping into the air, he swung his scythe around his body majestically. Bringing the blade down, he caught the vampire just as he looked up from his conquest. As the Wraith's blood still dripped down his face, the scythe slashed cleanly through the vampire's skull, just above his jaw. The monster paused, looking confused, just long enough for the top of his head to slide off. Its body crumpled atop the Wraith's body still twitching from the final electrical pulses sent by its now severed brain.

Thomas glanced up through the glowing embers that flitted around. His face became long with dismay. His people were dying in waves. The vampires outnumbered them almost three-to-one. Most of his charges were nothing more than mortals in Wraith's clothing. They had a limited amount of training, but they weren't ready—and tonight's battle proved that with their blood. Thomas lifted his head and sounded the retreat. But he knew it wouldn't be that simple. It wasn't a matter of just turning away from the vampires and running, they would pursue. And with mortals in the group, the vampires would catch them with their superior speed. Thomas could easily outrun them, but there was little hope for the others. He had to hold the line and give them time to escape. It was the only option.

Cradling his scythe in his hands, he let the cool metal of the shaft comfort him. His personal weapon reverberated with perfectly attuned power. It flowed up from his fingers through his arms and into his chest. As the energy washed through him, it brought peace and calm. Taking a breath into his lungs, he quickly exhaled and steeled his nerves.

It was now or never.

Twirling his weapon, Thomas charged into battle. His blade created a shimmering barrier of silver around him as he moved. Diving into the fray, he easily dropped another vampire with two quick swipes of his scythe. As the fire swirled around him, he was on the move again. Whipping his long black leather coat behind him, Thomas dashed deeper into the battle. Spotting another of his men, his preternatural eyes hardened. Three vampires were on his man, who was losing ground. His scythe flipped and danced around his body as he tried to fend off the powerful attackers. They slashed at him with their claws and their own melee weapons. Swords and knives flashed under the bright light of the moon as they pushed the mock Wraith back toward the alley wall. It was only a matter of time now. They had him.

Without planting his feet, Thomas lopped off the head of the nearest vampire and leapt forward. His momentum threw him into the back of another. Dropping his shoulder, he hit the monster like a linebacker instantly leveling him. As the small hairs on the back of his neck stood straight up, his instincts told him to drop. Complying, he somersaulted forward narrowly avoiding the third vampire's blade. Rolling to his feet, he stood up next to his soldier and sank down into a defensive position.

Holding his scythe horizontally, he glanced over to his man. He couldn't be much older than twenty with light brown hair and hazel eyes. Several streaks of blood ran down his forehead from deep gashes the vampires had inflicted. How he had held his own against three for so long was a miracle in itself. How he was alive was another. The man attributed it to his training, but mostly to his sheer will to live.

He was a relatively new recruit—but then again, they all were. "How you doing, Daren?" Thomas asked without taking his eyes off the approaching vampires.

Daren pulled his olive green army jacket tightly around his chest and twirled his borrowed scythe once. Holding it firmly, yet carefully in his bruised and battered hands, he winked at Thomas. "I would've had 'em if you hadn't showed up." He bent forward slightly and gritted his teeth. Slipping his hand inside his coat, he took a slow, labored breath. Pulling his hand free, Thomas saw deep, red blood glistening on Daren's fingers.

"You're supposed to keep that red stuff on the inside," Thomas joked, masking his grief. Daren was fading fast. It might already be too late. "You remember what I taught you?"

Daren wiped his fingers on his pants and returned his hand to his weapon. He looked at Thomas and nodded. "Ready."

Thomas focused on the two vampires standing just

91

beyond arm's length in front of him. Their golden eyes glowed in the low light as they stared ominously. Two black tribal tattoos twisted up the right side of their faces. These were Bane's foot soldiers. Each was holding a rusty, battered katana sword and was shifting their weight from foot to foot. Thomas could tell with a mere glance that neither was trained to use the weapons. They were relying solely on their vampiric strength and speed to gain the upper hand.

Thomas smiled. That wasn't going to be enough anymore.

Lunging forward, he twisted the scythe and pressed his attack. Daren mirrored his every move without a moment of hesitation. The two were in perfect sync as Thomas had taught. The vampires and Wraiths met in combat. As the battle raged on around them, Thomas used his advantage to carve through the two soldiers. Whipping his curved scythe horizontally, he carved through the poorly made katana blade and the vampire's stomach. He glanced right to see Daren completing the same move with similar results. As the two vampires fell back, their weapons clattered to the ground.

Thomas and Daren pushed ahead. They didn't have any more time to waste on these two. Twisting his scythe blade up, he snapped it horizontally and swung it clockwise down and up until it connected solidly with the vampire's groin. Using every bit of his supernatural strength, he lifted the vampire straight up and flipped him over his shoulder instantly ripping the blade free. The vampire erupted in blue fire as his body hit the wall, instantly exploding into ash and embers.

Twisting to the right, Thomas realized the mistake in

92

his plan. Daren's scythe was lodged in the groin of the vampire, but he had been unable to finish the move without the Wraith's supernatural strength. As fire exploded over the vampire's legs and torso, he had pushed forward and overwhelmed Daren. The vampire knew he was dead, but he wasn't going alone. Wrapping his arms around Daren, the vampire bit into the man's throat. The two toppled to the ground, struggling, screaming, engulfed in flames. Stumbling back, Thomas watched his friend burn to death in the hands of the enemy. He cursed under his breath. Snatching Daren's scythe off the ground, he turned back into the battle. There would be time to mourn later. He had to keep his mind on the living for the time being.

He turned and dashed toward the remaining vampires.

He spotted a familiar light brown blur in the heart of the storm—Master Verge. His heart skipped a beat as he watched at least ten vampires descend on Conrad. Without thinking, Thomas reacted on instinct alone. Leaping into the air, he flipped skillfully and landed just behind Conrad. Knocking down two vampires with his scythe, he dropped down just as Conrad's weapon whizzed past his head. Without a word, without even seeing his student, Conrad knew he was there. He could sense Thomas. The two warriors became one blurred ball of destruction as their weapons and bodies moved in perfect rhythm. A hellish blaze of blue fire erupted around them as vampire after vampire fell.

"How are we doing?" Conrad yelled over his shoulder to his pupil, his friend.

"The usual," Thomas answered glibly.

Conrad grunted as he ripped his blade from the chest of a vampire. "That bad, huh?"

Thomas swung his scythe over and narrowly missed his target. The vampire dodged and got inside his defense before Thomas could counter. Knocking the Wraith down, the vampire slashed his claws down Thomas' face opening two wounds that ran over his eyebrow and continued down his cheek. Ignoring the stinging pain on his face and the blood running into his left eye, the young Wraith kicked up and wrapped his legs around the vampire's. Twisting, he brought the revenant to the ground. Rolling onto his knees, Thomas slammed the wooden tip of his weapon into the vampire's heart. Thomas quickly rolled back to avoid the flames and recovered to his feet.

"We need to get out of here," Thomas said as he defended against another lunging attack. "We can't win."

"I couldn't agree more," Conrad said quickly.

Before the last word was even out of Conrad's mouth, the two Wraiths were on the move. Fighting back to the mouth of the alley, Conrad and Thomas were perfection. They turned and began to hold off the mass of vampires to give their men time to escape. Every attack, every blow was countered and returned. They broke the mass of vampires in two giving their men a safe corridor or passage.

As the last living member of their squad broke through the line, Conrad reached into his coat and pulled a small, circular object free. "I hate doing this," he muttered to himself. Lifting the grenade to his mouth, he grabbed the silver pin with his teeth and ripped it free.

"Fire in the hole!" Tossing the grenade underhand,

Conrad watched it roll into the center of the vampires.

Conrad and Thomas used every bit of their preternatural speed as they turned and charged away from the active grenade. A burst of golden light preceded the sound of the explosion. Shrapnel careened in all directions, shredding anything it came in contact with. The yellow eruption of fire shifted to light blue as the vampires' bodies were incinerated. The minor explosion created by the grenade was amplified, almost instantly quadrupling in size and obliterating everything in its path. Diving to the ground, Conrad and Thomas felt the blast singe the back of their coats and hair as it mushroomed out and dissipated.

Rolling onto his back, Conrad stared back at the devastation he had wrought. "That was good."

No sign of the vampires remained, but the area looked like ground zero at Nagasaki after the atomic bomb was dropped.

Thomas smiled and shook his head. "Next time, I come up with the escape plan."

***

She was barely alive.

She had long since gone beyond the need for sedatives and anesthetic as her body no longer functioned. Starved to the point of death, she was little more than a vegetable. She wished she had died in that alley all those years ago, instead, she had been dying every day over the past ten years. Her body ached and throbbed from the many invasive tests and procedures she had been forced to endure. As a vampire, she had a heightened regenerative system allowing her to heal more rapidly. It was, in fact, what gave her immortality—and kept her alive during this horrible, nightmarish experience. She had seen her entire left arm excised just below her shoulder, only to have it reattached months later. Her legs, hands, eyes, even her fangs had been systematically removed and reattached. She felt like a patchwork of pieces and thread, barely held together.

A light scar in the shape of a Y ran down from both shoulders, met above her sternum, and continued down her abdomen. Commonly known as the "Y Incision" to those who performed autopsies, she had watched two techs cut her torso open and remove each of her vital organs and study them. She was startled to see her heart continue to beat outside of her body and then resume its work once returned. Considering herself a very learned individual, she still didn't recognize two bulbous organs removed from close to where her kidneys should have been. The technicians commented that this was part of her enhanced digestive system and that they looked healthy, but she had no idea what function they served. She wondered for a moment how many human scientists would kill to get their hands on her unique physiology.

Her mind still worked, but weaved in and out of lucidity. Even her identity was gone. No longer did she have a use for a name, instead, she just existed with the others. Sometimes, she heard the attending lab technicians refer to her as "Patient Eleven Oh Four," but even that was fleeting. Whatever it was that made her her was nearly gone.

Her name was Kat.

At least she thought it was. It had been such a long

96

time since anyone called her that. She had a vague recollection of a man in a neat black suit standing over her smirking with satisfaction. Who he was or why he was there was gone from her mind but she knew she hated him. With every fiber of her being, she hated him. The sole thought that kept her going was his death at her hands. She wanted to scratch the eyeballs from his skull, and tear out his organs with her bare hands. She had dreamed of it many, many times. It would be hers.

She gnashed her fangs in her tired, aching mouth. It was nearing feeding time. She could smell it. Rolling her eyes to the left, she saw the first of the red fluid she craved begin to fill the clear tube that ran into her mouth and down her throat. A plastic guard installed between her upper and lower teeth kept her from biting the tube and severing it, but she was sure no vampire in here would willingly do that. This was their only source of relief. Once a day, the test subjects were fed just enough to sustain their bodies. It had been learned over the course of these tests that a vampire could endure starvation for up to six months before their body shut down, and even then, it refused to die. It would enter such a deep comatose state, that no amount of blood could awaken them.

As the blood rolled down the tube into her stomach, she felt a quick shudder of pleasure and release. It spread through her body like a wave. Her fingers and toes twitched as she regained the slightest control of her faculties. Her mind was instantly clear and focused. She remembered the man in the black suit again and suddenly her hatred was all consuming. Summoning all her strength and focus, she visualized getting off the table.

Muscle by muscle, she imagined lifting her legs, then her arms…if she could only get up. For a moment—the slightest moment—she felt powerful and alive.

But it was fleeting. The blood stopped and her body quickly sank back down into its near comatose state. A haze descended over her mind. Her consciousness fell back into her brain and was buried by the dust and cobwebs that had settled there.

She was lost again.

Chapter Eight

A roll of bills landed with a thump on the table in front of his half empty drink. Looking up cautiously, his old eye took a moment to focus in the low light—the fact his right eye had been lost five years ago didn't help. A thick scar ran down from the empty socket and cut across the bridge of his nose terminating above his right cheek.

He stared at the stranger hovering over his table. Completely clad in black, his olive skin looked nearly flawless, and his dark hair was slicked back against his scalp. A twisting, black tribal tattoo wound down from his left temple and terminated just above his strong jaw. A pair of rectangular, dark, smoky glasses covered his eyes.

"You are Neilson?" the stranger asked.

He hesitated. Unsure how to answer, he decided to play coy. "Who's asking?"

"The Crimson Syndicate," the stranger replied.

Neilson sat straight up at the name, as did the hairs on the back of his neck. He knew them well. Rubbing his bushy gray beard, he cocked his left eyebrow. He immediately knew what the stranger was. There was no need to play dumb, or avoid the truth. The stranger could easily see straight through that. "I'm Neilson," the old man answered.

"I need information."

Neilson looked at the stranger cautiously. Flipping up the collar on his dark green army jacket, he pulled it tightly around his chest. "I'm not in that business anymore."

The stranger's expression remained unchanged.

"I'm retired," Neilson said carefully.

"I'm looking for Talon Creed," the stranger insisted. He spoke softly but forcefully.

Neilson grabbed the wad of cash from the table and tossed it back to the stranger. "I told you, I'm retired. And even if I wasn't, I wouldn't go anywhere near Creed. And neither should you."

The stranger snapped his hand around Neilson's throat and lifted him easily from the table. Holding him off the floor, the stranger sneered exposing his glistening fangs. "Tell me what I want to know, old man," he sneered, "or you lose the other eye."

"Go fuck yourself," Neilson spat.

The stranger's face contorted in anger. Spinning, he threw Neilson hard over his shoulder. Neilson sailed across the dank bar and impacted against the far wall. Crumpling to the floor, he felt his body bruise and twist on the verge of breaking. Wiping a bit of blood away from his mouth, he rolled onto his back. "I'm too old for this shit."

A shriek of panic ran through the bar. Immediately, the other patrons leapt up from their tables and began to run frantically toward the exit. The bartender scooted quickly down the bar and disappeared behind a hidden door. It wasn't the first time this place had seen trouble, and most knew it probably wouldn't be the last. From his hiding position, the bartender seriously began considering finding a new line of work.

Before Neilson could move any further, the stranger was on him again. "Listen, you fucking blood-sucking leech," he said through gritted teeth. "I don't know anything."

"You lie," the stranger growled. He rubbed a bit of sweat from the man's forehead with his gloved hand. "I can smell it on you." Sliding his hand around the old man's throat, he slowly began to crush his windpipe with his thumb. "Tell me what I want to know," he repeated.

Neilson felt his air supply beginning to dwindle. "Why do you suckheads even need a bounty hunter?"

"That isn't your concern."

Neilson's vision started to blur as he suffocated. He didn't want to die like this in this place. No matter the twists and turns his life had taken, he deserved better than this. "All right," he croaked, "all right. I'll tell you."

The stranger lessened the pressure on Neilson's throat. Letting his hand fall away, the stranger sat back and waited.

Neilson rubbed his throat. "He usually hangs out at a bar down near the waterfront." Sitting up, he leaned back against the wall and stared at the stranger. "You have what you want. Now leave me the fuck alone."

The stranger smiled. Grabbing the old man and pinning him to the wall, the stranger dove in and sank his fangs into the man's throat. Neilson let out a muffled yelp as he died. Rolling back onto the balls of his feet, the stranger stared at the old man's dead body. Digging the rolled wad of bills out of his jacket again, he tossed it at Neilson's feet. "Thank you for your time," he said, wiping the excess blood from his mouth.

Moving back to the entrance, he stepped out into the cool night air. Looking up, he saw a few twinkling stars. Out of the corner of his eye, he watched two dark forms

101

materialize out of the night and approach him. Turning to face them, he held his position. The dark figures became vampires wrapped in black, hooded cloaks. Stopping in front of the stranger, the two vampires dropped to one knee and bowed their heads.

"Rise," the stranger commanded.

"Lord Bane," the two vampires greeted. "The Troika seeks an audience with you."

"Lord Black," Bane said slowly. He was wondering how long it would take for his presence here to arouse the local coven's attention. "I have business to attend to," he replied, "but I will meet with the Troika. When have they called for the meeting?"

"They wish to meet this time tomorrow night," the vampires replied. "They invite you to be their guest for dinner. You are welcome to bring as many servants as you require."

Bane nodded. "I will be in attendance. Go, tell your masters."

The two vampires stood, turned, and headed into the night.

"How stupid do they think I am?" Bane asked the night as the two vampires disappeared from sight. His human visage melted away revealing the twisted, scarred, rotting flesh of his face. His yellow eyes glowed ominously beneath his heavy black robe. Reaching into his robe, he removed a battered, rusted mask. Placing it over his face, he gazed out of the horizontal eye slits. The bottom corner of the mask was broken away—a souvenir from his battle with Saint inside the Wraith Academy—revealing a massive scar on his face just below it. It was from the only Wraith who had ever survived his wrath, and he would not soon forget.

"They seek to destroy you and claim your power."

"Of course they do," Bane said to the shadow over his shoulder.

A dark-haired woman in a tight red dress stepped out of the shadows and slunk up to his side. She placed her hands seductively on his back. "This is a precarious game you play, Lord. You have minions to handle this kind of thing. Why do you put yourself in unnecessary danger?"

"Because I enjoy it, Raquel," Bane growled at his aide. Spinning around, he slapped the woman hard across her face, knocking her to the ground.

Raquel crumbled to the sidewalk, but quickly picked herself up. To stay down would be an insult to both her and her Lord. "I apologize, Lord," she said quietly. "I had no intention of insulting you."

"Don't ever question my motives." His yellow eyes burned like fires behind his mask. "Do you understand?"

Raquel nodded, saying nothing.

"Now," Bane started down the sidewalk, "I have to meet with Mr. Creed." He smiled behind his mask as he disappeared into the thick San Francisco fog. "We have business to discuss."

***

"We have no choice! We have to act now or we face certain doom. The old ways have kept us alive for two thousand years. To abandon them now would be foolish!"

Thomas sat in the back of the meeting room, his arms crossed and his feet up on the back of an empty chair in front of him. He would've tried to catch a quick nap, but

Conrad hated when he fell asleep during the meetings. He would always say something about being disrespectful to the speakers, but Thomas felt that being a politician already earned these people a large amount of disrespect. Brushing a bit of his wavy hair out of his face with his gloved hand, he accidentally brushed the two deep cuts on his face. Flinching slightly, he swallowed a quick breath to fight off the pain.

They had convened in an old church this night. The reverend supported the Wraith and helped whenever he could. Deep in the heart of London, the vampire hunters hoped this place would dissuade any vampires from entering, although they all knew that religious places and artifacts held no actual sway against or protection from the creatures. Modern dogma—created by books, movies, and even the Internet—had become a weapon of the Wraith. Even vampires weren't sure if all the myths were true or false. The building was battered, it had seen better days, but at least it was a roof over their heads for the night. They had agreed to leave before the morning's first service at nine. It was half past midnight.

Returning his attention to the front of the room, he did his best to ignore the throbbing of his face. Two men, High Wraith Xavier and Wraith Alexander, were engaged in a heated argument over the fate of the Gwyliad Wriaeth. Xavier still wore his maroon vest signifying his rank as a High Wraith, and his sworn allegiance to the council—even though they no longer existed. Xavier had been one of the few Wraiths to survive the Academy's destruction, and had even fought against Vampire Lord Bane's forces valiantly. He had failed—losing his left hand in the process—and still wore the dishonor like a badge, yet he made it his goal to keep the teachings and will of the council alive. He spearheaded a group of Wraiths Thomas had come to dub the "Traditionalists." They wanted things to return to the old ways and a new council be formed.

Alexander, on the other hand, had been in a remote area of Russia when Bane struck and had only journeyed back when news of the council's demise had reached him. With strong new ideas about how the Gwyliad Wriaeth should move into the twenty-first century, he no longer felt that the Wraith needed to adhere to the "old" ways. Individual Wraith would be responsible for the acquisition, training and education of new hunters. It would be a more democratic order, with each member having a voice and vote in all matters. A Chancellor would be elected to oversee the order. Thomas knew Alexander's name would certainly be on the ballot if a Chancellor were deemed necessary. Alexander wanted to lead, and if he couldn't do it in the traditional way, he would change the system to make it possible.

Thomas didn't care for either ideas—or men, for that matter—but Conrad was engrossed in the debate. Sitting in the front row, he watched both men intently listening to every word they spoke. Thomas knew Conrad would probably fall into Xavier's camp of Traditionalists. His whole life had been spent upholding the ideas, and ideals, of the Gwyliad Wriaeth. In the aftermath of Master Quinn's death during Bane's attack, Conrad was considered the most loyal, wise, and well-rounded Wraith in the order. He was by the book, cover to cover. He wanted to make sure he knew the viewpoints and political platforms of both sides before he made a decision.

105

But there were those in the order—much like Thomas—who didn't care for politics. They simply wanted to do what they were trained for: kill vampires. And in this time of sweeping darkness, they felt their skills were needed more than ever. There would be time to rebuild the order later, right now, they needed to concentrate on stopping Bane. His army marched almost unopposed over Europe and was threatening to spread into Asia and Africa. Each day the Wraith hesitated, each day they argued about policy, Bane added another hundred soldiers to his ranks. Soon, it would be too late and all the debate and rhetoric would be pointless. The Wraith would be gone and Bane will have won.

Thomas didn't want to see that day.

Anger swelled in his chest. Shooting up from his chair, Thomas marched to the front of the room. "We need to stop arguing and do something!" he roared.

He saw Alexander begin to retort and quickly squeezed the Wraith's throat with his telekinesis just enough to make him choke. As Alexander tried to catch his breath, Thomas took the opportunity to face the full audience of forty to fifty Wraiths and humans who had assembled to hear the debate. He noticed her sitting in the third row for the first time. She frowned as he caught her gray eyes. Unfazed, he returned his attention to the crowd.

"The longer we sit here and argue about politics, the larger Bane's army grows," Thomas said condescendingly. "He is already almost too powerful for us. If we wait, the few of us who are left will have no chance against him."

"Thomas." Conrad stood up and walked toward his

student and friend, "Please sit down." He glanced over at Alexander, who still had his hands clasped around his throat. "And release the chokehold please," he whispered.

"No," Thomas spat. "We need to fight. This is pointless."

"Thomas," Conrad repeated, this time more sternly.

"Just in case you didn't notice, we're dying out there," Thomas said, pointing over his shoulder. "We need to stop this! Now!"

Conrad's temper flared. "Thomas! That is enough!"

Thomas shrank back from the verbal scolding. He lowered his eyes, then his head. Even though he was a full Wraith in his own right, he still felt like Conrad's young student. He obeyed, despite feeling the furnace in his heart ignite. "I'm sorry, Master." He spoke into his chest.

Releasing the grip on Alexander's throat, he turned and took a step back from the audience's critical stares. His eyes firmly planted on the floor, Thomas quickly made his way out of the room hoping Conrad wouldn't follow.

To his surprise, Saint was the next out of the door.

"Tommy?" she asked softly. "Are you okay?"

You are better than all of them.

It had been a long time since he had heard the voice...and it frightened him. The spark in his heart was threatening to blossom into an inferno. Thomas struggled against his inner demon, fighting to push it back into the cell he had created for it. As he worked to control his anger, Thomas took a slow breath in through his nose and exhaled it through his mouth. He felt his heart cool again as he started to feel better. "I'm okay."

107

He looked straight at her and remembered his first day in the Academy when she had been the first one to speak to him. Slightly different now, her brown eyes had transformed to a haunting bluish gray and she did her best to hide the fangs in her mouth. Her raven black hair was drawn into a loose ponytail, but a few strands escaped and fell down around her face. Her long, black leather coat—very similar to Thomas'—hung down over her black tank top and baggy khaki pants. Shorter than he was, the thick, chunky black boots she always wore made up for some of it.

Saint was a year younger than Thomas, and had gone through the final ritual of passage a year later. She had been part of the last "class" to graduate from the Academy, and along with Master Xavier, was one of the few to survive Bane's attack. She had even faced the fearsome lord in single combat deep within the bowels of the academy, and nearly lost her life. She had lost her Master—Ben Quinn—and most of her closest friends that day, yet she still found the strength to carry on.

There were rumors running rampant about Saint. Some said she was the Chosen One who would help create a new race of Wraiths, while others feared her. She was stronger, faster, and a better warrior than any Wraith alive. She was the perfect blend of vampire and Wraith, but some claimed she teetered more toward the darker side of her gifts. She had even begun to acquire her own group of loyal followers—though she wanted nothing to do with them. There were those in the order who wanted Saint to lead them, claiming that the Chosen One was best suited to bring the Wraith through these dark times. She was becoming something of a quasi-religious figure within the order.

The two had been friends since day one, and even with the changes, she was still Saint. Though they never shared anything like she and Miller did, he considered her his closest—if not his only—friend. Conrad was more of a father figure to him. Even though he could speak of just about anything with his Master, he never truly felt at ease. He never wanted to bring up a subject that might disappoint, or lower Conrad's opinion of him. He didn't have that problem with Saint.

"Good." Saint smiled. "What the hell were you doing in there? You had the patented Skywalker whine going full bore." She paused for a moment, then punched him squarely in the shoulder. "But I was going to Toshi Station to pick up some power converters," she joked, doing her best Luke Skywalker impersonation from the first Star Wars film.

Thomas stumbled back from the punch, which would have leveled an ordinary human, and wrapped his hand over his shoulder. Looking bemused at the Wraith, a smile crossed his face. "It was that bad, huh?"

"You looked like a spoiled brat up there," Saint barked. "Look," she said, placing her hand on his other shoulder, "the message was right, but you did it in the wrong way. I know you hate it, but you need to be more diplomatic. Throwing a tantrum in the middle of the quorum won't do you any good."

Thomas nodded. "I know. I just get so tired of all the politics." He stopped, "Daren died today."

Saint frowned. She had known the boy. He would have made a good Wraith. "How?"

"Fell in battle," Thomas answered solemnly. "There

109

wasn't anything I could do. I just," he stopped again, "watched him die."

Saint nodded. "So that's what this is all about? Is the mantle of leadership a little too heavy to bear?"

Thomas' eyes widened with shock. "What?"

"You've been pushing for your own command since the start of this war," Saint explained. "Now that you have it, you can't handle that your men are dying."

"That's not it at all."

"Really?"

Thomas' face grew long. "It's hard," he said finally.

Saint smiled softly. He was so powerful, yet beneath the leather and training, he was still just an insecure boy. "I know. You're doing a good job though."

"I'm trying." Thomas nodded, accepting the compliment. "I haven't been sleeping well lately."

Saint looked caringly at her friend. "Why?"

"Bad dreams," he admitted. "They keep recurring."

Saint took a step closer to Thomas. "What are you dreaming about?"

"A woman."

"Oh," Saint said with a laugh, "they're that kind of dream. I see now."

"No," Thomas said quickly. "It's not like that at all. I don't know who she is," he explained, "but I care for her deeply. She's slender, athletic, with beautiful blond hair, and the most incredible blue eyes I have ever looked into."

"What happens to the woman?" Saint's curiosity was piqued.

"She," Thomas paused, the emotions obviously causing him pain. "She dies." He swallowed hard. "I can

110

see her lying on a rooftop in a pool of her own blood. I'm too late to save her," he admitted. "No matter what happens in the dream, I'm always too late. She dies in my arms."

"Curious," Saint responded.

"Here's the weird part," Thomas said slowly. He glanced over his shoulder to make sure no one else was in earshot, "I think she's a vampire."

Saint took an uneasy step back. "You know that's forbidden," she breathed. "Don't even joke about that."

"I wish I was."

Saint took a slow breath and tried to process the new information. Dream or not, Thomas was treading on thin ice. This was not something the order tolerated at all.

"Dreams pass in time." She wrapped her arm around his waist and started to turn him back toward the door, "we should—"

"Saint!"

Thomas and Saint turned to see a familiar woman running up the hall toward them. She was out of breath and on the verge of total panic.

"Chris," Saint said, walking toward the mortal woman. "What's wrong?"

Chris wiped the rain from her face. Reaching into her pocket, she produced a clear jewel case with an unlabeled recordable CD inside. "The quorum needs to see this immediately," she said.

"What is it?" Thomas asked, snapping the CD away from Chris. He studied the disk in his hand hoping to glean some hint of information from it.

"This just came over the 'net," Chris answered. "Two of our scanners found it about fifty minutes ago.

They had to verify its authenticity." She looked at the two Wraiths in front of her with fear in her brown eyes. "It's from America."

Saint felt a lump in her throat. So far, the Americas had been left relatively untouched by Bane's march to power. Saint had a pretty good idea what she would see on the disk. Taking it from Thomas, she handed it back to Chris and started her toward the door. "It would be best if you presented this," she said wisely.

Twisting the handle, she threw open the door and maneuvered Chris inside. Glancing over her shoulder, Saint paused. "Thomas, are you coming?"

He hesitated. Thomas didn't want to go back in there and face the burning, accusing eyes but he knew this was an emergency. He wanted desperately to see what was contained on the CD.

"Yeah," Thomas breathed. "Let's go."

As Thomas rounded the doorframe, he saw Saint and Chris already at the front of the room. Sliding past a lone Wraith seated in the back row, he returned to the seat he occupied before the outburst. Sinking slightly down into the seat, he crossed his arms and glanced nervously over the crowd. No one had paid any attention to his return, thankfully because of Saint and Chris' distraction. He watched the two women explain the nature of the emergency to Xavier and Alexander. The two Wraiths turned politicians understood and gave up the floor. Saint took the CD from Chris and immediately began setting up a small laptop computer and projector.

Chris turned to face the audience. "Two of our best scanners intercepted this video feed fifty minutes ago. It was being uploaded to a police mainframe on the west coast of the Unites States. Initially," she explained, "we weren't overly interested in the footage, until they spotted something significant." She turned to look at Saint. The Wraith nodded at the scanner signifying her readiness. "The footage is no more than twenty-three seconds long and we've enhanced it slightly to take out some of the grain and lighten the image."

Saint activated the projector. A black and white image was displayed on the front wall of the meeting room. The time stamp on the image was from yesterday evening. Immediately, the audience began to sit forward to see better. They could clearly make out two men standing in a convenience store with a young clerk behind the counter. One of the men was pointing the barrel of a shotgun directly at the clerk's face. The video was shot from a security camera probably mounted on the ceiling and angled down toward the counter. The men's faces were obscured in the footage.

"Can someone get the lights?" Chris asked quickly.

Thomas turned and looked at the switch on the wall. Raising his hand slightly, he reached out with a tendril of power and snapped off the light before the closest Wraith could make it there. There were only two known Wraiths who could use their minds in such a fashion, he and Saint. With a smile, he turned back to the image.

"Thank you," Chris said, without actually noting who completed her request. "There's no sound on the video," she added apologetically. "What you'll see here," she paused, "well, it doesn't need an explanation. Roll the video please."

As the video began, the two men snapped into motion. Waving the shotgun at the man behind the
113

counter, the men were obviously holding this convenience store up. Racks of potato chips, candy, and other goods were knocked sloppily to the ground at their feet. The clerk, with his hands up, was trying to back away from the two men as the holdup continued. The audience could see the two robbers yelling at the man to stand still and open the register. The clerk was trying to explain something…probably the fact he didn't have much money in the till. Unfazed by his argument, one of the men reached over the counter and grabbed the man by the nape of the neck. Lifting him up and over the counter with one hand, the robber leaned in and bit the man's throat.

Dropping the clerk's dead body to the ground, the vampire hopped over the counter and ripped open the cash register. Digging the money out hastily, he stuffed it in his pockets while his accomplice turned and stood guard at the double glass doors. As the vampire jumped back over the counter, his body seemed to be stuck in midair. The vampire writhed as a blade appeared in the center of his chest. Materializing out of thin air, a tall being garbed in a black cloak stood with his arm blades extended. He held the vampire impaled on the end of his right blade, suspending him off the floor. Reaching out with the opposite blade, he easily lopped off the head of the second vampire with the gun. As his body fell to the floor, the weapon discharged accidentally hitting the camera.

As the video image crackled and began to fill with interference, the cloaked being turned toward it. His glowing eyes and metallic mask were clearly visible.

"Hold please," Chris requested.

The video progressed in the dead silence of the room.

"Hold!" Chris shouted.

Saint snapped herself away from the image and clicked the pause button on the computer. Turning back to the video, she stared at the mask. She knew it well. She glanced down at the left missing corner and her eyes hardened. "Bane," she growled.

Chris nodded. "That was our assessment as well. The local police come across this kind of footage occasionally and their first instinct is to hide it from the public as quickly as possible. Why this one was being uploaded to an unsecured server is a bit of a mystery in itself." She looked back at the video for a moment. "What we couldn't figure out is what exactly he's doing," Chris added.

"Looks like he's gone vigilante," Conrad offered from the front row.

"That doesn't make any sense," Saint said, shaking her head. "He doesn't care about that dead clerk, or that the vampires were robbing him."

"The answer is right in front of you," Thomas said from the back of the room. "Where was this footage taken?"

"San Francisco," Chris answered.

Thomas was silent.

Conrad stood and looked back at his student. "Are you planning to enlighten us with the answer?" he asked sarcastically.

"Bane's not interested with anything visible in that video," Thomas replied. "He's making a statement."

Saint snapped her fingers. "He's right."

Conrad glanced from one young Wraith to the other,

slightly confused.

"That area is controlled by a triumvirate of Vampire Lords," Thomas said, slowly adding the pieces together for the audience. "Bane is signaling his presence and his intent to take over the Troika's empire."

"They control much of the western seaboard," Saint added. "If I remember correctly."

"He's looking to make a big splash in America," Conrad breathed.

"We need to stop him," Xavier said, stepping forward. "We can't let him expand his empire any further."

"We can't even protect our own country," Alexander shot back. "How are we supposed to keep him off an entire continent?"

Saint walked up between the two bickering politicians and pushed them apart. "There isn't time for this. I understand the need to rebuild the order," she said, addressing both, "but if we don't stop Bane, there won't be any one left to rebuild it for." She turned and looked at the audience. "I'm going to stop him. This isn't an assignment, but I need help. We can end this war and stop the Wraith Purge." She stopped and let the words sink in for a moment. Taking a quick breath, she scanned over the audience. "Who wants to volunteer?"

"Right here," Thomas said, immediately standing up. Walking around the rows of chairs, he joined Saint in the front of the room.

Conrad shook his head. "I better go, too." He looked at his student. "Someone has to watch after you two."

Turning back to the audience, Saint watched more hands slowly lift into the air. She smiled approvingly.

116

Chapter Nine

Kat opened her eyes slowly to see three lab techs standing around her. Busily detaching her from the hub, two of the lab techs pulled needles and wires out of her skin. A third held a bag of murky red blood in his hands. As the two techs pulled away the final tube, they began to fasten restraints around her wrists, ankles, and chest. There had been no need for them before as her body was in a weakened state, but things had changed. With the restraints in place, the tech grabbed the remaining feeding tube and attached the bag of blood to it. Looking to the two other techs nervously, he snapped open the plastic valve. As the three took a step back, the blood began to flow down the tube and into Kat's mouth.

Her body twitched as the blood hit her stomach. As more and more poured in, she felt her body quickly recover from the years of starvation and abuse. Writhing in pure joy as the blood worked its way through her body, she pulled against the restraints. Her decaying, gray flesh vanished away as her mental projection reformed. She was healthy and pink again, wearing the same white dress she had been buried in. Blond hair rolled down in waves from her once bald scalp as her gold eyes melted to blue. As the last of the blood flowed from the tube, the techs removed it from her throat.

She was herself. She was Kat again.

Trying to sit up, she stared down at the thick, black restraints that kept her in place. Pulling with all her vampiric strength, she was barely able to move them. She felt better, but wasn't completely back to one hundred percent yet. Turning to look at the techs, a sneer rippled across her lips. Kat's eyes smoldered with rage. "Release me!"

The techs backed further away from the table.

"There's no need to shout."

Turning, Kat spotted a tall, gaunt man in a midnight black suit and tie. Rage instantly blossomed in her heart. She struggled against the restraints again, frantically trying to get free. She wanted to tear his heart from his chest and feed on it.

"I am in need of your services," Mr. Black said as he strolled casually toward her.

Ten years of her life were gone and he was to blame. Kat wanted desperately to get her hands around his throat. She stared unblinking at him hoping that one of her hidden vampire powers were laser beams that would shoot from her eyes and incinerate anything she looked at. At least her creativity was working again.

"I'm willing to make you a deal." Mr. Black stopped next to the table and placed his hand on her thigh. "If you work for me, I will grant you your freedom. The job is relatively simple. Interested?"

Kat didn't hear a word he said. Instead, focused on his face, she imagined her thumbs crushing his eyeballs back into his skull.

"I can find someone else," Mr. Black warned. He pointed to the ever-growing number of vampires suspended from the ceiling. "There are plenty in here who would be willing to help me to gain their freedom."

This time, Kat keyed on one word: Freedom. She pushed her anger back into her chest for a moment.

"What's the offer?"

Startled by her sudden clarity, Black had to take a moment to recompose his thoughts. "I have a very important guest visiting tonight, and I need a special operative."

"Operative?"

"This guest is a very prominent Vampire Lord," Black explained, "and I would very much like to see him eliminated." A devious smile broke across his thin lips. "I want his power. I want his army." He balled his fist. "I want him dead. That's where you come in." He paused and stared at Kat. "I need you to kill him."

Kat's mind whirred. She needed retribution against this vampire, but she couldn't do it trapped in here. She swallowed her pride. "What would I have to do?"

"My geneticists here in the Farm have created a special cocktail I want you to inject Lord Bane with," Black explained. "It can't be ingested, or I would simply slip it into his drink. It has to be added directly into his bloodstream."

Kat raised an eyebrow. "What does this 'cocktail' do?"

Black lifted his hand and examined his nails and cuticles as if he had little interest in the conversation. "It reverses the Vampire Virus."

Kat's eyes widened. It was everything she wanted…to be human again. The possibilities swirled through her brain. She could reclaim her life. Yet this vampire was using it as a weapon. He sickened her.

Kat eyed the Vampire Lord warily. "Then you'll free me?"

"If you survive." Black nodded.

"Why me?" Kat asked after a moment of thought.

Black considered lying to her, but decided there was no harm in the truth. "I have a trusted inner ring of servants. I don't want to lose any of them, especially if I am to take over Lord Bane's empire. You, on the other hand," he grinned from ear to ear, "mean nothing to me. You are expendable. I merely chose you at random from the hundreds of vampires contained here. Luck of the draw, I guess," he added with a cackle.

Kat gritted her teeth. "How do I know you'll honor your word?"

Black ran his hand a little further up her thigh until he was inches from her vagina. "You don't." Running his fingers over her dress, he could feel her pubic hairs beneath. Slowly drawing his hand away, he stood smiling at Kat. "So, do we have a deal?"

Kat wanted to tear herself loose from the table and grind every single bone in his body to dust. She felt repulsed and dirty at his very touch. It took every bit of restraint she possessed not to spit in his face. "You have a deal."

Black clapped his hands in excitement. "Very good. I'll call for you this evening. Remember to wear appropriate attire," he said with a smirk, "something black, lacey, and preferably extremely low-cut." Turning, he walked away from the table with a laugh.

Snatching a syringe from an adjoining table, one of the techs quickly moved to Kat's side. Jabbing the needle into her shoulder, he emptied the contents into her body. Taking a step back, he watched her eyelids become heavy and she started to fade out again.

The tech smiled. "Nap time."

***

"Talon Creed?"

The bounty hunter sat alone in the back of the dingy bar. Dressed in black denim, his head was cleanly shaven. His dark skin stretched over his bulging muscles and powerful frame. Dark glasses sat on the bridge of his nose while a chewed toothpick dangled from his lips. A black motorcycle helmet sat on the table beside a single shot of malt whiskey that didn't appear to have been touched. The front of the helmet was painted into the demonic grin of a skull with flames tapering off and wrapping around the sides. He would have been an imposing figure in any setting, let alone this smoky, dimly lit corner of a bar.

"Who's asking?" he asked in a deep, murky voice that matched his body perfectly.

Bane—once again assuming the visage of a stranger—sat down at the table opposite Creed. "The Crimson Syndicate."

"Not interested," Creed spoke slowly and evenly. "Now either buy me a drink, or get the fuck out of here, you Euro-trash looking piece of shit."

Bane smiled. He liked this man already. He knew exactly what Bane was, yet showed no hint of fear. His heart wasn't even beating any faster. Lifting his hand, he signaled the bartender for another shot for Creed. "We are in need of your services," Bane said, sliding into a chair opposite Creed's as the bartender brought the second drink to the table.

Creed stared at Bane without expression. He lifted his first shot from the table and gulped down the heavy

121

liquor. Spinning the glass in his meaty paws, he placed it gently back on the table upside down. "I told you I wasn't interested."

"Hear what I'm offering before you turn it down," Bane said, losing a bit of his patience.

Creed lifted his hand and pulled off his sunglasses exposing his extremely pale blue irises. Looking as if they had no pigment at all, they seemed almost completely white with only the dark pupil and the outline of the iris in the center. "You have sixty seconds," he stated. Reaching into his jacket, the bounty hunter pulled out a wooden stake and set it next to his glass.

Bane was amused. He could kill this man before his hand even made it to the stake. Still, the show of power was intriguing. "I need you to find someone and bring them to me," he paused, "a Wraith."

"I thought they were the good guys," Creed commented.

"Good, bad, it's all irrelevant," Bane dismissed the comment. "What matters is that this person is important to the fate of every Wraith and Vampire alive."

Creed ran his fingers over the top of the still full shot glass. "What's so important about this hunter?"

"That isn't your concern."

Creed tapped the stake. "I'm making it my concern."

"You do understand that I could kill you before you had the chance to use that." Bane nodded to the stake. "I'm only humoring you."

Creed laughed deeply with more than a hint of evil in his tone. "You think so?" He pulled off his glasses and set them on the table. "Feel free to try."

Bane accepted the challenge.

The vampire was up and out of his chair and inches from the man's throat before Creed even flinched. With a speed and power that surprised the Vampire Lord, Creed snatched Bane in the middle of his attack, spun his arm around Bane's neck, and slammed Bane's face to the table all without spilling his drink, or leaving his seat.

Crushing down on the vampire's throat with immense strength, Creed scooped the wooden stake up with his free hand and held it in front of Bane's face. "Looks like I had the chance to use this," he said mockingly. Sliding his arm free, he released Bane. "Never underestimate your opponent."

Bane slowly sank back down into his seat, staring at the bounty hunter. His respect had grown immeasurably for this human and he understood why he came so highly recommended. "We're prepared to pay you two hundred thousand dollars for your services."

Creed nodded, slowly considering the offer.

"Do we have a deal?"

"On one condition," Creed replied after a few moments.

Bane waited expectantly. "And that is?"

Creed leaned forward and lowered his voice, "I get to keep the vampire hunter's scythe."

"Why?"

"I want to add it to my trophy collection," Creed said, flashing a smile for the first time all night.

"Two hundred thousand to find and bring the Wraith to me." Bane smiled, "And you can keep her weapon."

Creed nodded. "Deal."

Bane stood up and let his mental projection melt away. Lifting his mask from a hidden pocket in his cloak,

123

he slid it onto his face. "The Crimson Syndicate thanks you."

"I think you should get out of San Francisco," Creed said, staring at the Vampire Lord in front of him.

Bane's eyes hardened behind the mask. "Is that a threat?"

"No," Creed laughed, "but if George Lucas sees you, he'll sue your ass for copyright infringement."

Bane neither understood the joke, nor cared to. "How much time do you need?"

"Depends on where this Wraith of yours is."

"I don't know," Bane answered.

Creed nodded. "Two weeks. Tops." He knew full well what he was capable of. There wasn't a man, woman, or child alive today he couldn't track.

Reaching into his cloak, Bane produced another rolled wad of bills and tossed it on the table in front of the bounty hunter. "Here's one hundred thousand. Consider it a down payment." Bane turned and started toward the exit. Stopping just shy of the door, he glanced over his shoulder. "I should very much like to finish our fight when this is all said and done."

Creed laughed, "Any time, suckhead."

***

The moon's ghostly face was partially hidden by rolling, heavy storm clouds. A smattering of rain trickled down from the sky around them. It was neither heavy nor light, but somewhere undecidedly in between. Several darkly clad figures weaved through the night toward their destination. Traveling light, none had more than a single

124

duffel bag slung over their shoulder. It would be dawn in less than an hour. They had to move quickly.

A single building occupied the nearly flat landscape. Well outside Pembroke, the small rural airstrip was in a state of disrepair. The runway was cracked and patched with jagged lines of asphalt as it stretched away from the small terminal. No longer in use, it had been of vital importance during the second world war to get supplies to war-ravaged London and the resistance in France. A single airplane sat quietly on the tarmac awaiting its passengers.

A figure stood next to the plane in the darkness, only the glowing red cherry of his cigarette visible. Still slightly groggy from being awakened at four in the morning, he rubbed his palm down over his face as he exhaled smoke into the night sky. Reaching over, he grabbed his Styrofoam coffee cup off the wing of the plane and took a heady sip of the thick, caffeinated beverage. Feeling the warmth spread down through his throat and into his stomach, he breathed a sigh of satisfaction. He flicked his cigarette away as the dark figures approached him.

"Tell that rat bastard Quinn that we're even after this," he said jokingly through a gravely, exhausted voice.

Saint stopped in front of the man and nodded. "I wish I could, Norm. Master Quinn died about a year ago."

Norm Bowie's jovial mood fell to the ground and shattered. "I'm so sorry, kiddo. I..." He paused and took a breath. "I didn't know."

Saint nodded.

"It's been a while since I've worked with Wraith," he tried to explain. Stopping, he knew it was pointless. "I never did get to properly thank you two for saving my ass," Norm said apologetically. "If you two hadn't been there, I would have been vamp food. Thank you."

Saint dropped her duffel bag at her feet. "Just doing our job. Are we ready to board?"

Norm nodded, understanding the quick change in topic. "Just topping off the tank," he said, pointing to a thick, yellow hose attached to the underside of the plane. "We'll be off the ground in less than twenty minutes. Go ahead and get your people loaded. I'll make the final preparations."

Saint turned and nodded to her squad of Wraith. Eight had decided to accompany her, Conrad, and Thomas on the mission. She frowned. They represented a major portion of the remaining Wraith protecting Great Britain. Without them…she stopped. There was no need to think of that right now. The mission had just begun. They didn't even know the size of Bane's army in America. It could easily be huge, or just a small scout force. She hoped for the latter. If that were the case, they might be able to stop an invasion before it even began. Reaching forward, she grabbed the hatch and pulled it open. The plane was just large enough to accommodate everyone and their sparse equipment, yet too small to make it across the Atlantic on one tank. Norm had told her a stop in Greenland and another one in Washington D.C. would be required to complete the flight. It was going to be a long trip, but she knew it had to be taken.

Wraiths couldn't really take a commercial flight anymore. Many of their weapons were constructed of metal, and in the post September 11th world, the airlines

126

frowned on that. Not that continent hopping was ever a major part of a Wraith's life, but sometimes, it was necessary. She was just lucky to have remembered that Norm owed her one. It beat the other option: a slow boat to America.

She was sure there was a joke in there somewhere.

Conrad and Thomas stood behind her watching the other Wraith board the plane. Saint turned and looked at the two. Conrad was obviously the most experienced leader on this mission, but he had abdicated to her. He explained this was her mission and he had no desire to take that away from her. He was as gracious and giving as ever. She appreciated his company and help.

Thomas on the other hand...

The two had grown up together at the academy. She had seen him grow from a sweet, quiet boy into the budding egomaniac he was today. He was good, there was no doubt there, almost as good as Saint herself, but there was no room for the ego and attitude in the Gwyliad Wriaeth—especially now. She wasn't sure she wanted his attitude, but she was certainly grateful for his assistance. He was a valuable warrior—if he would only learn his place, he could become one of the greatest Wraith to have ever picked up a scythe. Saint smiled at the two, barely exposing her fangs. She was, in the end, glad they were here.

"What are you smiling about?" Thomas asked with a smirk.

Saint laughed. "Just thinking about the time I kicked your ass in Basic Defense Class."

"I seem to recall Jeanie Gardner putting the smackdown on you later that same day," Thomas quickly retorted. "And if I remember correctly, she bloodied your nose, too."

Saint nodded with a chuckle. "Not my finest hour. Whatever happened to Jeanie?"

"Last I heard, she was on assignment in Japan with Master Yamamoto," Conrad interjected. "Haven't heard from either since before Bane's attack on the academy."

Saint nodded. She was nervous, and they could tell. She was making idle small talk to try and calm her nerves. She had led squads of Wraith into battle before, but this was somehow different. She was scared.

"I'm nervous, too," Thomas said.

A sly grin crossed Saint's face. "You were reading my thoughts again, weren't you?"

Thomas lowered his gaze, embarrassed he had been caught. "Sorry. It's almost become second nature. It's hard to turn it off sometimes."

She was continually amazed by his mental powers. They seemed to be growing by leaps and bounds every single day.

Thomas adjusted his long leather coat and moved past Saint toward the plane. Tossing his duffel inside, he stepped up and disappeared inside.

Saint took a step closer to Conrad and lowered her voice. "How's he doing?"

Conrad didn't take his gaze away from the plane. "Why do you ask?"

"He seems," Saint searched for the appropriate description, "different lately."

Conrad understood. "He's just going through growing pains. Thomas is struggling to find his place in the world, and it's a painful process. He doesn't always make the right choices, but that's part of growing up. You know."

Saint nodded in agreement. "Right there with you."

"He has a lot of power," Conrad added, "and sometimes, that frightens me. He could be too powerful for his own good." He stopped and thought about his student and his friend. "He just needs to learn control," Conrad assessed.

Saint was shocked at the raw honesty Conrad displayed. She bit her lip carefully to avoid puncturing it with her fangs. "I hope you're right."

Conrad turned to Saint and placed his hands on her shoulders. "I can't even begin to imagine the burden you carry. Just hearing the term 'Chosen One' bandied about makes me nervous."

"It's tough," she admitted. "But I just try and take it one day at a time. If I am the Chosen One." Saint paused to consider the statement and the ramifications. She had never referred to herself as chosen, let alone the key to an ancient prophecy. "I just can't think about that. I have to do my job."

Conrad smiled in a fatherly way at her. "Master Quinn would be very proud of you."

Saint let a soft smile creep onto her face. "Thank you." Spreading her arms, she leaned in and gave the Master Wraith a quick embrace. "That means a lot to me."

"We need to get going," Norm shouted from beneath the plane as he uncoupled the fuel hose. "We need to beat this storm out. Get on board."

Saint pulled away from Conrad and snatched her duffel bag from the ground. Turning, she and Conrad started to climb inside.

Thomas slowly turned away from the window where he had watched the whole scene. A dark shadow fell across his face as he considered Saint and Conrad's words. Leaning back into his seat, he felt a flame flare up in his heart. Closing his eyes, he gritted his teeth. He felt betrayed by his best friends.

They fear you…

Balling his fists, he pressed down hard on the armrests until he heard the metal support brackets begin to creak and groan in protest. Lifting his head, he took a slow breath and tried to calm down. He had to get control…the thought of the word angered him. How could he have spent so much time with two people and they barely knew who he was?

"Thomas, are you okay?"

He looked up into Conrad's concerned face. Unclenching his fists, he stuffed the anger deep down into a ball in his chest. "Yeah," he lied. "I'm fine."

Chapter Ten

Bane—beneath the "stranger" façade—walked slowly into the entrance with Raquel on his arm. She had chosen to have her dark hair very long tonight, falling down to her waist. Her almost porcelain white skin was offset by the silky black dress that dangled perilously off her shoulders by two thin straps and hugged every slender curve of her magnificent form. A tiny, swirling black tattoo emerged from the corner of her left eye and terminated in the center of her cheek. Bane, meanwhile, had chosen a black suit with a modern cut, a crimson tie, and a long black leather trench coat with a matching crimson silk interior. His tribal tattoo was tinged with crimson tips, as if they had been dipped in blood, and perfectly matched his attire and mood. There would be blood tonight. He would see to that.

Neither wore sunglasses, instead, choosing to reveal their golden preternatural eyes. There was no need to hide what they were tonight. All could sense it as they walked toward the tall, gothic building in the heart of San Francisco: this place was almost entirely populated by vampires. Bane laughed to himself. Ever since that idiotic work of fiction, Interview With The Vampire, came out, vampires flocked to the city by the bay to be part of what they considered to be the "scene." Most were fledglings that didn't know any better, or accidental creations that wanted to recreate their fantasy. Bane wanted to laugh in each of their faces. North America was relatively backwater in the vampire world. Most of the true lords had been born and risen to power before this self-serving, egomaniacal country had even been thought of. Europe was truly the place to be…and soon, it would all be his. Bane allowed a brief smile to wash across his face.

Three large goons moved slowly behind him, their faces blank as they kept a watchful eye on their lord. Each wore formal attire, dark glasses, and had concealed weapons beneath their coats. Flanking Bane and Raquel on the sides and rear, the goons attended to their masters' every need.

The Troika's guards lined the lobby of the building. It was a show of power and respect for the visiting Vampire Lord. Each stood fast in their assignments, never staring directly at Bane, nor altering their stance. The lobby was decorated with paintings Bane recognized for their historical value. Most—if not all—were originals as well. A fountain stood in the center of the room amidst the sea of marble floor. A stone angel stared up into the heavens as her wings partially wrapped around her body. She seemed cold, tired, and forsaken by her creator. Several streams of water, colored electric blue by lights in the fountain, arced over her back creating the illusion of rain around her. Bane knew this statue was very telling of the vampires he went to meet. Working around the fountain, Bane's party headed for the elevator bank at the rear of the room.

The guard who flanked the chrome doors immediately stepped forward to greet them. "Welcome, Lord Bane," he said evenly. "You are expected and everything is in order for your arrival." Reaching behind him, the guard tapped the elevator call button.

Bane nodded in approval.

The doors slid open with a chime and the guard stepped courteously out of the way. "Mr. Black, Mr. Yellow, and Mr. Blue are waiting for you on the observation deck, floor thirty-three." He motioned for Bane's party to enter the lift. "The doors will open directly onto the observation deck," he added in parting. "Enjoy your stay, Lord Bane."

One of Bane's goons tapped the top button on the panel. As the doors slid shut, they felt the lift slowly begin to rise. As the glowing blue numbers above the doors began to count up, they could feel the elevator accelerating.

"My Lord," Raquel breathed, "aren't you concerned that we're walking into a trap?"

Bane stood motionless, staring at the numbers. "No."

Raquel put her free hand on his chest. She knew she was skirting a severe reprimand by questioning him, but she needed to know. It was her life on the line tonight as well. "Why?"

"I know these men, this Troika," Bane replied. "I have encountered them before."

Raquel was surprised at the answer. "My Lord?"

"They are cowards," he answered quickly. "The Troika wasn't powerful, smart, or cunning enough to hold a coven together in Moscow, so they fled to America. Here, one needs only a pair of fangs to become successful."

"How do you know them?"

Bane turned to his aide and smiled, "I was part of the invasion force that pushed them out of Russia."

Raquel felt her heart fall into her stomach with a plop. Not only were they rival Vampire Lords, Bane and the Troika had a history together. This evening did not bode well for her survival.

She had joined Bane's campaign after the initial assault on the Wraith Academy. Her predecessor, a woman named Brigitte, had died in the assault by the hand of a High Wraith and a mere mortal. In death, she had disgraced her Lord. Raquel would not. This she had vowed to him, and herself.

A vampire for a mere twenty-eight years, she was still considered extremely young. Born and then reborn into darkness in the city of lights, Paris, Raquel had wasted many of her younger years as a revenant that rarely left the cemetery where she was buried. The small coven that took her into their folds believed that vampires should be the true monsters they were and not hide behind phony mental projections and disguises. Each was little more than an animated corpse in the rags they died in. To speak to a human, under any circumstances, was considered treason to the coven. Humans were merely a food source and nothing more.

But Raquel wanted more.

She would sneak out of her grave early in the morning before the sun came up to watch mortals laughing, loving, and enjoying being alive. Her life was little more than a chore at that point: wake, feed, repeat. She craved an actual life like the vampires from literature. She wanted to be beautiful, powerful, and seductive. It was these needs that led her to Bane. She heard rumors of a powerful Vampire Lord marching his army across the face of the continent, destroying all those who dared oppose him. They were everything she wanted to be, so she created an insurrection in her coven.

They would never let her go willingly. Her choice was life with them, or death. Either choice was death to her. As they sank into their dirty, musty coffins to sleep, Raquel put her plan into action. She had spent the previous weeks sneaking away from the cemetery and gathering the supplies she needed. Gasoline and dynamite were her weapons of choice. Dowsing each coffin in the gasoline, she carefully placed sticks of dynamite on their lids and taped them in place. Digging a trench away from the coven's coffins, she used the remainder of the gasoline to create a flammable channel.

Tearing off her ragged, filthy clothes, Raquel closed her eyes and activated her mental projection for the first time. She was once again the beautiful woman she had been in life standing in the middle of the cemetery just before dawn came. Draped in black satin, she bent down and tossed a match into the gasoline. She watched as the flames quickly spread and started to engulf the first coffin. As the lid broke open, a screaming vampire emerged only to be incinerated by the dynamite as it exploded. Turning, Raquel slowly walked away listening to the cries of her coven as they were either burned to death, or annihilated by the explosives. As the western sky began to turn pink, she knew the sunlight would kill any who escaped the flames. Moving out of the cemetery, she had to move quickly, or the sunlight would claim her, too. Finding the most lavish hotel she could, she used every power available to her and found herself in the most lavish suite she had ever seen.

She felt alive again, but she needed more. She wanted power. She sought out Bane in England after the fall of the Wraith Academy. Begging to join his army, he had accepted her as his personal aide after hearing her tale of triumph over her coven mates. She was everything he wanted in his second-in-command: ruthless, cunning, and vicious. She was perfect for the job.

Raquel turned and looked at the numbers above the doors rapidly approaching thirty-three. "Do we have a plan, Lord Bane?"

Bane nodded. "Wait for my signal," a terrible sneer grew across his lips, "and kill them all."

***

Her body felt groggy and tired, but her vampiric metabolism quickly worked to flush the remainder of the medication out of her system. Leaning over the black porcelain sink, Kat cupped her hands under the cool running water and splashed it on her face. Snatching a hand towel from its resting place to her right, she dabbed it on her face removing the excess water. Standing straight, she felt a shiver run down her spine. It had been ten years since the last time she looked into a mirror. This time around was no easier. She saw water droplets that seemed to be suspended in midair reflecting back at her, but she knew they were actually on her skin. Her lack of reflection just reinforced the fact she wasn't human anymore. Something she hoped to remedy if her plan came to fruition.

She had to focus. She was just hours away from her freedom.

Standing in front of the mirror, she felt inadequate somehow. In life—her mortal life—she had never been concerned with spending hours on her appearance. But now without her image, she felt as if she were missing a key component of herself. Closing her eyes, she imagined her long, blond hair pulled up with a wavy lock dangling down the right side of her face. She clad her frame in a slinky, black silk dress both sexy and seductive, yet still gave her the range of movement to complete her plan. Her fingernails were long and colored a deep shade of red that matched her lipstick. Slowly opening her eyes, she glanced down at her body to see it exactly as she imagined. She allowed herself a brief smile.

Being a vampire did have some advantages.

Stepping out of the restroom, she walked quickly across a small lobby and out onto the observation deck. It was a beautiful night in her hometown with the stars shining brightly overhead. Off the edge of the thirty-third floor, she could see the Golden Gate Bridge's red collision lights blinking on and off in the distance. The fog was beginning to waft in off the bay and to Kat, looked alive as it wound its way through the streets and enveloped buildings. A smattering of servants in white formal wear moved feverishly around a single, long table making last minute preparations. Three high-backed wooden chairs lined one end of the table for the Troika, while a matching—if not slightly smaller—chair occupied the opposite end for Lord Bane. Tasteful twinkling lights ran from the top of the lobby to the roof and created an almost magical feel. Three obviously vampire musicians sat in chairs on the far edge with their string instruments waiting to add atmosphere.

Turning, she watched the leaders of the Troika exit the elevator from the penthouse. All three looked identical in black suits except for their differently colored ties. Each wore a gold-rimmed pair of glasses with their blond hair slicked back to their scalps. Their gaunt, clean-shaven faces seemed almost elegant in the low light of the observation deck, but she knew monsters hid beneath. Tonight, she would make them pay and reclaim her life. She felt rage bubbling up in her chest as she stared at the three. Every movement, every word, every step they took just made her hate them more. She had to be patient though. Things were not in place yet. Mr. Blue moved to the table and took his seat to the right of the head chair while Mr. Yellow and Mr. Black stopped in front of Kat.

"It's good to see you again, Katherine," Mr. Yellow greeted. "I never had a chance to get an autograph from you before your unfortunate incarceration," he said with a smile. "Perhaps you could do so tonight."

Kat tried to fake a smile, even though she wanted to spit in the vampire's face. Her life as a writer seemed so far away, but it was pleasant to be reminded that she was more than just a monster.

"Your work has skyrocketed in value since your death," Yellow added. "Your novel has become something of a cult favorite. There's even talk of a feature film."

Of course there was. Now that her agent exclusively controlled the rights, she could do whatever she wanted. Plus, there was no need to send royalties anywhere except into her pocketbook. Kat gritted her teeth. She would have to kill her agent when this was all said and done. "Any casting rumors yet?"

Yellow nodded. "The buzz is that Brad Pitt is the frontrunner for the character of Simon."

Kat shook her head in disgust. That wasn't whom she

envisioned at all when she created the character.

Mr. Yellow reached over and placed his hand gently on her shoulder. "Please don't leave tonight before talking to me again. I have an idea for you about a possible sequel." He smiled softly, turned, and headed to join Mr. Blue.

Kat cocked her head slightly. He was so different from Mr. Black, yet she knew all three were cut from the same cloth. Maybe she would spare Yellow tonight. The night was young. She could decide later. She turned and focused her attention squarely on Mr. Black.

"Kat," he said slowly, "let's move to the opposite side of the deck." Placing his hand on the small of her back, he led her away from the ears of the others. Kat felt her flesh ripple with disgust at his touch. "We need to discuss tonight's operation. Are you prepared?"

Nodding, Kat took a step away from Black without making it look like she was trying to escape his touch. "I'm as ready as I'm going to get. What's the plan?"

Black reached into his jacket and pulled a silver cylinder free. It wasn't more than four inches long with a glass tube on the end filled with an amber colored fluid. The opposite end had a plastic cap over it, but she could clearly see a quarter inch long needle jutting from the tapered end. Holding it in his open palm, he presented it to Kat. "This is the weapon. Every drop of this toxin must make it into Bane's system or the plan will fail. Do you understand?"

Kat accepted the cylinder. Lifting up her dress, she placed it in the red garter she wore around her right thigh—a gift from Mr. Black and the one piece of real clothing on her body. "How do I deliver it?"

"That's up to you," Black breathed, staring at her exposed leg, "but I would suggest waiting until Lord Bane becomes comfortable and relaxes. Up until that point, you will act as my aide for the evening. You may sit at the table. Allow an appropriate distance between you and the rest of the Troika, but do not sit too far away, as it will seem suspicious."

Kat understood. "Is there a certain area on Bane's body I should inject?"

"Try for the upper arm, shoulder area," Black suggested. "That should introduce the toxin into his bloodstream fast enough."

"What then?"

"The virus is fast acting. Once he's human again, my men will descend on Lord Bane's party," Black sneered viciously, "and kill them all."

***

Eleven figures moved cloaked in the darkness at the base of the building. Sticking to the shadows in this urban jungle, each moved with speed and purpose. The war could end tonight right here. Thousands of Wraith had so far been claimed by Bane's march to power. The eleven were determined no more would join them. This would end here.

They were the best and the brightest warriors the order had left to offer. Each had seen more death than they cared to admit. They were guardians of life, after all, not bringers of death. Thomas often wondered if this was how it felt to be one of God's angels. What an odd dichotomy they must be, one hand lifted piously to the heavens, while the other was dipped in blood carrying out their Lord's commandments. The Wraith were much the same way: they sought to protect humanity from the waves of darkness it didn't even know existed, yet they were cold-blooded killers when necessary. It was the way it had to be. They knew it to be true, and tonight, they would continue a dance that had begun innumerable centuries ago. Before time had a name or system to be counted and measured, the two sides had fought. It was more than good versus evil, as those labels had become useless almost as quickly as they had been created.

It was life versus death.

And life was losing.

Coming to a stop, the eleven spread out and became motionless. They could clearly see several heavily armed vampires patrolling the entrance. Floodlights on the front of the building killed every shadow, while a nearly invisible laser alarm grid protected the perimeter. Barren of landscaping or anything that could be used to mask their approach, the building was designed to be impenetrable.

"They'll see us coming from a mile away," Thomas assessed.

Conrad, Saint, and Thomas crouched behind a large, blue dumpster opposite the vampire's building amidst a sea of concrete and asphalt. The remaining eight members of their squad were scattered across the parking lot, motionless.

Conrad nodded. "Maybe that's what we want."

Thomas looked at his master oddly for a moment before Conrad's idea became clear. "A diversion?"

Conrad nodded.

"It'll cost us Wraith," Saint said with disdain.

"I don't see that we have much of a choice," the Master Wraith concluded. "We have to get into that building and I don't see any other options. This is your party though."

Saint ran her fingers through her hair with a solemn look on her face. "What's the plan?"

"Split into three teams," Conrad started quickly. "Team One will be the diversion. Teams Two and Three will split up and assault the building." He looked into the eyes of the two young Wraiths. Both wanted a shot at Bane. He wouldn't deny them that. "I'll lead Team One. Saint, you take Two, and Thomas, Three. Each of you take two other Wraith with you, and I'll keep the extra two men down here to help. Understood?"

Saint and Thomas nodded. Reaching into his pocket, he produced three small two-way radios. Handing one to both Saint and Thomas, Conrad kept the third for himself. "I'm on channel five," he said, glancing at the black dial on the top. The two young Wraiths made the proper corrections to their radios. Conrad patted his apprentice on the shoulder, then quickly crawled off to inform the remaining Wraith of the plan.

Saint took a quick breath and looked at Thomas. "What's your plan?"

Thomas reached down and pulled his scythe hilt from his belt. "Find every vampire in that building," he smiled devilishly, "and kill them all."

Chapter Eleven

The three leaders of the Troika stood as the elevator chimed, announcing its arrival. They quickly straightened their jackets, ties, and brushed small bits of lint from each other like monkeys grooming each other in the wild. A last minute wave of worry crashed like waves through them. Tonight marked either the beginning of the Troika Empire, or the end of it. Each knew Lord Bane was more than a formidable opponent. To face him in single combat signaled one's doom, but tonight, they had an ace up their collective sleeve. Not above cheating, they would find a way to bring down Bane. Even if a thousand Wraith could not, they would find a way.

They signaled the half a dozen guards standing around the observation deck. There was no reason to hide snipers, or highly trained assassins. Some unseen tether of energy allowing them to sense one another connected all vampires. To try and hide any living thing from such a creature was pointless and often insulting. This tether extended from vampire to Wraith, but the binding was not as strong. Something about the way the virus mutated in the hunters weakened it. They could sense each other to a degree. To the hunters, it felt like little more than a disturbance. Yet it was there.

As the silver doors slid open, two of Bane's goons stepped quickly out and surveyed the area. Glancing from one Troika guard to another, the goons assessed the situation. They were hopelessly outnumbered. Just the way they liked it. Stepping to the side, they allowed their lord to exit. Bane and Raquel moved like spirits, not seemingly moving their legs, nor did their feet seem to touch the ground. They swept majestically from the lobby onto the observation deck and waited silently.

The Troika stood from the table and cautiously walked toward Bane. "Lord Bane," Mr. Black greeted with open arms, "thank you for accepting my invitation. I am Mr. Black, and these are my associates Mr. Blue, and Mr. Yellow."

"The Troika," Bane said. "A group of Russian vampires who fled the old world to conquer the new."

Black was slightly taken aback by Bane's knowledge of them. "Um yes." He paused, unsure how to proceed gracefully. "Would you care to be seated?"

Bane nodded.

Black snapped his fingers toward Kat. Getting up from her seat, she walked quickly—but gracefully— toward Bane's party. "My name is Katherine," she said with a smile. "I am Lord Black's aide."

Bane's hand on Raquel's arm loosened slightly at the sight of Kat. Perhaps he would have to get to know this woman better tonight.

"If there is anything you need," Kat added, sensing his interest, "don't hesitate to ask." She turned and extended her arm to the vampire lord. "Allow me to show you to your seat."

Abandoning Raquel all together, Bane slipped his arm around Kat. "Thank you, Katherine," he said in his deep, gravelly voice.

As Kat led Bane to his seat, she could feel the cold metal of the syringe against her leg. Pulling out Bane's chair, Kat allowed the lord to sit before she seated herself to his right. Raquel shot the woman a venomous glance as she sat down to her lord's left. Carefully adjusting her dress to cover the syringe, Kat smiled politely at Bane ignoring Raquel. She was inconsequential to Kat's plan, but would still have to be dealt with. She knew Bane's concubine would complicate the situation as she fought jealously for his attention. Kat didn't need this tonight. She had no interest in anything but her freedom.

The Troika moved to the other end and seated themselves with Mr. Black assuming the seat at the head of the table. "Perhaps we are seeing a new step in our evolution tonight," he offered. "Two Clans breaking bread together, as it were. Perhaps this is a taste of the future?"

Bane smiled at Black's empty toast. They both knew why they were here, and it wasn't to further relations between their two covens. Bane lifted an empty glass from the table and held it up. He watched everyone else at the table lift their glasses as well. "To the future."

"To the future," they all repeated honestly. It was the one thing each was actually thinking about.

"So, Lord Bane," Mr. Blue said casually, "you've made quite a name for yourself in Europe over the past year. Care to share any of your secrets?"

Bane nodded with a laugh. "The secret is actually quite simple." He steepled his hands in front of his face and stared at the Troika. "Kill all who stand in my way."

Black let the thinly veiled threat fall away without retort. "What brings you to the United States?"

"I had to make a personal visit to arrange a special job. Decided to take in a few of the sights while I was here."

Yellow's eyebrow jutted up slightly. "Special job?"

"It's nothing of consequence," Bane dismissed the question quickly.

The party fell into an uncomfortable silence.

Several of the Troika's servants emerged from a separate door in the lobby carrying bottles of what looked like wine on silver trays. As two moved to attend the Troika, one turned and walked cautiously toward Bane. "Drink, sir?"

"What's on the menu tonight?" Bane asked to Black more than the servant.

"It's from my private stock," Black answered smugly. "I think you'll approve."

Bane pushed his glass toward the edge of the table and nodded to the servant. He could see beads of sweat forming on the human's brow and became suspicious. "Katherine," he said as he reached over the table and snatched her waiting glass, "care to drink with me?"

Kat smiled politely. "I would love to."

Bane set her glass next to his on the table. As the steward uncorked the bottle, the vampires caught the scent of blood. Tipping the green glass bottle down, the man carefully poured the fluid into the glasses. Twisting it, the man stopped the pour perfectly and held the bottle in his arms. Moving to Raquel's glass, he repeated the process.

Raquel quickly snatched the drink and raised it toward her lips. Bane's hand shot out and grabbed her free hand stopping her. One quick glance from his burning golden eyes told her everything she needed to know. He turned back to Kat and smiled politely. "To the future," he echoed his earlier toast. The two vampires clinked their glasses lightly together.

"To the future," Kat said with a seductive smile. The scent of the blood was almost overwhelming her senses.

Lifting the glass to his lips, he watched Kat do the same. She took a deep drink of the blood and set the glass back on the table. Her blue eyes flashed gold for a moment as the blood ran down her throat. A wave of pleasure washed over her body at the taste of human blood again. Grabbing the edge of the table, she dug her fingernails into the wood and waited for the nearly orgasmic sensation to ease.

Satisfied that the blood wasn't poisoned or drugged, Bane lifted the glass to his nose and took a heady sniff. This was indeed quality stock. No trace of drugs—legal or illegal—or alcohol could be detected. He had found that the more mind and body altering substances humans injected, the more the taste of their blood soured. Tipping the glass back to his lips, he took a sip of the blood. He didn't like it cold, but it was of exceptional quality. He removed his hand from Raquel's to let her drink.

"Spectacular," Blue smiled, "isn't it?"

Bane swallowed down the rest of his glass in agreement. He had tasted blood similar only once in his life. On a pilgrimage to the Far East, he had encountered and killed a group of monks who were just as pure. "May I ask where this came from?"

Black nodded. "As I said, we have our own private stock. We keep a rotating stock of about ten humans in the cellar for drinking purposes only. It took quite a few years to figure out how to keep them in a comatose state without the use of drugs, but it was worth it."

Bane leaned forward as the steward poured him a

147

second glass. "How do you do it?"

Black turned and looked at his two companions for approval. As they nodded, he leaned back in his chair and lifted his half full glass of blood and began to swirl it gently. "Genetic engineering." Black waited to see Bane's expression change. When it didn't, he continued half-heartedly. "We breed our humans specifically for this purpose. All higher brain function is severed so basically, they're vegetables. This allows us to keep taking blood from them without sedating them. We keep them on a strict diet of proteins and vitamins to keep them healthy and alive."

Bane nodded in approval.

"Once a subject turns thirty-five, they're immediately killed so a new, younger donor can be brought in," Black continued. "Call it personal preference, but we just don't enjoy the taste of older blood."

Kat was horrified at the revelation. Pushing what was left of her glass away, she felt a knot growing in her gut. She imagined helpless, brain-dead babies and infants trapped in a darkened basement below them with blood tubes running out of their tiny arms and legs...all to feed these sadistic monsters. She wanted to be human again now more than ever. She gritted her teeth in anger but kept her cool.

"That seems like a lot of work just for some blood," Raquel interjected.

"To each their own," Black responded with a nonchalant shrug. "Our position affords us this kind of luxury. And since it's not us drawing blood from the veggies, who cares?"

"You are wasting your existence," Bane countered.

"You've taken everything that signifies being a vampire and sanitized it away. You're nothing more than overglorified humans." He scooted to the edge of his seat and stared intently at the Troika. "Do you remember what it feels like to use your fangs? To hunt your prey?"

Black erupted from his seat and slammed his fists against the table. "How dare you insult us?"

Bane quickly tried to hide his smile. He was trying to get a rise out the Troika, and apparently succeeded. Dinner was just about over. "I meant no insult," he said diplomatically, "I just wanted to point out what I saw as obvious."

"Which is?" Black remained standing and was joined by the two other members of the Troika.

Bane's three goons took positions around their lord. Folding their hands behind their back, each settled in and became motionless. Their expressions were blank, but they were ready. Behind their dark glasses, they eyed the Troika guards warily. They could sense the guards becoming agitated.

Kat lowered her hand under the table and began to hike up her dress. Rolling her fingers gently around the syringe, she pulled it free of the garter. She cradled it in her hand.

Bane slowly stood from his seat and smiled broadly at the Troika. It was time. He'd had enough of them. "That you three have become, completely and utterly, a useless waste of vampires and deserve to be wiped from the face of the planet."

Just then, all hell broke loose.

***

149

Conrad's team of four stood just beyond the laser perimeter. Behind them, Saint's and Thomas' teams of Wraiths stood ready for battle. Drawing their weapons, each hunter activated their scythe.

Thomas looked at Conrad and extended his hand. "Good hunting, Master."

Conrad took his apprentice's hand and shook it firmly. "To you as well." He paused. "You're buying when this is finished."

"The hell I am," Thomas protested with a chuckle. "I bought last time and I had more kills. It's your turn."

Conrad laughed. "Fine. Drinks are on me." He looked at the young Wraith's face for a long moment. He had seen Thomas grow from a boy into a young man and a capable, powerful warrior. If he were guilty of anything, it would be pride in his student. He had known since the beginning Thomas would become a powerful hunter. Letting go of his student's hand, he nodded and turned back to the perimeter.

Thomas stepped to the right and checked the duffel bag over the shoulder of one of Conrad's men a final time. Making sure everything was in place, he nodded to his master. They knew they were already visible to the Troika guards, but the Wraiths were also aware the vampires wouldn't attack and abandon their posts. As long as they stood there, the Wraiths were in no danger.

But that wasn't the plan.

Conrad set his jaw and took a step forward. As his leg broke the laser beams of the alarm system, the area was suddenly flooded with even more light and the grinding sound of klaxons. Spinning his scythe around, he leaned forward and charged toward the oncoming onslaught of Troika guards.

As the Wraith cut a swath into the volley of guards, the team of four separated into groups of two. Holding back the waves of clawing monsters, they opened a path for Teams Two and Three to the entrance. As Saint and Thomas made a dash for the doors, Conrad's men turned and continued to hold off the guards. They had to buy the other teams more time to get inside. All knew they would face heavy opposition once inside. They didn't need to worry about more guards spilling in from outside. It was an entire building of vampires loyal to the Troika.

This wasn't going to be easy.

Silver scythes twirled and sparkled in the bright lights as they cut through the bodies of vampires. A hellish blue blaze of fire began to grow around the five Wraiths threatening to engulf them. A scream sliced through the sound of the alarms as the first Wraith fell. With no time to look over his shoulder to see who had fallen, Conrad continued to fight. Whipping off the head of the nearest vampire, he reversed his swing and buried the blade of his weapon in the torso of another attacker between the neck and shoulder. Tearing it free, he swung his whole body around and chopped the vampire in two.

"Regroup!" Conrad yelled as the vampires forced him back.

The sound of a shotgun blast drew his full attention. Snapping his head around, he saw another of his Wraith spill to the ground, a huge, bloody hole in his chest. Cursing under his breath, Conrad stepped over the dying Wraith's body and charged toward the attacker. A large vampire with platinum blond hair sneered at the Wraith.

151

Conrad heard the weapon cock. Lunging forward, he swung his weapon over his head and felt it hit solid metal. Deflecting the barrel just as the vampire pulled the trigger, Conrad whipped the end of his scythe forward and smacked the monster hard across the temple. The Master Wraith pressed his attack as the monster stumbled back. Completing the circle around his body with the light and powerful weapon, Conrad twisted the blade up at an angle and connected with the vampire's chest. Using all his preternatural strength, he continued to cut through flesh and bone until the vampire's head and left arm fell away.

He felt the sting of four claws rip down the flesh of his back. Stifling a grunt of pain in his throat, he leapt backward into the air just as the vampire attacked again. Conrad somersaulted and came down directly onto the monster, crushing it to the ground. Stabbing his weapon down into the cranium of the vampire, he heard a faint gurgle as the creature died. Spinning, Conrad vaulted out of the center of the ravenous pack of revenants and landed next to his last remaining Wraith. A long bloody gash ran across the Wraith's nose and cheek completely splaying the soft flesh open. Blood poured from the wound. Turning back to the vampires, he watched at least thirty pairs of golden eyes bearing down on him. He knew in that instant the two of them couldn't hold the vampires off any longer. He had to sound the retreat.

Conrad hoped he had given Saint and Thomas enough time.

***

As the Troika's guards advanced on Bane, a large smile grew across his face. He had been patient, but this was what he had been longing for. His three goons stepped forward and easily held off the poorly trained Troika guards. He had time. Dropping his mental projection, Bane quickly lifted his mask and slid it over his face. Tossing his long, billowing cloak back over his shoulders, he revealed two long, curved blades attached to his forearms. He pressed an unseen button with both hands and the blades snapped forward ready for battle.

Turning to his right, he watched Raquel's mental projection change. She was suddenly swathed in black, much like Bane. Drawing two compact submachine guns she had hidden on her back, she snapped off the safeties. Grinning at her lord, she immediately turned toward Kat and lowered her weapon. Leveling the other at the three shocked Troika still standing at the head of the table, she pulled the triggers.

Kat dove under the table just as the bullets shredded the chair where she had been sitting. Holding the syringe carefully, she snapped her head to the right just in time to see Bane's legs disappear. She had to get out of here. Slipping the syringe back into her garter, she summoned all her courage and strength. Diving forward, she wrapped her arms around Raquel's legs knocking the woman to the ground.

Bane landed on the balls of his feet on the table. Charging forward with near lightning speed, he lunged at Mr. Black with his dual arm blades pointed directly at the Vampire Lord's chest. To his amazement, Black rolled back avoiding the attack. Snapping his arm blades back, Bane landed on his hands just beyond the Troika and

153

vaulted up onto his feet like an Olympic gymnast. Spinning, he snapped his arm blade back out just in time to block Mr. Blue's lunge with a broadsword. Holding the vampire at bay, Bane turned to see Mr. Yellow and Black pulling similar swords from a hidden cache beneath the table. He laughed out loud in sheer joy.

This was getting better and better.

***

Pushing through the front doors, Saint's and Thomas' teams immediately assaulted the remaining Troika Guards in the lobby. The two best and brightest warriors in the order easily cut a swath of death through the resistance. Blades spun too fast for the human eye to follow as they pushed through to the back of the spacious room. Vampires fell to the ground one after another in an inferno of unholy blue flame. Those behind Saint and Thomas had little to do but avoid the carnage.

Hitting the edge of the fountain with his booted foot, Thomas leapt high into the air, somersaulted, and perched perfectly atop the back of the stone angel. His black coat billowed around him like an unholy demon expelled from Hell as he held his glimmering silver scythe across his body. Fire burned in his heart. It was not of rage or anger, but of pure pleasure. He was engulfed by it, becoming one with the battle. His movements, his actions were no longer his own. He was controlled by the moment. Letting go of his conscious mind, he became the perfect engine of destruction. Standing tall on the statue, he shot forward like a diver, arms wide and chest pushed out. Snapping his scythe into both hands, he executed a controlled flip and landed directly in the center of five waiting vampires. Before they had a chance to attack, Thomas had already ended their existences with a quick swipe of his weapon.

Saint, an equally powerful warrior, was nowhere near as flashy as Thomas. Her moves were concise, controlled, and perfectly timed. Each attack used only the minimum amount of energy required, as she knew she had to conserve for the long battle ahead. But while she knew her limits, she couldn't say the same about Thomas. He seemed like a nuclear furnace that never tired in battle, no matter how much energy he expended. Her style was much more like Conrad's than Thomas'. She was technically proficient in every fighting form the academy taught, but not an ostentatious or brassy warrior. And that was exactly the way she liked it.

Carving through the final vampires in the lobby, the two teams stopped just short of the elevator's polished doors. Thomas snapped his head around and stared at the main entrance. He waited.

"I'm sure he'll be here any minute," Saint assured him.

Thomas nodded.

"We should go back and help them," one of Thomas' Wraiths spoke up.

"We don't have time," Thomas barked as he continued to stare at the empty doors. "We have to stay on mission."

"Suggestions?" Saint asked, staring at the elevator. "If we load up into the elevator, they'll lock us down and trap us."

She was correct. Measures were already being taken

by Troika security to lock down the building.

Thomas motioned to his right, then left. "Stairwells on both sides. That'll give us access." He finally turned his attention away from the entrance and looked at Saint. "Where is he?"

Saint closed her eyes for a moment and reached out with her senses. Her brow furrowed, "I can't tell." She felt a shooting pain in the center of her forehead. Snapping her eyes open, she pulled back quickly. "They have psychic blockers on premises." She lifted her hand and rubbed her forehead gently. "I can't sense him."

"We're going to have to do this the old-fashioned way," Thomas said with a grin. "Search and destroy."

Saint agreed. Patting her friend on the shoulder, she leaned close to his ear. "He'll be okay."

Thomas tightened his jaw.

Turning away, Saint pointed toward the right stairwell. Snapping her weapon open, she led them up and around the first corner disappearing from sight.

With one final glance to the main entrance, Thomas activated his scythe as well. Taking point, he charged toward the left stairway with his two Wraiths in tow. He pumped his legs hard up the stairs steadily increasing speed. The fire in his heart had been fundamentally changed. No longer pleasure, it burned with raw emotion...teetering on the edge of pure rage.

Chapter Twelve

Saint poked her head slowly around the corner. Ahead she could see several Troika guards hovering at the end of the connecting hallway. Motioning to the two Wraiths behind her on the stairs, she indicated silently there were four vampires and what direction they were in. The two nodded understanding. Turning back to the hall, she peered in the opposite direction just in time to see Thomas' team dash across and disappear into a connecting hallway like shadows. Her team had no such luxury. The only way to go was directly toward the vampires.

It was time.

Snapping her scythe closed, she attached it to her belt. Pulling off her leather trench coat, she tossed it to the floor revealing the tight, midriff length tank top she wore. A pair of formfitting, low-rise, black leather pants covered her legs and terminated in the heavy black boots she favored. Tossing her long, black hair over her shoulder, she cocked her head to the right, then the left. As her spine popped and crackled, she lifted her scythe off her black studded belt. Glancing over her shoulder, she checked her two Wraiths for readiness. As they nodded, she took a step into the hallway.

She hit a dead sprint as she charged toward the vampires. Activating her scythe, it sprang open quadrupling in length. Whipping it across her body, she excised the first vampire's head before the others even knew she was upon them. As the vampires turned to face her, two more were cut down by Saint's Wraiths. Winking at the final Troika guard, Saint jabbed the wooden tip of her scythe into his chest as his golden eyes widened in horror. Pulling her scythe back and snapping it closed, she reattached it to her belt as the vampire crumbled to ash around her.

Turning to face her two Wraiths, she heard the first gunshot.

Blood splattered on her as the Wraith fell forward and crumbled to the ground. Lifting her head, she stared into the empty hallway. Saint couldn't see, or sense, anything. Her head whipped to the left as two more gunshots echoed through the confined space. She watched in horror as the second Wraith slammed against the wall and slowly slid to the floor leaving a thick blood trail behind. Saint reached for the scythe on her belt but felt it knocked away by some unseen force. A vicious jab to her jaw snapped her head back. A second bloodied her nose while she was still stumbling. Bringing her arms up defensively in front of her face, she took two hard punches to the ribs that nearly knocked the wind out of her. A final blow to the head sent her spilling to the ground.

Looking up, she saw her attacker materialize above her. Tall and powerfully built, Talon Creed's cleanly shaven head glistened with a few drops of sweat. Clad in a pair of black jeans and a tight black t-shirt that seemed to barely stretch across his strapping chest, he slid his pistol into the holster strapped to his thigh. A pair of black oval sunglasses covered his eyes. His face was expressionless as he glared at the young Wraith.

Reaching up, he grabbed a small talisman that hung

158

around his neck. Pulling it free, he tossed it down next to Saint. "I'll have to thank the witch doctor," his low voice rumbled, "his masking spell worked perfectly."

Saint wiped the blood from her nose on the back of her hand. "Who are you?" She wasn't sure she expected an answer, but she wanted to buy herself some time. Her body throbbed with pain. She sniffed the air and instantly understood. Danger signs in her mind flashed a single word: werewolf.

"Doesn't matter," Creed answered. Digging into his pocket, he produced a small, glittering object wrapped in what looked like a plastic bag. Unwrapping it with his meaty paws, he was careful not to touch the surface. Creed held it up in front of his face by the edges. He looked at the roughly silver dollar-sized object. Almost perfectly round and no more than a quarter of an inch thick, it was intricately carved with symbols and pictures Saint didn't recognize. "Ever seen one of these?"

Saint said nothing. Slowly, she pulled herself into a sitting position as the pain subsided.

Creed smiled. "Why don't you take a closer look?" He tossed the object to the young Wraith.

Out of instinct, Saint snatched the object out of the air before it could hit her body. A tingling sensation shot up her arm like electricity. Her mind screamed to let the object go, but the message was lost somewhere before it reached her hand. As a tremor ran over her body, she felt paralysis set in. It was as if her brain was somehow disconnected from her body, floating in the distance unable to communicate. Her hand still clamped around the coin, she flopped to the floor helplessly.

"I'll have to thank the witch doctor for that, too,"

Creed said as he knelt down next to her. Snatching her scythe from the ground, he held it in his open palm and admired the craftsmanship. Bands of gold wound around the silver skin beautifully like a wild vine. Rolling it over, he looked at the activation button located in almost the exact center of the hilt. He wanted to touch it, to see the weapon spring to life, but he denied himself. There would be time to admire his new trophy later. He still had work to do.

Placing his hand on Saint's leg, he tested the good doctor's work. The talisman in his pocket was working. The coin had no effect on him. Grabbing the Wraith around the waist, he slung her over his shoulder and stood up. As he walked down the stairs, Creed snatched Saint's coat and flipped it over his opposite shoulder. Turning, he headed for the exit.

***

Bane blocked another attack with the edge of his arm blade. Instead of retaliating—which would have been the logical move—he pushed Mr. Yellow back easily. He didn't want to kill them yet. He was enjoying the dance too much. "You are all just as clumsy as you are stupid," he taunted as he dropped down into a defensive posture. "You disappoint me. I'm sure you can do better."

The Troika glanced at each other, then to Bane. Holding their broadswords with both hands, all three lunged forward simultaneously and attacked. Parrying the blades, Bane knocked them down and held them in place. Using his free arm, he swiped his blade across Black's chest. The attack, only meant to insult, cleaved Black's tie and splayed open his finely tailored white shirt. Releasing the Troika's weapons, Bane stepped back and stood tall. He had no reason to fear them.

He was in total control.

The situation quickly began to bore him. He wanted a challenge. This was too simple. Deciding it was best to end this, he lifted his blades and went on the offensive again. Pushing forward, he listened to the clink and clatter of his blades meeting theirs. Almost musical to his ears, he pressed harder and faster. The three were easily overmatched by Bane's superior skills. Snapping his curved blade over and under, he knocked Mr. Yellow's sword free from his hands. Using a similar move on Mr. Blue and Mr. Black, he disarmed the Troika. Kicking their swords away, Bane loomed over the three vampires like death itself. His yellow eyes burned behind his golden mask as he moved in for the kill.

Throwing his blade toward the nearest target, Bane jabbed straight into Mr. Blue's chest. To his surprise, nothing was there to stop his forward momentum. Stumbling completely through the Vampire Lord, Bane snapped his head around and looked in confusion. His eyes widened, then narrowed as he understood. Standing tall again, he turned and faced the three lords...or rather, one Vampire Lord. "Interesting tactic."

Mr. Black smiled as he faced Bane. "I was hoping it would come to this."

Bane nodded. "When did your brothers die?"

"You should know," Mr. Black answered. "You were there."

"Ah," Bane said slowly. "They were killed when Lord Atreus drove you from Moscow."

"Atreus was a fool," Black spat. "He lived in his little corner of Europe for centuries until you showed up." His anger was bubbling over as his voice turned into a roar. "What exactly did you have to whisper in his ear to make him attack me? What promises of grandeur did it take to make him want to claim my homeland? Why did you take my brothers away from me?"

"I was a bit of a troublemaker back then," Bane said dryly. "No offense, I just wanted to raise a little hell."

Black's eyes flared like fireballs in his skull. Opening his arms wide, Mr. Blue and Mr. Yellow turned and walked straight into Black's chest. With a roar that sounded more animal than human, Black leaned back just as an intense white light shot from his mouth and eyes. Black's body twisted, contorted, snapped and transformed as he roared in pain. His human visage melted away revealing a twisted, decaying corpse that was more skeleton than human. His entire mouth was filled with row after row of razor sharp teeth that would look more at home in a great white shark than in a vampire. Two black horns sprouted from his forehead and curled back around his head like a ram's. Arching forward, he roared again as two huge, batlike wings sprouted from his back and fanned out.

Bane held his ground.

"I know you made a deal with the Devil to attain your army," Black accused. His voice sounded like three tortured souls trying to scream and moan together. "So I made a deal of my own." He stepped toward Bane. "Tonight, you'll pay for everything you took from me." Black lunged forward and slammed his massive fist into the floor, just missing Bane and creating a huge crater.

Leaping backwards, Bane flipped in midair and landed on the table. A hidden smile crept across his face. Launching into the air, he attacked the beast head on.

***

Thomas and his two Wraiths surged through a pack of Troika guards. Blades spinning, the three neither slowed, nor stopped. As blue flame, ash, and cinders surrounded them, they kept moving forward. As the last vampire fell under the scythe's blade, the three Wraiths slowed and finally stopped. Looking back at the damage, they saw the blue vampiric flames spawning bright yellow and red ones on the floor, walls, and ceilings. The fire was spreading…and blocking their exit. There was nowhere to go but up. A loud bell began to sound on the floor as the fire alarms were tripped. Sprinklers emerged from the ceiling and tried to dowse the flames, but the fire had already taken hold. Thick clouds of smoke were beginning to form along the ceiling and moving quickly through the hall.

Lowering his head, Thomas wiped the water from his face as the smoke stung his eyes. He gritted his teeth. He didn't have time for this. His eyes narrowed. With each moment that passed without a signal from Conrad, the fire in his heart grew more intense. He would find retribution in this place, even if he had to tear down the very walls with his bare hands to get it. Flipping up the collar of his jacket, he hunched slightly, his wet hair obscuring his face. A dark shadow seemed to fall over him.

Motioning over his shoulder, he and the remaining

Wraiths continued on. Turning the corner, Thomas spotted a form moving in the distance. He couldn't quite make out what it was as the water washed into his eyes. Picking up his pace, he held his scythe firmly in his right hand. He saw it again. Stopping, he pointed up the hall. His two men nodded having also seen it. Holding up his hand, Thomas motioned for the two to hold their position.

Moving lightly, he saw the form dart across the hall in front of him and disappear into an adjoining hallway. Pressing his back to the wall, he inched closer to the door. Stopping at the frame, he carefully peeked inside. He could make out no more than three men. He glanced back to his two Wraiths and motioned for them to continue holding. He could take care of this himself. Holding his scythe tightly in his hands, he dove around the corner and was on the attack. Whipping the blade over his head, he felt it hit the first figure satisfyingly in the chest. Ripping it free, he watched blood splatter on the wall as the body slumped to the floor…but no blue flames. No ash.

He was human.

"Wait! We're not vampires!" one of the men shouted in defense. "Please don't kill us!"

Thomas turned and glared at the remaining two men. His eyes were cold and hard. "You serve the Troika?" His voice sounded disconnected, as if it weren't him speaking.

The men nodded nervously, unsure what the Wraith wanted to hear.

Wipe them out, Thomas. All of them…

Thomas paused, his conscience screaming through the haze of anger in his brain. Quickly, the fire in his heart exploded, annihilating any trace of a conscience. It

164

didn't matter if these were mere servants. They helped the vampires who killed his Master, his best friend, his father…

"You serve the enemy," Thomas growled. Using his telekinesis, he slammed the door shut behind him and raised his scythe.

Stepping outside, he closed the door and locked it from the inside using his mind. Turning, Thomas came face to face with his two Wraiths. "Nothing in there," he said quickly. "Let's keep moving."

The two Wraiths turned to each other, then back to Thomas. Moving past him, they continued deeper into the compound. Thomas slowly turned and followed.

"Come in, Thomas. Do you copy?"

Thomas excitedly fished the two-way radio from his pocket. "Master?"

There was a pause and some static.

"Yes. Heavy losses outside," Conrad reported. "What's your situation?"

"We're on the sixth floor," Thomas answered, "heading up."

"Get to the elevators," Conrad instructed. "I have control of the security room. We need to get to the observation deck."

"We're heading to the elevator, Master."

"I'll meet you in the elevator. I'm on my way up right now. Conrad out."

Thomas smiled from ear to ear. Glancing down at the black and yellow two-way radio in his hand, he saw a smudge of blood across the front from his fingertips. He suddenly realized what he had just done. Guilt washed over his body like a waterfall. He felt weak, as if he were about to crumble to the ground.

One of his Wraiths grabbed his arm and supported him. "Are you okay?"

Thomas wanted to scream no, but instead, nodded his head with his best fake smile. "Just a little overwhelmed, I guess."

The Wraith nodded. "It's good to know that Master Verge is alive." He paused. "We should get going."

Thomas agreed. Standing straight, he found his strength. Glancing over his shoulder, he looked back at the locked door one last time. Doing his best to shake off the nausea, he looked away and started down the hall.

***

The two vampires crumbled to the ground. Raquel ripped her leg free of Kat's grasp and kicked the woman hard in the nose. Sitting up, she leveled her machine guns at Kat's head and slipped her fingers into the trigger guards. Kat reacted without thinking. Lurching forward like a cat pouncing on its prey, she threaded the needle between the two guns just as Raquel fired. Kat's hands snapped around Raquel's head. Using every bit of her immense strength, Kat slammed Raquel's skull into the floor repeatedly until she heard a gratifying crunch of bone.

Bringing the weapon in her free hand up, Raquel pressed the barrel into Kat's side. Smiling at her opponent with burning golden eyes, Raquel pulled the trigger. Two bullets ripped through the soft flesh of Kat's side and out her back. Screaming in pain, Kat punched Raquel solidly in the face. As her head snapped back against the ground again, the machine guns tumbled from Raquel's hands. Lunging forward, the two vampires struggled for control of the weapons. Kat focused all her strength as her nails dug into Raquel's flesh. Rearing back, Kat delivered a quick one two combo to Raquel's eyes and finished by crushing down on the vampire's throat. As Raquel coughed involuntarily, Kat leapt ahead and snatched one of the lost machine guns.

Her hand wrapped around the handle just as a searing blast of pain ripped through her left thigh. Glancing back, Kat looked in horror at Raquel biting into her leg. Swinging the weapon around, Kat hastily aimed at her attacker and squeezed the trigger. A volley of bullets tore into Raquel's head and shoulders. The vampiress screamed in pain. While not deadly, Kat knew it hurt like hell. Taking the opportunity, Kat kicked out, her foot connecting just below Raquel's chin. The force of the impact sent Bane's aide skidding back a few feet. Rolling up onto her knees, Kat cradled the black machine gun in both hands and fired again. She watched in delight as bullet after bullet shredded Raquel's torso.

Letting the weapon fall to her side, Kat watched Raquel lay motionless. She wasn't dead, but it would take some time to recover from that. Her side throbbed with pain but she could feel her vampire chemistry healing the wound. Looking down, she saw that the bullet holes had almost closed completely and the bleeding had all but stopped. Running her hand over her lower back, she could feel no trace of the exit wound. She was relieved as the pain started to subside.

Pulling up her dress, she wrapped her fingers around the syringe. Feeling moisture on her fingertips, she pulled the syringe free of her garter and stared at it. She uttered a curse under her breath as she stared at a long crack that ran down the length of the glass tube. Over half of the amber fluid was gone. Lifting the syringe to her left shoulder, she popped off the safety cap and pressed it hard into her flesh. Tapping a button on the sheath, she heard a hiss and an immediate burning sensation as the fluid emptied into her body.

She started to feel light-headed as the chemical worked its way through her body. Her face flushed and her vision became blurry as she took an uneasy step back. Pain ripped through her side again. Looking down, she pressed her palm to her side where the wound had been. Pulling it away, she stared at the crimson blood smeared across her hand. The wound had reopened. Reaching out for the edge of the table to steady herself, the tablecloth gave way sending her spilling to the ground. Drawing a painful breath into her lungs, she felt a gurgle at the bottom. Kat coughed hard. Wiping her hand across her lips, she cringed as more blood was smeared there. She was dying.

Again.

Something went wrong. The injection wasn't working correctly. Black had lied to her. She was sure it wasn't working to make her human again, but rather destroying her from the inside out. Rolling over in pain, she wrapped her arms around her chest. Her eyes caught the glimmer of something silver lying next to her. It was one of the sterling silver serving trays the steward had used to deliver the blood during dinner.

Her eyes widened.

She could see her reflection in its polished surface.

168

Reaching over, she snatched the tray and pulled it close to her face. She stared at her vampiric features in shock. As the world darkened around her, she saw her blood spilling over her lips. She ran her shaking fingertips gently over the reflection, welcoming it as if it were an old friend.

Dropping the tray, Kat rolled onto her back and laughed.

The now familiar sound of the elevator chime caught her attention. Rolling her head to the right, she saw the polished doors slide open and several men and women in long, dark coats charge onto the observation deck. Her genetic memory told her exactly what they were: Wraiths. It didn't matter anymore. Closing her eyes, she took another labored breath and lost consciousness.

Chapter Thirteen

Thomas' eyes widened as he stared across the observation deck.

There she was, lying in a pool of blood. A sudden memory hit him like a landslide. It felt like his dream. It was exactly like his dream. Every detail matched perfectly from the color of her hair, her blue eyes, to the trickle of blood that ran down her cheek from her lips. As the remaining Wraiths—including Master Verge— charged toward Bane, Thomas stumbled forward as if drugged. His feet and hands felt like bricks of concrete dragging him down. His world suddenly seemed out of sync, as if he were no longer in reality. The color bled away leaving only her lying before him. His scythe fell from his hand and clattered to the floor as he dropped to his knees beside her. He slowly lifted his hand toward her face, but couldn't bring himself to touch her. Steeling his nerves, he gently placed his fingertips on her pale skin. Cool to the touch, he felt his heart sink.

He was too late.

Running his fingers down her face, an overwhelming curiosity gripped him. He had to know, once and for all. Placing his thumb on her upper lip, he carefully pushed it back revealing her teeth below. With a gasp at the sight of the two perfect fangs, he yanked his hand away as if burned. She was a vampire... Sliding one hand under her neck and his other around her waist, he carefully pulled her onto his lap. Cradling her in his arms, he felt a deep sense of pain and loss. He had dreamt of her for years. He knew she was meant for him and yet the fates had conspired to give him a glimpse of his possible future and quickly yank it away. He felt empty inside, hollow. A single tear rolled down his cheek and dropped onto her face.

He saw her eyelids flutter slightly.

In that moment, he decided to change fate. He would not lose her. Reaching into his coat, he retrieved a small pocketknife and snapped open the blade. Drawing it across his wrist, he felt the metal sting as it sliced through his flesh. Blood welled up in the cut. Thomas balled his fist several times to get his blood pumping. Pressing his wrist to her mouth, he waited.

Nothing.

Another tear ran down his cheek as he started to feel panicked. Still, there was nothing.

Leaning over, he placed his forehead against hers and whispered gently to her, "Please…"

He felt her lips move.

Sitting up, he watched her mouth open around the cut. He began to feel suction on his flesh and in his veins as she drew the blood into her mouth. She swallowed for the first time. And again. She was building strength. He felt her breath moving in and out as his life flowed into her. Lifting her hand, she pressed it firmly to Thomas' arm holding it in place. He let her drink. He would let her take every drop if he knew she would survive. He wanted to let go completely. He wanted to live in this moment forever.

Stopping, her head fell back and her golden eyes snapped open. Trying to focus, Kat looked at the man holding her in his arms. An expression of recognition washed over her. She knew him from somewhere. Her mind struggled to comprehend. Her eyelids felt heavy. She was still very weak. Smiling at the man, she rolled into his arms feeling completely comfortable and safe.

Sliding his hand beneath her legs, Thomas lifted Kat from the ground and stood up. Staring across the observation deck, he saw his fellow Wraiths fighting not only Bane, but also a horrible monster. He had to help. It was his duty, but he wanted to turn and take her away from here. He resolved himself. Turning away from the battle, he rushed Kat to a far, dark corner of the deck. Placing her gently down on the floor, he couldn't manage to take his gaze off her. He ran his hand over her cheek. "Wait for me."

Kat didn't respond.

Standing, Thomas looked over her one more time. Emotions he didn't fully understand rushed unchecked through his brain. Nothing seemed to make sense. He had to fall back to the one thing he did understand: battle. Turning, he lifted his hand and summoned his scythe to it. He walked slowly and deliberately toward the battle. His face was calm as his black coat wafted around him.

Soon, this would all be over.

**

As one of Thomas' Wraiths crumbled dead to the ground, Conrad lunged forward and slashed at the beast. Missing, he continued the spin of his weapon over his back until he connected. Following through, he sank down into a defensive position as a chunk of the beast's horn clattered to the ground.

172

That was his first mistake.

The beast charged, throwing his massive frame at Conrad. Launching into a countermeasure, Conrad whipped his blade around and back slicing across the monster's chest. Flipping backward, he kicked up hard with his booted feet and connected with the creature's chin. The Master Wraith landed solidly and attacked again. He brought his scythe over and down, but this time, the beast anticipated him. The curved blade missed the beast's head, but still connected. The beast roared in anger as the blade pierced the flesh of his arm. Snapping its hand up, it grabbed the weapon with the Master Wraith still attached and lifted him into the air. Even with being shaken side to side, Conrad refused to let go.

That was his second mistake.

The beast whipped the Master Wraith over his shoulder and slammed him hard into the floor. He felt his leg break under the impact. Conrad struggled to take a breath as the wind was knocked out of him. Managing to roll to the left to avoid the beast's next attack, Conrad watched as one of Thomas' Wraiths threw himself into the battle to engage the monster's attention. Charging in, the Wraith dropped his shoulder and hit the beast solidly in the chest like a professional linebacker. The beast stumbled slightly but wasn't amused by the effort. Snapping his huge, clawed hands around the Wraith's head, the beast snarled. Lifting the Wraith off the ground, he sneered at Conrad and easily flipped the Wraith off the roof.

Conrad leaned forward in shock and watched his comrade sail into the night to his inevitable death.

Like a shadow in the night, Bane materialized

173

directly behind the beast. As his eyes glowed and his dark cloak wafted around him, he snapped his arm blades forward. The Wraith would not take credit for this kill—if they even could—this was his victory. He would destroy the Troika, and then the Wraith. Leaping toward the beast, Bane brought his blades across and sliced off one of the batlike wings. Rearing back as blood sprayed from the excised appendage, the beast spun and knocked Bane to the ground. Diving forward, the beast slammed into Bane with every ounce of his strength. The Vampire Lord felt his rib cage start to give way.

"You don't have the power to destroy me," the beast hissed. He leaned close enough to Bane's mask to see his breath on the cool metal. "Tonight, I take command of your army. Look around you, they're all dead."

The beast was right. Every one of Bane's and the Troika's men had fallen in combat. Even Raquel and Kat lay dead or dying. The casualties had been heavy on both sides.

"They mean nothing to me," Bane admitted. "I came here to kill you, Black." He glanced quickly over the beast's shoulder at the approaching shadow. "When I walked through those elevator doors tonight, you were already dead. And now," he watched the shadow raise his shimmering weapon, "it ends."

The beast cocked his head slightly. "Overconfidence will be your undoing." He pressed harder on Bane's chest feeling his rib cage crack beneath his fingers. "I will see to that."

Bane grunted and laughed through the pain.

Thomas erupted into raw, unbridled power. From a near standstill, he hit a dead run and became a dark blur as he charged. Leaping off the creature's calf, Thomas flipped in the air. Landing between the beast's wings on the balls of his feet, Thomas brought his scythe over his head in one clean swing and buried the curved blade deep in the beast's skull. Dropping down to his knees, Thomas held on like a bronc rider working for his eight seconds. The beast bucked, spun, and twisted trying to get the Wraith off his back.

Thomas was calm and focused. He saw what he had to do moments before it happened. Precognition of this level was rare—even for him. He let himself go and let intuition and training take over. Reaching out with his mind, he called Conrad's scythe to his hand. Spinning the weapon in his leather-gloved hand, Thomas reached into the beast's body with his telekinesis. Using an invisible tendril of power, he crushed several of the monster's vertebrae in its neck. As the beast let out a shrill shriek of pain, Thomas delivered the deathblow. He brought the blade down and across and sliced cleanly through the beast's damaged neck.

As the monster slumped down to the ground, Thomas slid off its back and landed lightly as the beast's head tumbled toward the edge of the roof. Wiping some of the blood off his leather trench, he turned and looked at his Master with a smile of satisfaction. Conrad was reaching toward him with fear on his face. Confusion hit him. Thomas saw the attack in his mind, but it was too late.

He felt the slash of cold steel down his back.

Turning quickly as he stumbled, he saw Bane loom above him like darkness itself, his blades glistening with Thomas' blood. The Vampire Lord's eyes burned with glee as he pressed forward.

Thomas managed to block the next attack and parry the third with Conrad's scythe. He gritted his teeth and attacked. He had talked with Saint many times about Bane's fighting style. He knew what to expect. Or so he thought. Diving in under one of Bane's swings, the young Wraith slammed his weapon into the Vampire Lord's ribs and heard a crunch. Reversing his attack, Thomas was determined to slice through the vampire's torso but a quick flash of steel stopped him. Bane blocked the scythe and quickly began his own attack. Bringing his right blade over and down, Bane barely missed Thomas' thigh.

Skittering back, Thomas lowered his body into his standard attack posture. He stared intently at the Vampire Lord. His blue eyes were steeled with icy focus.

"I've heard the name Thomas Cross uttered with such reverence and awe on the battlefield," Bane commented. "They think you're some kind of hero." He paused, "but we know the truth, don't we?"

Thomas' mind reeled. Could Bane know what he had done? Or was the vampire simply bluffing? Thomas didn't care. His calm and cool exterior was quickly melting away as the fire inside his soul burned brighter and hotter than it ever had before. He lifted his hand and sent out a tendril of power toward Bane.

To his amazement, the vampire waved off the attack. "You'll need to do better than that, boy." Bane started to slowly circle Thomas. "You claim to be one of the best the order ever had to offer, but we both know that isn't so. You're just a scared little boy hiding behind the couch," Bane growled, "watching your family die."

Thomas' face turned white. It felt like the vampire was inside his head, reading his every thought. He knew.

"You are a coward."

Thomas yelled at the top of his lungs and charged toward Bane. The two became a swirling hurricane of silver and black as they pushed each other back and forth across the observation deck. Each attack was blocked or parried while every move was countered, yet neither would give up. Bane could feel the anger growing exponentially inside the young Wraith. He wanted to see how far he could push the boy, but didn't want to see this ticking time bomb detonate. Not just yet.

Bane pressed his attack again. Blow after blow, strike after strike, he looked for the weakness in Thomas' form. Driving in again, he finally saw the hole. Knocking the Wraith's scythe up, Bane slashed across Thomas' side. Thomas grunted in pain as Bane's blades layed his flesh open. With Thomas stumbling, off balance, Bane attacked again. Swinging hard horizontally, he connected first with Thomas' shoulder, then his upper thigh. They were merely flesh wounds, but it was enough.

It was time to finish the fight.

Thomas fell back to the ground. Fear rushed through his mind for the first time tonight. Bane had bested him, and now the vampire meant to destroy him. He held up his scythe in defense. Bane lifted his weapons and started the downward swing... Pain shot up Thomas' left side like lightning. Too in shock to scream, Thomas merely turned and looked at his severed left hand lying on the ground, Conrad's scythe still grasped in it.

Thomas' body and mind became numb. Lifting his right hand, he summoned every ounce of his remaining strength and detonated an intense blast of psychic energy that blew the two combatants apart. Thomas crashed angrily into what was left of the Troika's dinner table as Bane sailed off the edge of the roof.

Trying to lift himself from the ground, Thomas felt weak and crumbled back to the floor. His entire body ached. Every inch of it screamed in pain. He felt burned from the blast and every last ounce of his strength was gone. He gasped in pain as it even hurt to blink. He had never attempted to use his power in that way before…and if he survived tonight, he never would again. His mind wandered back to his mystery woman. He wanted to get up, to go to her, and comfort her but he was in no condition. Soon, the sun would be up. If she didn't find shelter, or was unable…Thomas' mind started to ramble into the void that preceded death. He was slipping.

Conrad rushed to his student's side. As he dropped down next to Thomas, he rolled the young Wraith onto his back and looked into his unblinking eyes. Thomas's pupils were dilated as if he were staring off into some unseen fate. Conrad placed his hand gently in the center of Thomas' chest. "Hold on, my friend. Hold on."

Thomas' world faded to black.

Chapter Fourteen

His mind slowly became aware. Groggy, a heavy haze sat on his brain. A dull ache lived in his left arm from the elbow down. Opening his eyes slowly, the light blinded him. His vision struggled to adjust but didn't seem to be able to cut through the fog in his mind. A tube ran over his upper lip with two small prongs up his nose feeding him a constant supply of oxygen, while another one ran down and attached to a thick needle embedded in his right hand. He could hear the constant, rhythmic beep of the heart monitor to his left and the hiss of the oxygen in his nose. He felt like he hadn't eaten in days but the pungent smell of antiseptic was turning his stomach.

Blinking his eyes rapidly, the grogginess started to lift. Shapes stared to become clearer and his mind became more cognizant. Slowly turning his head, he glanced around. It looked like he was in a small hospital room— although he hadn't seen one since he was little. Large rectangular banks of lights were recessed into the ceiling, while creamy white paint dominated the walls. A complex bank of monitors and computers sat to his left and a table filled with water bottles was to his right. He was covered from foot to chest in a white sheet and gray wool blanket. A white hospital gown with tiny blue dots was strapped across his torso. His head was propped up slightly in the bed, just enough to see a television suspended from the ceiling in front of him. To his right, he could see the doorway to the tiny restroom cracked slightly, while the entrance to his room just beyond was wide open.

Amidst the pain and haze, a single thought surfaced. He saw her face with a single bead of ruby red blood running down her pale cheek.

Lurching straight up, he felt the stitches in his side and back stretch in protest. He groaned as pain radiated out like electricity in all directions from the wounds Bane inflicted on him. He was in no condition to find her, or get out of bed, for that matter. Thomas slowly sank back down and pulled up the sheets. With a sigh, he turned and stared out the window. The sun cast a beautiful orange haze across the city as it rose over the horizon. It seemed peaceful, almost serene. He wouldn't know a war was raging between two species who were older than recorded time.

Lifting his left arm, he expected to see a stub where his hand once was, but instead, found five digits protruding from heavy gauze wrapping. He stared at the hand and wiggled his fingers. He felt a twinge of pain in his wrist. It didn't feel right. It wasn't his. It wasn't even human.

"They couldn't save it. I'm sorry."

Thomas looked up to find Conrad hovering just inside the door. With crutches under both arms, he hobbled on his broken leg. "It was created especially for you. It took quite a bit of conjuring."

Thomas looked at his hand in dismay. He'd heard of this procedure before, but had never seen it done. He knew it existed in the realm of very dark magic and more often than not, Wraiths turned down the operation to replace a missing limb. He looked to his master and frowned. Since he was unconscious, he didn't have a choice. He placed it gently on the bed and returned his attention to his master.

"With time and rehabilitation, you should feel as good as new." Grabbing a chair from the corner, Conrad pushed it next to Thomas' bed and sat down. Propping the crutches against the wall, a soft smile grew on his face. "It's good to see you awake."

Thomas remained quiet.

"When I brought you in, they told me that you had lost a lot of blood. They weren't sure you were going to make it," Conrad said.

Thomas' mind flashed back to the image of her lips wrapped around the open wound on his wrist. He hadn't lost the blood; he had given it willingly. He let his gaze fall away from Conrad's. He had betrayed his Master and the order with his actions. The guilt in his mind almost hurt worse than the physical wounds.

"Are you all right?" The Master Wraith sat forward slightly with a concerned look. "Should I call a nurse?"

The young Wraith shook his head slowly.

Conrad leaned forward in the chair. "What's the matter?"

He didn't know how to respond. Thomas wanted to tell his Master, his friend, everything. He had never spoken to Conrad about the dreams. To tell his Master now that Thomas had found his mystery dream woman seemed rather obtuse. Stranger still, she was a vampire. The very idea sent chills down his spine. Wraiths were not to fraternize with vampires. They were the enemy, killers, and to see them in any other way was an affront to everything the order stood for.

But the order barely stood now.

He knew he was grasping at straws. To fall in love with a vampire and claim that it was "okay" because there was no more Esgobaeth was idiotic, and childish at best. This secret was his alone to bear. There were still times he saw flashes of fear in Master Verge's eyes when he looked at his student, although Conrad tried his best to hide it. To admit that he loved a woman from his dreams—whom he had only met once, and who just happened to be a vampire—was a conversation he didn't want to have. He felt it best to bury it deep within his mind and throw away the key. He felt his heart sink. She was probably dead anyway. He couldn't save her in his dreams. What made him think this would be any different?

"Where am I?" he asked, finally breaking his silence.

"San Francisco General Hospital," Conrad answered. "This is one of the few Wraith friendly hospitals on the West Coast. We were just lucky to be here."

Thomas nodded once. Turning slowly, he looked down at his left arm. He didn't feel right. His mind wandered. "How long have I been here?"

"Six days."

He paused. The inevitable question was on the tip of his tongue. He just didn't want to hear the answer. "How many Wraiths made it out alive?" Thomas asked finally.

Conrad sighed. "Just you and I."

Thomas cocked his head. "Saint?"

Conrad shook his head. "Never found a body. It's like she just vanished. I found the two Wraiths in her squad though. Both were dead."

"Vampires?"

"Gunshot," Conrad replied.

A deep sadness washed over the young Wraith. Besides Conrad, Saint was his closest friend. "And Bane?"

"Gone. I brought you here and went back to look for him," Conrad admitted. "After you blew him off the roof, he just seemed to vanish."

"Then it was all for nothing," Thomas summarized grimly. "We lost a lot of good Wraiths and didn't manage to take out the target."

"I wouldn't call it a total waste," Conrad corrected. "We did shut down one of the biggest covens on the West Coast. The Troika is no more. The building is being demolished this morning."

Thomas nodded. It was a small victory compared to the sacrifices. He slowly lowered his eyelids and took a deep breath of the oxygen in his nose.

"We did find something interesting," Conrad added. "Apparently, the Troika had been working on some kind of biological weapon. It's a drug that counteracts the vampire virus."

Thomas looked at his mentor. "What does that mean?"

Conrad smiled. "It can turn vampires human again, and perhaps Wraiths as well. We're taking it back to England to study."

Thomas let his mind assess the possibilities. This discovery had the potential to change everything. Including his life. And hers. If he could get a hold of the drug and find her again, they could start over. If she was even alive... His excitement was suddenly lost in a tsunami of pessimism.

Grabbing his crutches from the edge of Thomas' bed,

Conrad slowly stood. "You should get some rest."

"Apparently, that's all I've been doing," Thomas replied sarcastically. "When do I get out of here?"

"Be patient," Conrad advised. "We all have to heal." He frowned. "The war will still be there when you get better." Turning, he hobbled out of the room and pulled the door shut behind him.

Chapter Fifteen

The air was crisp and cool as it swept in through the window. The first rays of morning spilled over the city and into the room casting a warm orange glare across the floor. The bedsheets were crumpled and spilling off the bottom of the bed while static filled the television screen. The room was a reflection of his mental state. He searched everything he could get his hands on, accessing every memory while ignoring the physical. There was an answer…there had to be.

His limbs felt heavy and useless.

Even though no painkillers remained in his system, his mind felt groggy and tired. The world around him seemed gray, as if it were devoid of any emotion or pleasure. The color had drained away leaving only the hard black edges and shadows that threatened to suck everything down into a never ending chasm of despair. A ball of darkness spun around his heart, undulating and changing. Tendrils of despair and anguish shot throughout his body. He could feel it as if it were a shadow quickly falling over him. Lifting his black leather clad hands, he stared at the stretch of exposed skin just behind the fleshy mounds of his palms. White gauze wrapped around his left wrist where the new hand was connected. It would be so easy to open his veins and let his life drain away. Then it would all be over.

Thomas wanted to give up. He wanted to lay his arms down, but he was tired and no amount of rest would fix him. He had lost her before he even knew she existed.

There was no sense in going on. His fate had been destroyed on that rooftop. Standing quietly at the foot of his hospital bed, Thomas lowered his hands and wrapped his new black leather trench coat—a gift from Master Verge—tightly around his chest. He felt cold as if ice raged through his veins. The temperature in the room was a constant seventy-eight but he couldn't stop shivering. In the two weeks he had spent convalescing, his thoughts had grown increasingly morose. He was sure his mystery dream woman was dead.

Now she was only a dream.

He wanted to sleep if only to see her face again. He would gladly sleep eternally if it meant dreaming about her, but the fear of what lay beyond sent shivers down his spine. He had a sinking feeling that this—his life—was all there was. He couldn't bear to stand the thought of nonexistence. He didn't want to live without her, but he couldn't fathom the idea of dying. He could see the silvery blade of his knife being drawn across his wrists splaying open the flesh. He imagined the dark blood pooling and dripping off his arms as he lost consciousness. It seemed such a simple action in his mind. He thought back to that night on the roof. He had done it for her, why couldn't he do it for himself?

He was a coward. That's why. He had faced snarling demons without so much as a twinge of fear, yet he couldn't perform this one, simple act. He had stood toe-to-toe with the Vampire Lord who had almost single-handedly wiped the Wraith from the face of the Earth and not even flinched. He knew the truth: he didn't want to die. He would rather live out the rest of his days pining away for her instead of facing the unknown country of

186

death.

Reaching into his pocket, he produced his small, black pocketknife. Locking open the blade, Thomas sank down into one of the padded chairs in his hospital room. This was probably the worst place in the world to attempt suicide, but he didn't care. Maybe he wanted to be caught. Perhaps this was "a cry for help," like all the television commercials claimed. Turning his back to the door, he pulled back the cuff of his jacket and held the knife just above his wrist. As it hovered, he saw a reflection on his skin as if it was highlighting the area it wanted to cut. Slowly bringing the knife to his wrist, Thomas balled his fist and started to apply pressure. He felt a bead of sweat form on his forehead. He knew all it would take was one stroke, one quick pull. He pushed firmly feeling the blade biting harder into his skin.

He didn't want this, but he didn't see any other option. His world was crashing down around him. The woman of his dreams had come and gone too quickly, Saint was dead, and the Order was losing its battle. There was nothing left to live for. He didn't feel useful anymore. His field of vision narrowed into a single point on the horizon and to his dismay, he didn't find anything there. Nothing awaited him at the end of his journey.

It scared him.

He flexed the muscles in his arm and started to pull the knife—

"Thomas Cross?"

Yanking the knife away from his arm, he felt it nick his flesh. Glancing down, he watched a small bead of blood well up from the cut. He peered over his shoulder to see a large man standing in the open doorway. He didn't recognize the man. He slowly turned in the seat. "Yes?" He held his pocketknife tightly in his hand...just in case.

The man, extremely muscular with short, messy, dark hair, was wearing clothes that would look more at home in a second-hand store. A heavy blue and white flannel jacket covered a stained white t-shirt and blue jeans. His blue eyes had the slightest tinge of red around the irises. Thomas knew immediately what he was. He had been forced to dispatch several of his kind a year earlier after they went rogue. He hoped this wasn't one of their kinsmen looking for retribution. He wasn't in any condition to fight a werewolf. Thomas tensed waiting for the wolf to make the next move.

"She's alive," the wolf said, taking a slow step forward.

Thomas' mind immediately flashed to his dream woman. He felt raw excitement crash through his body at the mere thought. He paused as the excitement was replaced with concern. How could this creature know about the vampire woman? He became wary. "Who?"

"Saint."

Thomas stood up. It wasn't what he wanted to hear, but it was almost as good. "How do you know?"

"She's in the possession of a bounty hunter called Talon Creed," the wolf answered. "He's also a werewolf."

"Who are you?"

"Ben," the wolf replied.

Thomas cocked an eyebrow suspiciously. "Why do you care if a single Wraith is alive or dead? Werewolves and Wraith don't usually have the best relationships."

188

"I," he paused. "I helped Saint once." Ben had a guilty look on his face. "I watch after her."

"Why?"

Ben shook his head. "That's none of your concern. Time is of the essence. We need to move quickly to save her."

Thomas stared at the werewolf. "How do I know you're legit?"

A smile flashed across Ben's face. "You'll have to trust me. That's all I have to offer."

Thomas nodded and took a breath. There was an air of true urgency in the wolf's voice and Thomas could smell the anxiety in the man's sweat. The lycanthrope was taking a huge risk walking into a public place like this. The creatures tended to be more primeval than even vampires. Crowds and stress had driven more than one werewolf into an uncontrollable feral frenzy. In Thomas' estimation, werewolves were like people who had a social anxiety disorder. The only difference being werewolves didn't want to crawl into a corner and hide; instead, they would unleash their beast and kill everything in sight. This wolf meant business.

He thought of the strangeness of life for a moment: A few seconds earlier, he had been ready to commit suicide; now he was contemplating a rescue mission. Reaching down, he wiped the blood from wrist and dug his hand into his pocket to hide the wound.

Thomas slipped his knife back into his jacket. "We need to find Master Verge."

***

Saint's feet were bound tightly together and attached firmly just above the base of the wall. Heavy steel shackles at the ends of thick chains suspended from the ceiling held her arms above her head. Her body arced forward pushing her spine to its limits while the muscles in her arms twitched and shivered in protest. Her long, black leather coat hung off her back and licked the floor. She had been here longer than she cared to think about. With no food or water, her body was on the verge of breaking down. The only thing to do was fight the fatigue in her body and mind. There was no comfort to be found. Someone would come for her.

They had to...

But they didn't even know she was here, or alive.

Saint slid out her tongue and licked her dry, cracked lips. Taking a breath into her lungs, the muscles in her ribs and back cried out in protest. She closed her eyes firmly and stifled a yelp of pain in her throat. Exhaling, the pain slowly subsided. She was being tortured by her captor, but for what reason she didn't understand. She didn't know this bounty hunter from Adam or what his motives were—or why she was still alive.

Her surroundings were tastefully decorated with the finest things money could buy. Silver, glass, and black marble dominated her view. Tall glass shelves stood on both sides with various objects that didn't seem to mesh with the decor. Necklaces, a lock of hair, and a human eye encased in an airtight plastic cube were just some of the items. Then she saw it: her scythe. Closed and sitting on a display case in the exact center of the case, it gleamed under the lights installed in the top of both shelves. Polished and cleaned to immaculate perfection, it looked as it had the first day she received it from Master Quinn. Even one of the decorative gold vines that wrapped around the hilt—scarred from an old battle—had been refinished. She understood what the shelves were. It was the bounty hunter's trophy case and she was part of the collection.

"Comfortable?"

Saint looked up slowly at the sound of the booming voice to see her captor standing in the open doorway opposite her. He was dressed in an immaculately tailored charcoal gray suit. A white tie knotted at his throat stood out amidst the sea of black that was his shirt, while a pair of black sunglasses covered his eyes. A lone, red handkerchief in his breast pocket gave the bounty hunter some color.

Creed smiled. "Like the suit?"

Saint ignored his question.

"Usually werewolves dress more," Creed rolled his hand in front of his face as he searched for the proper word, "shabbily. I, on the other hand, have taste and culture." He knew he was wasting his breath, but he was enjoying his latest acquisition. "It's Armani. Spent a small fortune on it," he continued as he walked toward Saint, "but my daddy always said every man should own one good suit." He leaned over slightly and peered into Saint's eyes. "I own a hundred of these." He threw his head back and roared with laughter.

Saint gritted her teeth.

Creed took a slow breath and straightened his posture. He eyed the Wraith slowly. "Some people just have no sense of humor." He turned and walked past her to his trophy cases. Clasping his hands behind his back, his eyes settled on his latest acquisition. "Magnificent weapon. The craftsmanship is simply amazing. How is a Wraith scythe created?"

She remained quiet. She slowly opened her mind, unaware if Creed could sense it. She started to reach for her scythe.

"There has to be a mystical element," Creed mused. "It's light as a feather and has no seams. This can't be human made." He found himself enthralled by the silver and gold weapon. He wanted desperately to rip it from its display, activate it, and slice through the spine of the Wraith...just to test it out. He smiled. There would be time for that later.

Saint knew her window of opportunity would be small. A werewolf's reflexes were more enhanced than her own. She felt her tendril wrap around the hilt of the scythe. Almost immediately, it began to reverberate with power as it recognized her touch. She waited.

Creed turned back to the Wraith but didn't step away from the weapon. "My client is late," he informed. "He's lucky you're preternatural, or you'd be dead by now."

Saint's eyebrow rose slightly. This was the first mention that she was a job. She had to find out more. "Lucky me," she said slowly. The dryness of her throat and mouth almost prevented the words from escaping.

Creed stopped and looked amused at the Wraith. "So you do speak? I thought maybe a vampire got your tongue."

He placed his fingers gently on Saint's chin but she quickly pulled away.

"I've seen it happen," he added with a smile. "I watched a pack of vampires catch a Wraith a few years ago and torture him. They bit off his tongue and fingers one by one. Gruesome." His deep voice made the story sound that much more horrific. "Took hours." He was enjoying Saint's discomfort.

She looked the wolf straight in the eye, all the while keeping her mind trained on her scythe. "Who hired you?"

Creed grinned. "That would be telling."

"I'm going to find out anyway," Saint argued. "Might as well just tell me, so I know if I should curtsy or bow."

The bounty hunter laughed out loud. "If my client doesn't show up soon," he ran his fingers down her face, "you'll be a permanent addition to my collection." He turned and started toward back toward the door.

Saint took the opportunity. Ripping her scythe from its stand, she watched it sail through the air toward her. Using her mind, she activated the weapon. The curved blade sprang to life and cartwheeled toward the chains that restrained her feet. Just as the blade was about to connect, she saw an ebony hand swoop out of thin air and capture the weapon and disappear again.

Saint looked up to find Creed standing in front of her with her scythe in his hands. The long weapon looked tiny in his massive hands. She sighed and let her head drop. He wouldn't make the same mistake twice.

"So," Creed said, twirling the perfectly balanced weapon in his hand, "you have psychic abilities as well. Very uncommon in a Wraith."

Her emotions sank as exhaustion overtook her.

Creed looked down at the scythe and deactivated it. Opening his jacket, he slipped it inside. "I think I'll keep

193

this with me for the time being. Wouldn't want you hurting yourself with sharp objects." He laughed again. "Or me."

Turning away from the Wraith, he walked casually back to the entrance and shut the door behind him. As the lights in the room dimmed automatically, Saint was once again enveloped in darkness.

***

Master Conrad Verge tentatively placed weight on his leg. His Wraith physiology had helped the broken bones knit much faster but he wasn't completely healed yet. The thick white cast that had helped support his weight just half an hour earlier was now split in half on the table next to him. Holding his hands on the edge of the examination table, he felt a twinge of pain shoot up his calf. Easing off quickly, the Master Wraith transferred his weight to the opposite foot. He looked down at the doctor and forced a smile.

"Still a little tender?" she asked, still amazed that it had only been two weeks since she set the break and wrapped it.

Conrad reached over and patted the small Asian woman on the shoulder. "It'll be fine in a few days," he assured. "Thank you, Doctor."

Doctor Akemi Tan nodded. Saved from a vampire by a Wraith several years earlier, she committed herself to helping these unsung, noble warriors. She couldn't count how many stitches and casts she had applied, or trips around the world she made to save dying Wraith, but they continued to astound her. She handed Conrad the cane he had chosen to use until his leg was completely healed. She knew he didn't need it, and perhaps it would hinder his recuperation a bit, but she was starting to think the Master Wraith was feeling his age—whatever that may be. He had spoken to her of fighting vampires during the Nazi bombings of England in the second world war, yet he didn't look a day over thirty-five. The scientist in her was piqued.

Tan stood and placed her hand on the Wraith's chest, "Conrad—"

"You already know the answer to that request," the Wraith cautioned. "It's too dangerous."

"For whom?" Tan cocked an eyebrow, slightly perturbed that she could be read so easily.

"The world," Conrad replied quickly. "They can't know."

"I wouldn't tell anyone," Tan honestly promised. "I just have to know. The possible medical applications here are immense. You can't keep denying me this."

"I have to. You know the conditions," Conrad reminded. "Full access if—"

"If I join the academy's research facility," Tan finished. "I know, I know. I just can't give up everything I've worked so hard for that easily. And even if we did unlock some medical miracle, I still couldn't release it to the public."

Conrad nodded solemnly. "Those are your options."

Tan nodded with a smile. She had to try. She would have to be content with patching up soldiers and sending them back into the battle. At least then, people like her would stand a fighting chance against the oncoming darkness. "You're all done," she said finally, taking one last glance at his leg. There was nothing more she could do. "I wouldn't recommend battle anytime soon," she cautioned, "but you should be fine."

"Thank you, Doctor," Conrad replied courteously.

He looked up to see his student—he really should stop thinking of him that way. Thomas has been a full Wraith in his own right for quite some time—standing in the doorway. His face was drawn, but there was a hint of excitement brewing behind his eyes. The Master Wraith moved past the doctor toward Thomas, favoring his leg slightly. Using the black cane, he quickly became self-conscious of his weakness. Picking it up, he slid the curved handle over his forearm and did his best to ignore the tingling pain in his shin.

"Master," Thomas greeted.

Conrad nodded, but his attention was turned to the man standing a step behind Thomas. His lips drew into a smile. "Ben!"

Ben stepped past Thomas and wrapped the Master Wraith in a friendly embrace. "How've you been, Con?"

"Con," the Master Wraith repeated slowly. "Now that's a name I haven't heard in a long time," Conrad said, pulling away. He slapped the wolf on the shoulder with a laugh. "I haven't seen you in years."

Ben took a breath and nodded. "It has been a while." He tried to recall the last time the two fought together but couldn't seem to remember that far back. It had indeed been a long time.

Conrad turned to look at Thomas with a grin. "How did you fall in with this old dog?"

"He came to me," Thomas answered quickly, not showing any of the exuberance of the other two. He cut right to the chase. "The wolf claims Saint is alive."

Conrad's smile fell away as he turned back to Ben. "Is this true?"

Ben frowned deeply. "The bounty hunter has her."

"Talon Creed?" Conrad asked immediately, hoping he was wrong. He knew there were very few bounty hunters who specialized in preternatural beings, and Creed was the best.

To Conrad's dismay, Ben nodded. "Creed."

The Master Wraith cursed under his breath.

"Who is this Talon Creed?" Thomas asked innocently. "Sounds like you two are talking about the Devil himself."

"One of the best bounty hunters to ever stalk the creatures of the night," Ben answered.

"When demons and vampires have nightmares," Conrad continued the thought, "they're about Creed." He twisted the hair of his goatee between his thumb and forefinger. "I've never heard of a case of Creed hunting Wraith before."

"Not his style," Ben agreed. "Something must've changed."

Conrad let out an uncomfortable laugh. "Everything's changed." He was right. This wasn't the same world they knew only a year ago. "How did you come by this information?"

"Before the Troika's building was demolished, I sniffed around a bit," Ben admitted. "I could smell him. I tracked the scent inside from the entrance to where his and Saint's paths combined. He killed the two Wraiths and took Saint. I'm sure of it."

Conrad became suddenly suspicious of his old friend.

"What were you doing in San Francisco?"

"I," Ben paused uncomfortably. "I followed you from England."

"Why?" Conrad raised an eyebrow. His hand slowly lowered to his belt and hovered just above his scythe. His muscles tensed.

Ben shifted his weight slowly, aware of the Master Wraith's sudden unease. It was thick on the air. "I promised to look after her."

Conrad let his hand fall away from the weapon. "Promised who?"

Ben looked from Conrad to Thomas, then back. He hadn't told anyone the details of his promise. Not even Saint. He took a deep breath. "Master Quinn."

Conrad's mouth fell open. "Saint's Master? But he's—"

"Dead," Ben acknowledged. "He died in the explosion that destroyed the Wraith Academy in England. His spirit came to me shortly after that and asked me to keep her safe. He loved her and knew her importance in the grand scheme of things. We all do. A werewolf cannot ignore a plea from the spirit world. I've been with her ever since."

"The grand scheme?" Conrad echoed.

"You Wraith aren't the only ones who believe in the prophecy," Ben said quickly. "If she is the chosen one, we must protect her at all costs. This could affect not only the future of the Wraiths, but all werewolves as well."

"I don't follow you," Conrad admitted.

"The prophecy states that a saint's blood will create a new race," Ben recited from memory. "Werewolves believe this new race will be the perfect hybrid of all preternatural species." He paused. "Ours included."

"My god," Conrad breathed. "Imagine the power such a creature would have. Werewolf, demon, vampire, Wraith..." He let his sentence trail off. "It would be utterly unstoppable."

Ben nodded. "That's why I've been tasked with protecting her. We have to make sure this being will be brought about on the right side of good and evil." He took a breath. "I don't know if Creed knows about the prophecy. He cut all ties with his clan a long time ago," he added with a hint of anger.

Conrad detected the change in Ben's voice and understood. "He was a member of your clan, wasn't he?"

The wolf nodded. "He was like my brother. But that was a long time ago," he repeated, more to himself than the two Wraith.

Thomas was getting impatient with talk of boogeymen, ghosts, and moldy, five thousand year old prophecies. He wanted action. "We're going to go get her, right?"

"It's not that simple, kid," Ben cautioned.

"Why can't it be?" Thomas shot back. "There are three of us, one of him. We can do this."

"Ah," Conrad said slowly, "my brash, young Wraith. Subtlety isn't your strong suit." He paused and considered the options. "Don't let our apprehension fool you. We are going to rescue Saint. But we need to be cautious."

"We need a plan," Ben agreed. "But we'll have to make one on the way. Time is running short."

Conrad nodded. "We'll meet you in the hospital lobby in five minutes. I need to talk to my apprentice."

Ben nodded and turned away.

Conrad waited for the wolf to disappear from sight before addressing Thomas. He reached over and placed his hand on the younger man's shoulder. "Thomas—"

"I'm really not in the mood for a lecture, Master," Thomas interjected quickly.

Conrad frowned, slightly agitated by the comment. "This isn't a lecture." He shook his head. "I just wanted to tell you that I'm proud of you. I know I don't say it enough, but you've grown into a respectable young man, and an exceptional Wraith."

Thomas cracked a brief smile at the compliment, but he allowed it to vanish quickly.

"I know you lost your scythe during your confrontation with Bane." Conrad reached into his battered, brown leather jacket and pulled a dark object free. He handed it to Thomas. "This is for you."

Thomas cradled the cylindrical object in his hands and stared at it in awe. The weapon reverberated with energy. Already attuned to his biorhythm, it felt as if it were singing in his hands. It was a scythe hilt, but like none he had ever seen before. Instead of the traditional silver, it was a glossy, midnight black. Gold and red vines wrapped around the hilt beautifully making the weapon look more like a work of art. Holding it away from his body, Thomas thumbed the activation stud and felt the scythe spring into a full-length staff with wooden tips on both ends. Hitting the button again, he saw the familiar curved blade snap open at the top. Looking down, he noticed a matching curved blade open on the bottom facing the opposite direction. He had read of double-bladed scythes while at the Academy, but had never seen one. His face lit up in a wide grin. Hitting the activation button one final time, the weapon snapped shut and returned to its original size.

"I had it specially designed for you while you were recuperating," Conrad admitted. "There isn't another one like it in the entire world."

"Thank you, Master," Thomas said graciously as he slid the weapon onto his belt.

"May it serve you well," Conrad smiled and patted his friend and student on the shoulder. Turning, he guided Thomas toward the door. "Come on, we have work to do."

Chapter Sixteen

A nearly full moon hung in the cloudless sky above them. Though all three knew that the waxing and waning of the moon held no sway over a mature wolf, they couldn't help the ominous feeling the silvery light was casting down on them.

In myths and lore, a werewolf could only transform during the three nights of the full moon. Perhaps this was just a bit of disinformation that had been passed down over the generations, or the true story had been lost through the countless oral retellings. With the exception of the first change in a werewolf's life, the transformation was completely voluntary.

That didn't make them feel better.

Ben—using his heightened sense of smell—took the lead while Conrad and Thomas followed closely behind. The three moved like shadows in the darkness. Quickly and quietly, they slithered unseen toward their target. Ben picked up Creed's scent about forty minutes earlier and had been following it almost haphazardly through downtown San Francisco. Winding around, back, and through the buildings, Ben could only assume that Creed had been a busy man, or overly cautious. It seemed as if the bounty hunter was doubling back to confuse trackers. From Conrad's point of view, it was working.

"Do you know where you're going?"

Ben shot an angry glance over his shoulder at Conrad.

"I'm just saying," Conrad defended, "it seems like

we've been walking in circles."

"We have," Thomas confirmed quickly from the back of the group.

Ben stopped. Turning, he stood tall over the two Wraiths. He looked at both accusingly. "Perhaps you would like to take the lead, Conrad?"

Conrad lifted his hands to assuage the wolf. "No disrespect," he said carefully, "but Saint's life is hanging in the balance."

Ben gritted his teeth. Conrad had no reason to remind him of their mission. His face flushed as anger welled up inside him. Taking a slow breath, he closed his eyes and concentrated on the moment as the wolf clawed at the inside of his chest. "I just need a little more time," he said finally.

"Time is the one luxury we don't have," Conrad argued in frustration.

Ben lashed out and grabbed the Master Wraith by the throat. Lifting him easily off the ground, the werewolf's eyes shifted to red. A guttural growl escaped from his curled lips as his teeth sharpened to fangs.

Conrad struggled against Ben but was unable to break the wolf's grip. He reached clumsily for his scythe.

Pulling the Wraith close, Ben stared into his eyes. "I have had my fill of you," he warned.

He saw Thomas draw and activate his scythe. "He would be dead before you could attack, boy," Ben warned.

Thomas held his position, unsure what move to make.

Assessing the two Wraiths, Ben knew he would have a fight on his hands if he chose to continue down this path. Perhaps one he couldn't win. Ben slowly lowered Conrad to the ground and released his grip. The Wraith stumbled back gasping for air. Rubbing his throat, he looked through bleary eyes at Ben.

"Don't you dare presume to tell me the importance of this." Ben's red eyes looked luminous in the moonlight. "If it wasn't for my information, you two would have left her to rot in Creed's hands. You would have let her die."

"Saint is one of my oldest and dearest friends," Thomas breathed. "But she knew her duty when she walked into the Troika building. We all take the risk of death every time we do our jobs. As far as we knew, we lost her that night," Thomas defended. "Yeah, it hurts," he admitted, "but we can't go on personal crusades every time a Wraith gets killed. There just aren't enough of us left."

The wisdom with which Thomas spoke surprised Conrad.

"I think you need to examine your priorities in this matter," Thomas added. "If it were anyone else, I don't think we would be here."

Ben shrank back from the undeniable logic. "I can't let her die." He sounded hurt and weak.

Conrad shook his head. "We won't." He stepped forward and placed his hand firmly on Ben's shoulder. "That's why we're out here."

"She would certainly come after each one of us if the situation were reversed," Thomas concluded. "We owe her that much."

Ben slowly let the wolf recede and his head fall forward. "I apologize, Con."

Conrad nodded. "Emotions are running high. I would

expect nothing less." He stopped and rubbed his throat. "Just don't try to kill me again."

Ben scowled as he turned away from the Wraiths. "No promises."

***

Creed stood with his meaty paws clasped behind his back. His legs were spread shoulder-width apart as he stared out the enormous plate glass window in front of him. His demeanor was calm, even though he had caught their scent almost ten minutes ago. He knew they were coming and there had been no word from Bane. Creed found himself torn. He had not been fully paid for his work. The Wraith meant little to him, and he had already collected his trophy. He had the inclination to simply set the Wraith on the front stoop and let her go, yet his overwhelming sense of greed wouldn't allow it. She was his until the money was safely in his possession.

Turning, he stared at the immense aquarium that dominated the opposite wall of his office. So large that most aquariums would be jealous, it housed several species of fish and a single tiger shark. The seven foot predator glided slowly through the water, it's toothy mouth pulled up into a perpetual sneer. Its black, lidless eyes stared unblinking out of the tank as if it were biding its time until it could kill its captor and be freed. Creed respected the shark. For most species, to stop swimming was to die as they needed to constantly move water over their gills to breathe. The bounty hunter felt the same way. He had to keep swimming, and he realized he had to protect his investment. The Wraith was his. Creed would have to fight to keep her. There was simply no other option.

Pulling off his suit jacket, he tossed it over the back of his leather couch. Unbuttoning his shirt cuffs, he started toward the door. He had to prepare for battle.

Stepping into the adjoining room, he stood in the darkness for a moment. Creed reached to his right and flipped a series of switches on the wall. Recessed lights in the ceiling flickered on displaying case after case of weapons. Another portion of his collection, this was more—this was his arsenal. Walking straight through to the opposite side, he paused and placed his fingers lightly on a pane of glass. Behind it was his history. He stared at the weapons hung with great care amidst the crushed red velvet lining. There in the center was the implement of his exile.

Opening the case, Creed pressed his fingers cautiously to the weapon as if it would strike on its own. Several decades had passed since the last time he touched it, but even now, it still held the same draw. It was beautiful. He could hear the weapon softly calling his name as it had done so many years ago. It was meant for him, even if no one else believed it. As he wrapped his hand around the shaft, he felt a vibration of pleasure run down his arm. Lifting it off the hooks that held it in place, the bounty hunter watched the blade glimmer in the light. Oversized—built for a werewolf to wield—the dual axe blades on the head were nearly perfect. Nary a scratch could be seen on the surface, even though it had been used in battle numerous times. The crest of his clan was chiseled into the metal between the blades. Crimson strands of unknown composition stretched down from the blades and wrapped around the shaft like veins.

This was a powerful weapon.

He knew the moment he ripped it from the clawed hands of his chieftain and buried it deep in his leader's ribcage. As he watched the wolf revert into a frail, old man and die, he understood. The blades were etched with pure silver. It had been created for one purpose: to kill werewolves. It made him desire the axe even more. It had cost him his future among his clan, but none of that mattered.

It was his now. And it would be the implement of the Wraiths' destruction.

A familiar scent lingered on the cool night air. It had been some time since it filled his nostrils. Intermingled with that of the two vampire hunters was another werewolf, and one he knew very well. Tonight would go beyond professional and deep into the realm of personal. Creed had an old grudge to settle tonight. Nothing would please him more than to see his axe buried in the skull of this werewolf. It would be fitting.

Ben would die at his hands.

***

Ben, Thomas, and Conrad stood in awe. It occurred to each that perhaps they had gotten into the wrong line of work as they looked at Creed's opulent residence. Situated on the beach, it was no more than a stone's throw from the ocean. Two stories in height, the second floor was almost completely dominated by immense glass windows. Of course, if it meant burning the house down to retrieve Saint, that's exactly what they would do.

207

"Anything in terms of a plan?"

Conrad addressed Thomas, then turned back to the house. "Rescue Saint."

Thomas laughed uncomfortably. "More specifically?"

Conrad smiled wryly. "Rescue Saint. Kill Creed."

Thomas nodded. He glanced over to see Ben solemnly staring at the massive house. "Thoughts?"

Ben remained focused on the house.

"Ben?" Thomas asked with a little more force in his voice.

Ben snapped his head around and glared at the young Wraith.

Thomas was slightly taken back by the look. His trust in the wolf had already been shaken earlier this night. He slowly lowered his hand to his weapon and looked at Ben warily. "Are you okay?"

Ben's gaze softened. "Just distracted for a moment." He rubbed his hand down his face as if trying to physically clear away the cobwebs in his mind. "I'm with you."

"We're a team," Conrad interjected. "I don't want either of you going rogue thinking you can take Creed alone." He looked at the wolf, then to his student. "Understood?"

"Agreed," Ben replied softly.

Thomas just nodded.

And Conrad knew it. The Master Wraith took a slow breath and drew his weapon. "Let's go to work."

Chapter Seventeen

Thomas' booted feet crackled and popped as he tried to navigate the heap of broken glass before him. Glancing over his shoulder, he watched Conrad and Ben step through the temporary entrance he had just created from one of Creed's large picture windows. Kicking one of the larger shards of glass away, Thomas snapped his scythe shut and returned it to his belt.

Walking across the large, second floor room, he quickly surveyed his surroundings. A complete gym with machines of all shapes and sizes, the room was completely swathed in black and silver. Even the dumbbells were chromed. A personal shower was installed to his right while a massive plasma screen television occupied the opposite wall. Thomas had the overwhelming urge to destroy everything in the room out of spite. No man responsible for such evil deeds deserved this level of luxury. Biting his bottom lip, he knew it would be a waste of energy.

"Don't you think we should be a little quieter?"

Thomas turned and looked crossly at his master.

"He's going to know we're here," Conrad added quietly. He stared intently at the only entrance into the room expecting the bounty hunter to appear at any moment.

"We're here to kill him," Thomas pointed out, making no attempt to subdue his voice. "I don't think it matters."

"Not necessarily," Conrad corrected, slightly taken

back by his student's blood lust. "If we can find Saint and get out of here without a confrontation, we will. We aren't assassins."

The comment struck Thomas as odd. Brushing it off with a shrug, the Wraith let the conversation die. He knew why he was here and it wasn't just to rescue his friend. Turning away from the Master Wraith, he focused his eyes on the exit. He could feel Ben move to his side. Thomas knew the wolf's motives were similar to his own. There would indeed be bloodshed here tonight, whether Conrad wanted it or not.

"We have to move quickly," Ben said. "He'll move her and we'll lose our chance."

Thomas turned and looked at the wolf. "How do you know?"

Ben smiled wryly. "It's what I would do."

"Is he even here?" Conrad asked from behind the two.

Ben lifted his head slightly and sniffed the air. He looked over his shoulder at the Wraith with a nod. "He's here."

Conrad started toward the two. "We should probably—"

Ben bolted out of the room before Conrad could finish the thought.

Conrad looked angrily to Thomas. "What the hell does he—"

Thomas snapped his scythe off his belt and charged after the wolf without waiting for his master to register a protest.

The Master Wraith took a slow breath in through his nose and slowly exhaled it. "And here I am talking to myself." Pulling his scythe, he thumbed the activation stud and charged out of the room.

***

Creed stood silently in his trophy room staring at the Wraith. She hung limp in the shackles as if her body had finally given up. He felt a flicker of remorse. This wasn't the first time his greed had claimed a life, and she was far from innocent, but she was technically one of the good guys. He assumed that made him one of the bad. "Good" and "bad" were merely labels to him. He considered himself neither in the grand scheme of things. He was just trying to make a dollar in the only way he knew how. His biology precluded him from keeping a normal day job.

The bounty hunter held his axe lightly in his hands. He knew he could end her suffering with one swift blow. He took a step forward. The Wraith made no movement. She didn't even acknowledge his presence. She was nearly dead. Even these near superhuman beings had limits. He focused on an exposed patch of skin at the base of her neck. Creed slowly lifted the axe.

But stopped.

The battle was on his doorstep. There was no choice now. Even if he chose to spare the Wraith, it wouldn't stop the onslaught.

He had to fight.

Spinning on his heel, he moved toward the door with purpose now. Reaching up, he pulled his dark sunglasses off his shirt collar and snapped them open. Lifting them to his face, he slowly slid them on. The dark plastic fit the bridge of his nose perfectly while the convex lenses stretched out into ovals creating the appearance of black, alien-shaped, almond eyes.

He had his game face on.

Moving swiftly down the hall that joined his trophy room to the foyer, Creed gritted his teeth. They were already inside. He could smell them. Their scents were strong through the home's recirculated ventilation system. That also presented a problem: he couldn't track them effectively with their scent spewing out of every vent he passed. They hadn't even tripped his security system. He made a mental note to kill the salesman who assured him the system was foolproof...if he survived.

Turning the corner, the werewolf skidded to a stop. There, amidst the moonlight spilling in through the large windows, was a shadowy figure. Creed's muscles tensed as he held the axe. He reached out with his heightened senses. His eyes hardened.

His head snapped around as a loud crash grabbed his attention away from the shadowy figure. Turning back, he felt a momentary twinge of fear.

The intruder was gone.

***

He lost sight of both his student and the wolf. Propping himself against the wall, he took a slow breath into his lungs. His leg was throbbing in pain. Gritting his teeth, Conrad pushed the feelings deep into the back of his mind. He didn't have time to stop and whimper. Rolling his thumb gently across the activation stud on his scythe, he cradled the hilt in his hand.

Pressing his free hand to the wall, he carefully slid

toward the nearest doorway. This house was equally impressive inside as it was out. Craning his head around slightly, he peered through the open doorway. Completely empty, the room was nothing but bare floor and walls. It seemed that not even the great bounty hunter had a use for every room. Turning his attention back to the hallway, Conrad started past the door.

But paused.

Some unseen force pulled at him. As if an invisible hand reached down and forcefully turned his head, he peered inside and noticed a flicker of silver in the darkness—something he hadn't seen before. Stepping fully into the room, he felt his mouth fall open. Quickly regaining his composure, he turned off his emotions and focused on the scene with his analytical side.

There, stuffed into the corner of the room that had been obscured by the door, heavy shackles hung from the ceiling. The drywall was shredded exposing the wooden studs, pipes, and wires that were the internal organs of the house. Several of the electrical wires were ripped free of the wall and the leads exposed. Stepping closer, he could see numerous gashes in the wall and floor, obviously made by claws. The faint odor of charred hair lingered in the air, while a dark stain stretched out on the floor.

Reaching out, Conrad placed his fingertips gently on the dangling shackles. He knew the purpose of this room. A werewolf had died here. Creed had imprisoned it, tortured the creature, and eventually killed it. The reason was unclear, but the Master Wraith knew the creature had been in great pain before it died.

Letting his hand fall away from the shackles, Conrad felt a deep sense of dread wash through him. Creed was not above torturing a prisoner to death. He wondered if it was already too late for Saint. Activating his scythe, he turned and moved carefully back into the hallway. He had to find Thomas and Ben before Creed did. Looking ahead, he saw a descending staircase. Searching his feelings, he stopped at the top. Looking down into the open, lavishly decorated floor below, he felt the same tug as before. Someone was guiding him. There was no choice but to follow.

***

Ben's mood darkened. He was her savior, her protector, and he had failed. He could sense her life force somewhere in the building, but it was dwindling quickly. She was on the very edge of death's doorstep. He knew she was holding on, but he could feel her fatigue. It had been two weeks under these conditions. A normal human would probably have succumbed after only seven or eight days. She had held on for fourteen so far. Tonight would decide her—and the Order's—fate. There was more saddled on her than just her hopes and dreams.

The werewolf had personally read the prophecy. Numerous times. Pouring over every arcane word, each masked syllable, he had tried to find a deeper meaning to the words. Using every text available, he had translated the parchment and ultimately came up more confused than before. Each volume of lore seemed to have three definitions of the same word. With no cipher key, no Rosetta stone, there was no true translation. Only interpretation.

It stated A saint's blood will create a new race,

according to the most popular interpretation. But the prophecy was written long before the quaint Christian idea of "Saints" came into being, so the actual focus of the text was unclear. It could be translated as saint, however that was a modern view of the word. The writer, or writers, probably had no notion of what that word would mean in the 21st Century. One thing had become clear though, Saint's particular condition seemed to fit. However, Ben noted that this notion had never been tested. He—and he was certain the scholars in both the Wraith and werewolf communities—had no idea what her blood would do when introduced into another, human or not. It could kill instantly, for all they knew. Her blood could be the plague that spread from creature to creature wiping the Earth clean of all supernatural beings, or it could be the most powerful mutation of the virus ever recorded. There was no telling—

Ben stopped and straightened his spine.

Flaring his nostrils, he caught Creed's scent stronger than ever before. He knew the wolf bounty hunter had spent considerable time marking his territory, but suddenly, his musk was overwhelming. Ben felt his wolf stir within him. Narrowing his eyes, he stared down the pitch-black hallway with his hybrid canine vision. There, standing silently in the darkness, was Creed. Ben balled his fists as he caught sight of the weapon in the bounty hunter's hand. Rage welled up from his heart and spread over his body like fire.

Slamming his hands against both walls to steady himself, he felt his fingers dig into the drywall and the studs beneath. His head snapped back as the wolf overcame him. The beast roared through Ben's open

215

mouth as his body began to contort and transform. Leveling his blood-red eyes on his target, he saw the bounty hunter begin to charge. Ripping free of Ben's flesh, the black-haired beast stood to its full height, barely fitting in the hallway. Dropping down on its clawed hands, the werewolf sprang forward.

The two wolves met with a thunderclap that rattled the house down to its foundation. Knocking the bounty hunter to the ground, Ben wrapped his meaty paw around Creed's chest and lifted him easily into the air. Slamming him into the floor repeatedly, it finally gave way. Shards of wood sailed into the air as Creed's body crashed into the substrata. Creed brought the axe up and cracked Ben solidly on the lower jaw with the flat area between the blades. As Ben's head snapped back, Creed recovered quickly. Rolling onto the balls of his feet, he sprang into the wolf's midsection. As the two tumbled over, Creed pressed the handle of his weapon solidly into Ben's throat and vaulted off the wolf with surprising agility and grace. Flipping in the air, the bounty hunter landed lightly on his toes without a sound. He spun the axe playfully in his hands as Ben lifted himself from the debris the two had created.

Creed sneered as he stared into Ben's burning red eyes. "Is that all you've got, puppy?"

Ben lowered to the ground, coiling his powerful body. His lips curled back into an evil sneer revealing his razor-sharp teeth. "How dare you wield the weapon of my clan? You have no right to even look upon it."

Creed looked down at the axe in his hands. Lifting his thumb to the blade, he carefully wiped a smudge away mocking the wolf. "It's my clan, too. I have every right to

216

this axe."

Ben growled and gnashed his teeth. His claws started to dig into the floor in anger. "You gave up those rights when you betrayed and murdered the chieftain!" Ben took a deep breath and roared, "You killed my father!"

"Ah, Daddy," the words oozed from Creed's mouth. "It did take quite some time to get his blood off my axe," he said, looking at the weapon lovingly. "But that was a good move for you, right? You're the chieftain now. Isn't that a promotion?"

Ben snapped.

Lurching straight up, his massive, muscled arms shot out and dug into the walls of the hallway. Ripping massive chunks of the house free, he hurled them at the bounty hunter. Creed easily dodged the raining debris, or knocked it away with the weapon. An evil grin spread across his face. Ben couldn't see that behind the dark glasses, Creed's eyes had shifted to red.

***

Nowhere near as plush as the top two levels, the hardwood and accents gave way to bare concrete floors and walls. Lights hung silently from the ceiling with a single bulb in each saucer-shaped fixture. Light spilled down onto the drab gray, barely able to keep the shadows at bay. They seemed to be slowly encroaching on the illumination as if unafraid.

They would reclaim what had once been theirs.

Thomas held his weapon firmly in his hand. Spinning the scythe with an unnecessary flourish, he stopped just short of an open door. Separated from Ben and Conrad,

217

he had followed the hallways down from the second floor to the basement.

She was near. He could feel her.

He felt a powerful thump somewhere above him. Dust and particles of wood and insulation flitted down from the ceiling, loosened by the impact. Instinct pushed him back against the wall, careful to avoid any falling debris. He knew the battle had begun. Time was running short.

Placing his hand on the edge of the doorway, he extended his senses inside. Opening his mind, he scanned the room for any threat of danger. Working back across the center of the large room, Thomas' eyes snapped wide open. Without a second thought or hesitation, he whipped around the doorframe and marched inside. Deactivating his scythe, he slid it onto his belt and stood staring at the sight before him. Anger welled up in him then. The furnace in his heart ignited.

She hung lifelessly from the ceiling, her hands and feet shackled. Her back arced forward painfully, her body having given up. She wasn't fighting anymore. She was just waiting for death. Her leather trench coat slid off her back to one side and pooled on the ground next to her. Her usually well-kept hair was a mess of sweat and tangles. Thomas knew she had fought, but Saint was close to death now. Taking a slow step forward, he pressed his hand to her shoulder. Still warm. Moving up to her throat, he checked for a pulse. It was thready but it was still there. He carefully placed his hand on her cheek and lifted her head. Staring into her tired, icy blue eyes, he felt her pain stab him in the chest like a dagger. Her eyes were unresponsive. No pupil dilation.

218

"I'm gonna get you out of here, Saint," Thomas said, reaching for the iron shackles around her wrists. "Don't die. Please don't die," he pleaded.

Holding her firmly against his chest, he snapped open the first shackle. Saint's arm fell lifelessly down over his shoulder. Reaching up, Thomas released the second restraint and felt her full body weight pressed against him. Slowly spinning her in his arms, the Wraith set her down gently on the floor. Moving to her feet, he stared at the caked blood around the restraints. They had been cutting into the flesh of her ankles. Her skin was raw and bloody around them. Wrapping his fingers around the iron, Thomas easily broke them open. Tossing them aside, he scooted on his knees and lifted her into his lap. He ran his fingers gently over her face, her eyes still staring off into nothingness. Unsure what to do, the anger in his heart grew more intense. He wasn't sure he could get her to the hospital in time, even with his preternatural speed. He felt helpless to do little more than sit in the middle of the floor and watch her die.

"Saint? Can you hear me, Saint?" He took a breath. "Emily? Don't you leave me. Don't you die on me."

He saw her eyes shift for the first time. She tried to focus on his face.

"Emily," he said with a new excitement in his voice, "can you hear me?"

Saint nodded slightly.

His heart was racing. "What do I need to do?"

Her mouth opened, but no sound came out.

"What did you say?" Thomas leaned closer to her face. "Emily?"

Saint's hand slowly lifted. As if trying to touch

Thomas' face, her fingers uncurled, but fell away. She just didn't seem to have the strength to do it.

Thomas quickly took her hand into his. "What is it? What can I do to help you?"

Her lips moved again, still no sound.

Thomas moved his ear closer again until he was barely above her lips.

Saint licked her lips. "Your blood," she whispered hoarsely.

Snapping her arms around his neck and chest, Saint moved with a speed and strength that seemed to come from nowhere. Opening her mouth wide, she bit deep into Thomas' throat and felt the two warm fountains of blood on her tongue. Rolling him over, she pinned him to the floor while she drank. Her instinct had taken over. She wasn't the Wraith Thomas knew anymore, she was now the product of thousands of years of genetic memory and evolution. She had reverted to the most primal level. She was no longer the protector; the vampire side of her had fully taken over. Creating two more punctures with her fangs, she took even more of his blood into her body. With each swallow, she felt his heart slowing. He was dying.

Something inside her snapped.

Sitting up, she felt confused and disoriented. She stared around Creed's trophy room, slowly becoming aware of what had happened, and where she was. Glancing down at Thomas below her, Saint quickly lifted off the Wraith. Lifting her hand, she ran it across her mouth and pulled it away. The blood on her hand instantly sickened and repulsed her. Her eyes fell back down to Thomas. She saw the numerous punctures on his neck and understood what she had done. The urge to retch gripped her, but she couldn't force her body to release any of the blood it had just taken. She felt warm, stimulated, and slightly groggy.

Falling back to the floor, she felt her conscious mind fighting for control over her baser instincts. She wanted to finish the job and feed off Thomas, but wouldn't allow herself to. Closing her eyes and gritting her teeth, she fought to suppress her vampiric nature. It wasn't who she was, she told herself. Writhing on the floor in pain, she felt Thomas' blood coursing through her body. He was charging through her veins. She could feel his emotions, his care—his love—for her. She had to focus on that. She couldn't let him die. He was here for her...

Her icy blue eyes snapped open as she regained control.

Ripping off her leather coat, she scooted next to Thomas and placed her hands tenderly on his face. His head fell back in her arms. He was close to death because of her. She understood what she had to do. Feeling down his trench coat, she felt a familiar shape in his pocket. It was exactly what she was looking for. Digging into the pocket, she produced Thomas' pocketknife. He never went anywhere without it. A gift from her, Saint had given it to him on his sixteenth birthday. She ran her fingers along the black hilt and down to the silver blade. It wasn't anything special, she thought as she locked open the blade, but it was about to save his life.

Pressing the blade firmly to her wrist, she closed her eyes and took a quick, shallow breath. With one pull, she layed open the flesh of her wrist and the veins beneath. Her blood started to flow. Dropping the knife to the floor, she turned her arm over and placed it on Thomas' mouth. She waited.

"Drink," she whispered slowly.

She had no idea if this would work. The same virus was already in their veins. It could only work if she was indeed the Chosen One...if she was different from the others. She uttered a silent prayer as she ran her fingers through his hair. He was unresponsive. Her mood began to darken as she watched her blood spill helplessly over his face and run down to the floor. She slowly exhaled and started to pull her arm away.

She wasn't the Chosen One. And her best friend was dead.

She started to reach for something to wrap around her wrist when she felt his hand grab onto her forearm. Turning back, she watched oddly as Thomas licked her blood off of his lips. Opening his eyes slowly, Saint stared at his deep brown eyes. She pumped her fist twice to get the blood flowing again and returned her wrist to Thomas' waiting mouth. To her relief, she felt him start to suck on the cut. A mixture of discomfort and sexual arousal washed over her body as his lips pressed tighter and tighter to her wrist. Staring into his eyes, she was horrified. She watched them change from dark brown to gold.

Immediately, she started to reach for his scythe. Ripping it free of his belt, she stared at the immaculate design of his new weapon. Thumbing the activation stud, the weapon sprang to life. Tapping it again, she watched with satisfaction as the scythe blade snapped open. Lifting the blade across Thomas' body, she moved slowly and carefully so that he could see she was ready—with no uncertainty—to end his life should this go wrong. His hands tightened around her arm. She started to feel weak as her life drained out of her.

His eyes were staying gold.

Saint cursed under her breath. Tightening her grip on the weapon, she prepared for the killing stroke. He had saved her life and now she had to kill him. Life wasn't fair. But then again, she already knew that. She dropped the blade down against the side of his neck. One quick pull and this would all be over. She stared at his gold eyes in horror. The prophecy was true. She was the Chosen One. But her blood wasn't going to create a new race of Wraiths; it was creating a new species of vampire. She watched Thomas' skin become pale, the veins in his face easily visible beneath the flesh. The transformation was almost complete. She had to act now. She started to pull—

Thomas…

Thomas' arm shot up like lightning. His fingers wrapped like steel bands around Saint's throat. Standing up with one fluid motion, the former Wraith lifted Saint and knocked the scythe from her hand. Rushing across the room, Thomas smashed Saint into one of Creed's trophy cases. As the relics smashed around her, she felt several shards of glass slice into her back. Thomas ripped her free of the case and threw her like a rag doll across the room. As her body crumpled to the floor, he was on her again. Sneering at her, she saw his new fangs. He wrapped his hand around her throat again.

That's it, Thomas. Let the evil flow through you.

"Thomas," she croaked, trying to catch her breath. "Thomas, don't do this. This isn't who you are."

Don't listen to her, boy. Become who you were meant to be!

He listened to the voice echoing loudly in his ears. It was right. He didn't want to fight it. Thomas smiled and ran his tongue over his newly created fangs savoring every bit of her blood that remained there. "It is now." Lifting her by the throat, he pinned her against the wall and started to lean in toward her throat.

Good! Destroy her!

Saint lurched forward and crushed the bridge of his nose with her forehead. As Thomas' head snapped back, she wrapped her hands around his chest and sprang off the floor. The two slammed into the ceiling creating a huge crater. As they fell to the floor, debris rained down around them. Jumping to her feet, Saint grabbed Thomas' coat and returned the favor he had given her just a few moments before. Using all her strength, she hurled him into the concrete wall. Before his body could even hit the floor, she was on him again.

Pinning Thomas to the wall, she stared into his golden eyes. "Damn you, Thomas! Fight it!" She saw his eyes flicker blue for a moment. Hope rose up in her.

"Saint," he breathed slowly. "It's me. It's Tommy. I'm okay."

Her grip loosened slightly. "Thank God."

Thomas looked at Saint as a wicked smile crossed his face. "Trick or treat?"

Saint felt the color drain from her face. "What?"

"Trick, then!" His eyes washed over gold again.

Saint's heart sank.

Kicking out, Thomas smashed his foot into Saint's kneecap. As the Wraith crumbled to the ground, he threw a savage right cross into her chin. Pulling back his balled fist, he hit her again. He drew back for a third, but she was ready for him this time. Ducking back just before his fist could connect, Saint grabbed Thomas' arm and pulled him down, sending him into an off balance spin to the ground. Rolling onto his back, she ignored the throbbing pain in her knee and pinned his arms behind his back.

"I know you're still in there." Saint grunted in pain. "You have to fight it, Thomas. God damn you, Thomas! You selfish bastard!" She slammed his head into the floor with her free hand. "I said fight it! You are better than this! Don't make me kill you!"

Thomas bucked Saint off and rolled to his feet. The sneer faded from his face as his eyes flickered to blue for just a moment. The evil seemed to melt off him as his expression became sorrowful. Falling to his knees, he slapped his hands to the sides of his head and roared at the top of his lungs. Tumbling to the ground, he curled his knees up to his chest and wrapped his arms around them.

Saint lifted her hand and summoned Thomas' scythe from the floor. The metal hilt slapped into the palm of her hand and instantly activated. "I'm only going to give you one more chance, Tommy," she warned.

Thomas stopped moving.

Saint took a cautious step closer, her weapon poised to strike. "Tommy?"

Thomas…

Thomas slowly rolled onto his back. His skin was flushed with color. "Saint?"

She cocked her head slightly and stared at Thomas. Saint couldn't be sure if it was another trick. She took a tentative step. Her eyes widened. His eyes had changed completely. No hint of gold remained. Once a deep brown, they were a pale—almost unnatural—blue, just like hers. His skin was returning to normal as well. She reached out with her senses. A smile flashed across her face. Dropping down next to Thomas, she placed her hand on his chest.

He slowly reached up and wrapped his hand around hers. Thomas smiled tenderly. "Thank you. You saved me."

"Thank you," Saint echoed.

Thomas chuckled softly. "Who owes who what in a situation like this?"

Saint let out a sigh and closed her eyes. "I think we'll just call it even."

A sound like thunder filled the room. Both Thomas and Saint snapped their heads up to see the roof collapsing above them. Grabbing Thomas by his jacket, Saint threw them both out of the way as debris started to slam to the ground around them. Using his coat, Thomas wrapped it over himself and Saint to try and protect them. As the dust started to settle, they looked up to see two werewolves standing in the middle of the floor.

Chapter Eighteen

Conrad skidded to a stop in front of the gaping crater in the floor. Boards and pipes jutted in hard angles from it like ribs broken through flesh. Staring down through the cloud of brown dust and particles that hung in the air, he saw the massive forms of two werewolves staring each other down. Sliding around the edge, he spotted Thomas and Saint watching in horror from the far corner. The two wolves held their positions, unmoving, as they stared at each other. Their chests heaved as they drew in breath. He could see several dark patches of fur that seemed to glisten in the flickering lights. He knew it was blood.

Holding his weapon tightly in his hand, he stared down into the potentially explosive situation. Conrad shook his head. "This is not a good idea." Without a second thought, he jumped.

Sailing through the air, Conrad's booted feet slammed squarely into Creed's shoulders. The werewolf was crushed to the ground under the Wraith. Leaping off the creature, Conrad somersaulted in the air, spun, and landed solidly to face the two wolves. Before he had a chance to attack again, Creed was on his paws and charging with a roar.

Conrad gritted his teeth. "Oh, so not good."

Creed's massive, curved claws reached for Conrad's head. Centimeters before they dug into his flesh, he saw a black blur hit Creed and knock him away. Snapping his head back slightly to avoid the snarling teeth and claws, Conrad watched the werewolves writhe on the floor.

227

Biting, clawing, tearing, the wolves wrestled for dominance.

The Master Wraith quickly turned and charged toward Thomas and Saint. He paused at the sight of blood on both of their mouths. "Are you two okay?"

Thomas nodded. "I feel," he paused, "fantastic."

Conrad stared at Thomas' pale blue eyes and pristine fangs. He had questions, but now wasn't time. He turned and looked at Saint. "We need to get you out of here."

Saint placed her hand on Conrad's shoulder. "I appreciate the gesture, but I'm not going anywhere. I have a score to settle."

Conrad shook his head vehemently, "I have to protest. You are far too important to—"

Thomas dove forward and knocked Conrad to the ground just as a massive paw of claws sliced through the air above them. Before Creed could continue the attack, Ben was on him again. Latching onto Creed's back, Ben used his hind legs to dig into the other wolf's back. As Creed howled in pain, Ben bit into his opponent's throat. Reaching down, Saint snatched Conrad's scythe. Bringing it up with a flourish, she carved the blade across Creed's chest. Letting the weapon's momentum carry her around, she brought the blade around and down burying the silver blade in the wolf's chest.

Creed knocked Ben away and stumbled back. Blood poured from around the blade, spilling onto the floor around him. Wrapping his massive hands around the hilt of the scythe, Creed tossed back his head and howled in agony as he pulled it free. The weapon hit the floor with a clatter as Creed lost his footing and tumbled backwards.

Wiping some of the blood from his muzzle, Ben

228

watched Creed with satisfaction. As a silver glimmer beneath the rubble caught his eye, he knew what he had to do. His clan's honor was about to be restored. He took a step forward and slid his massive hand into the debris and pulled his clan's axe free. He cradled the ceremonial weapon in his paws, savoring the moment. It had been years since the last time he touched it, yet it felt completely familiar, as if it had never left his hand.

Ben turned and looked at the three Wraiths standing behind him. "Leave."

The three understood.

Turning, Thomas quickly scooped up his and Conrad's scythes from the floor. Deactivating his Master's, he tossed it back as he slid his own firmly onto his belt. With his hand on the small of Saint's back, Thomas led the three toward the door. Partially obscured by fallen wreckage, there was still enough room to squeeze through one at a time. Turning to look back over his shoulder, Thomas saw a dark form hovering near the edge of the crater the two wolves created.

He placed his hand on Conrad's shoulder. "Wait."

Before the Wraith could act, the black form shot forward into the hole and floated down to the ground. Its cape was outstretched like a raven's wings. Touching down gently on the top of the wreckage, its golden eyes flashed with satisfaction. Lifting its black clad hand, he pointed toward Ben. A thin, silver tether launched from some unseen device and latched onto the wolf's chest. A bolt of blue electricity shot along the strand and slammed into Ben's body knocking him to the ground. As his body lay involuntarily convulsing, the wolf's hair quickly started to fall away revealing the pink, human flesh beneath. Snapping the tether with its opposite hand, the black form turned to the three Wraiths.

Saint's face contorted into a sneer. "Bane."

The Vampire Lord's dark cloak appeared unearthly in the flickering lights as it wafted around his body, almost as if it were alive. His rusty mask was almost invisible in the darkness, only two glowing yellow slits that were his eyes could be seen. Tossing back his cape, he revealed his long, curved arm blades. Without a hint of emotion from his masked face, he snapped the blades forward across the back of his hands. Letting his arms fall to his sides, his massive cloak enveloped his entire body, making him look less like a figure and more a shadow that had somehow come to life.

Bane bowed his head slightly allowing his massive hood to fall around his head. Extending one of his hands from the cloak, he threw a thick roll of bills onto Creed's dying body. "Should you live," his deep voice crackled metallically from the mask, "you have my appreciation."

Creed writhed on the floor. Scooping the money into his hand, he understood. "You used me," he managed finally.

"Everything is as I foresaw," Bane admitted. He looked one final time to Creed. "You were merely a pawn."

Thomas ripped his scythe from his belt and activated the sleek, black weapon. As his dual blades sprang to life, he stepped toward the Vampire Lord. "You won't get away this time, Bane." His glistening fangs flashed in the iridescent light.

Bane smiled behind his mask at the sight.

Conrad and Saint stood with Thomas in defiance.

230

Thomas spun his scythe over in his hands and dropped down into an attack position.

Bane's eyes flashed. "I don't intend to escape."

Conrad activated his scythe and leaned close to Thomas. "We'll go in slowly, and together. You take the left—"

"He's mine!" Thomas charged headfirst toward Bane. Spinning his scythe over his head, he brought a blade down toward the vampire.

The Vampire Lord transformed into a swirling mass of black and silver as he deflected Thomas' attack and countered. Knocking Thomas' weapon down and away, Bane's hand flashed out and snapped around the Wraith's throat. Lifting him easily off the ground, Bane flung the boy away like used tissue paper. Thomas' body hit the wall with a terrible crack. Sliding down to the floor, he crumbled into a heap unable to focus his eyes on the black form approaching him. Bane glided across the pile of rubble as though his feet weren't even touching it. Tossing back his cloak, his glistening arm blades were fully exposed.

Bane lifted his arm to strike.

"I wouldn't do that." Conrad clamped his hand around Bane's wrist.

"Brave," Bane said, turning his attention to the Master Wraith, "and foolish."

A sly grin crossed Conrad's face.

Slashing across his body, the Vampire Lord narrowly missed Conrad's midsection as the Master Wraith jumped away. Blocking Bane's second slash with his scythe, the two became a swirling mass of silver, black, and brown—each strike was parried, each attack was blocked. As the two moved back and forth across the uneven floor, it seemed as if Bane were growing in size. His massive cloak reached out like tendrils of darkness toward Conrad. Golden sparks flew in all directions as their weapons repeatedly crashed into each other. Conrad brought his scythe down and jabbed toward Bane's knees. The Vampire Lord scissored his blades across the scythe and held it in place.

Bane stared through his golden eyes at the Wraith. "Master Verge," he said the name slowly and deliberately, his evil voice oozing through the slits in his mask. "How disappointing. The Order holds you in such high regard." He released the hold and knocked the Wraith back with a swift kick. "Let's see if you can do better."

Conrad remained silent as he regained his footing. His face was stern. Spinning his scythe once, he dropped down into one of the classic Wraith defensive positions. As Bane attacked, he easily deflected the blows and held his ground. Out of the corner of his eye, he could see Thomas slowly lifting himself off the ground. He had to hold on for a little longer.

Saint skidded across the floor and landed next to Ben. She instinctively ran her hand over his head and across his ears as she would a beloved dog. His red eyes appeared tired, blurry, and distant. She slowly rolled his head to face her. "Ben?"

He seemed to gain a moment of clarity. Lifting his massive paw, Ben carefully ran his fingers down her face. "Saint," he breathed slowly. "It's so good to see you alive." He looked down at his body. "I can't feel my legs."

232

"It's okay," Saint said softly. "We'll get you out of here."

His hand paused at her mouth. He stared at the blood running down from her chin. His eyes widened. "What have you done?" His tone was a mixture of horror and dismay.

"I," the words jammed in her throat. "We don't have time for this. I need to get you out of here."

Ben shook his head as his muzzle reverted to human form. "The tip of whatever that was Bane hit me with," he took a labored breath, "was filled with silver nitrate." Blue veins erupted onto his face, tearing through his flesh. Saint knew the nitrate was coursing through his body, destroying his werewolf biology. "Take this," he said, handing his clan's axe to Saint. "Return it to my people. Please."

"Ben," Saint breathed sorrowfully. She watched his flesh turn ashen as the silver worked its way into every one of his cells. Leaning over, she gently kissed her protector on the forehead. "Hold on a little longer. I won't leave you."

Resting Ben's head on the floor, she took the massive axe in her hands and stood up. She turned toward Bane and gripped the weapon tightly. Anger rose up in her heart at the sight. The Vampire Lord had taken everything away from her: her Master, her lover, her home, and now, her protector. The anger melted into pure rage. Channeling all of her aggression, she lifted the axe high above her head and charged.

Leaping off her toes, Saint lifted high into the air and attacked. Bringing the heavy weapon over her head, it sang as it sliced through the air. The blade tore deep into the flesh of Bane's shoulder. The Vampire Lord grunted in pain and stumbled forward, barely missing Conrad's continued attack. Whipping his blades around, Bane hit Saint solidly in the stomach with the dull side knocking the breath out of her. As her hands slipped from the axe handle, Saint fell back clutching her chest as she gasped for breath.

Using his free hand, Bane ripped the axe free and tossed it angrily to the ground. Blocking another of Conrad's attacks, Bane felt the pain reverberating through his body. He missed Conrad's parry and felt the sting as the scythe blade sliced across his chest. As he fell back, he saw Thomas rising to his feet and moving in for the attack. He was outnumbered, but his plans had been accomplished.

Snapping his blades back, he focused his energy and leapt straight up through the crater in the roof. Landing on the edge, he perched and stared back down at the three Wraiths. Standing tall, he whipped his cloak around his body and vanished.

Conrad looked to Thomas. "Everyone okay?"

"No." Saint charged across the floor and dropped down next to Ben.

Conrad and Thomas turned and looked at their werewolf companion. Completely human, the large gashes from Creed's savage attack were readily apparent on his naked body. A large, purple mass in the center of his chest showed where Bane's weapon had hit him. Small bits of silver around the wound glittered in the flickering light. Sliding her hand under his head, she could feel his life quickly draining. She had to get him out of here. Lifting Ben in her arms, she walked carefully

234

toward the wreckage in front of the door. Saint knew what she had to do: she had to get him back to his clan. They would know what to do. Reaching out, she grabbed the debris and threw it away from the door as if it were nothing. Without another look at the two remaining Wraiths, she left. She had to save Ben.

"Not so tough when you're facing down a Vampire Lord, are you?" Creed laughed hoarsely. Still clutching the wad of cash Bane tossed him, he was somewhere between man and wolf. As he laughed, it turned into a wave of coughing. Blood from his mouth splattered on his chin.

Thomas lifted Ben's axe from the ground and twirled it in his hands.

Conrad grabbed Thomas by the shoulder. "You don't have to. He's already dying."

Thomas ripped free of the Master Wraith's grip and walked slowly toward Creed.

Standing over the werewolf, Thomas looked at Creed with a sneer. Lifting the axe high over his head, he paused. He stared into Creed's blood red eyes looking for any sign of remorse.

Nothing.

Gritting his teeth, he brought the axe sailing down squarely on Creed's neck. As his head rolled free, the money in his hand fell to the floor.

He had lost his prize after all.

***

Thomas stared at the axe's discolored head. Containing blood from Creed, Bane, and Ben, the blade seemed to have somehow lost a bit of its luster. This once proud symbol had been perverted. He thought about tossing it away, but Ben would want it back to return to his clan. If he survived… Slinging the axe over his shoulder, Thomas turned back to Conrad. His face was solemn and drawn. "Do you think Ben will survive?"

Conrad didn't know the answer. "If Saint gets him to his clan in time." It was all he could think of to say. Conrad stood staring at Creed's magnificent home. "We need to get back to England. We're only days away from the vote." He paused, seeming lost in thought for a moment. "This could very well determine the fate of the Wraith. We should be there."

He turned and looked at Thomas. His dark coat was billowing around him as the breeze swept in from the water. Little more than a silhouette, Conrad could see a difference in the way his former apprentice held his body. He seemed fundamentally changed somehow. He seemed older now and powerful. Conrad felt his blood run cold. Thomas had always been counted among the most powerful Wraiths. Now, Conrad took a quick breath, it was almost unfathomable.

Walking slowly down onto the beach, Conrad couldn't take his eyes off Thomas. The urge to draw his scythe pulled hard on his conscious, yet he fought it. He had known this boy—this man—since he was twelve years old. On more than one occasion, he had trusted his life to Thomas, who had done the same in return. Yet he couldn't ignore the nagging feeling at the back of his mind that something inside Thomas had changed. He felt an air of unease surrounding the Wraith as he neared.

"Thomas," Conrad breathed.

The young Wraith made no attempt to acknowledge his former Master.

Conrad stopped short of Thomas, well out of arm's reach. "Are you okay?"

Thomas stared silently into the ever-brightening sky. The sun was slowly dawning behind them painting the sky various shades of pink, red, and orange. A column of glittering water stretched off as far as he could see. It was stunning, and it was as if he were seeing it for the first time. Taking a breath of the salty air in through his nose, he felt it roll down his windpipe into his lungs. His perception of the world had changed. Saint's blood not only included more power, but a basic change to his entire being. He was not the same man he was an hour ago.

Finally turning away from the view, Thomas looked on the Master Wraith with his new, icy blue eyes. "I'm not going back."

Conrad wanted to be surprised at the response, but wasn't. He felt it coming. There was only one question that came to his mind. "Why?"

Thomas turned back to the ocean. "He's out there."

"Who?"

"Bane," Thomas replied quickly. "I intend to track him."

"And then what?" Conrad asked incredulously. "Try and fight him alone? You'll get yourself killed!"

"Maybe," Thomas offered with a nod, "but maybe I can bring an end to this war." He turned and faced his Master fully for the first time. "You're right. You need to be there for the vote. The remaining Wraiths count on your guidance. You belong there." He let his gaze fall away. "I don't."

Conrad was confused and angered by the statement. "How can you say that?" He continued without waiting for the response he knew wouldn't come. "Are you trying to tell me that you're leaving the White Guard?"

Thomas drew a deep breath into his lungs and slowly exhaled. "No," he said finally. "I'm just trying to explain that my path goes in a different direction than yours now." He placed his hands on Conrad's shoulders. "You've been an excellent teacher but it's time for me to fly on my own now."

Conrad tried to hide the hurt he was feeling at Thomas' words.

"I'm not a politician or a leader," Thomas added. "I'm a warrior. I only understand one thing." He smirked. "Battle."

The Master Wraith nodded. He knew his student spoke the truth.

"I'm not asking for your permission," the young Wraith added with a streak of defiance. "I'm telling you."

Conrad found himself speechless.

Thomas let go and took a step back. He had a soft smile on his face. "Don't worry. I'll see you again."

Nodding, Conrad extended his hand. "Good hunting, Thomas."

Thomas accepted the gesture and shook Conrad's hand. "And to you, too, Master."

Turning, Thomas started down the beach.

Conrad watched him slowly disappear from sight. As the darkened sky began to light, the Master Wraith couldn't shake the ominous feeling that gripped his soul.

238

PART THREE

The darkness is patient.

The darkness is all consuming.

As the impurity overrides the liquid, it reaches out to the shoreline and into every tributary. What was once pure is now tainted. The darkness strives even before the stars grow cold.

It must wait no more. The light begins to dim as the blackness stretches like raven's wings across the sky.

Its time has arrived.

It always wins.

Chapter Nineteen

He stood quietly amidst the filth. Trash littered the corners, the wallpaper curled to the floor, and the windows were so stained that almost no light filtered in. But this was to be the beginning and the end. It would be here, in this disgusting apartment, that mankind's reign as the dominant species would end. It seemed fitting somehow to the vampire. Everything in this place had been used and tossed aside, even him. It was the human's shortsightedness that allowed this to happen.

He would not be tossed away like useless rubbish.

He held his hands on the sides of the altar. Thirteen white candles lined the back of what used to be a podium, the exact number the ritual called for. Digging into his green army coat, he pulled a silver Zippo free. He stared at his former company's logo emblazoned on the front and angrily flipped open the top. All of those men—good men—were long since dead. They deserved better than their fates. They deserved more from the race they had chosen to protect. He flicked the lighter with his thumb and watched a yellow flame jump to life. Moving it from one candle to the next, he carefully lit each one, pausing just long enough to make sure the flame didn't go out.

A thick black book sat in the center of his makeshift altar. Sweeping a shock of his long, black hair out of his face, he ran his fingers gently over the worn cover. It had taken him some time to find this book. He needed this exact one. This, and only this copy, contained the exact specifications of the ritual. Cracking open the heavy tome, he breathed in the musty smell of the paper. He had marked the pages he needed with a thin, red ribbon.

This was his moment of triumph. All was in readiness. He must begin the process. Lifting a slender knife from the altar, he held his right hand, palm up, over the book. Using the tip of the blade, he carved a symbol into the flesh of his hand as he chanted in a long since dead language. A triangle within a circle…he carved the pattern carefully as his blood welled up from the wound. Setting the athame aside, he turned his hand over and held it directly in the flame of the nearest candle. He could smell the symbol being seared into his flesh.

He was now marked as the Vessel.

Turning away from the altar, his eyes settled on the beautiful young woman lying unconscious on the floor. Her face was beaten and bruised, yet there were no cuts. None of her precious blood had been spilled. Snatching her from the floor, the vampire pinned her against the wall. Her body limp, he wasted no time. Diving forward, he dug his fangs into her throat and began to drink. The woman's eyes snapped open in terror. She tried to scream but her voice was lost in a deep, crimson gurgle in her throat.

Behind him and in front of the altar, a black sphere appeared out of thin air. The sphere began to spin. Faster and faster it spun until gravity flattened it like a pancake. An arc of electricity flashed out from the center of it as it snapped, popped and hissed angrily. The flattened sphere grew in size as the Vessel drank. With each gulp of her ruby life, the blackness became larger. As he took the final swallow of her blood into his mouth, the flattened sphere imploded inward, then doubled in size.

The Vessel dropped the dead body to the floor, turned and looked at its creation. No longer a flattened sphere, it looked like a black hole floating freely in the center of the apartment. The vortex churned and swirled pulling energy into itself, but this was not enough. It needed more blood. It needed to be fed.

The Vessel knew what must be done.

***

Conrad stared in horror at the ruins of the Wraith Academy in England. The broken, charred walls jutted into the gray sky above like ribs that had burst savagely through flesh. The academy lay open like a rotting corpse. More than just the loss of the original academy, it was a symbol of the times. The Wraiths were losing the war. This was a harsh reminder that no one, no place, was safe anymore.

If Bane could strike with such precision in the heart

241

of the order, what hope did they have of defeating this monster?

A light rain was falling on the British coast. Conrad pulled his battered brown leather jacket around his chest and crossed his arms. Lowering his head, he felt overwhelmed by the loss. He could hear the echoes of dying Wraiths and students as Bane's vampires marched into the school and slaughtered them without remorse. The clatter of scythes falling to the ground in defeat was almost deafening as he began to walk slowly through the ruins.

He didn't want to be here.

Only his second visit to the academy since its destruction, Conrad didn't like it here. He had trouble focusing on the task at hand as a riptide of emotion washed over him and threatened to pull him out to sea. He felt lost and confused. This had once been the shining jewel of the Gwyliad Wriaeth. It was the center of all knowledge, and home to many, many, many generations of hunters. They were the secret guardians of humanity, the silent protectors fighting back the darkness.

Now it was gone.

Conrad mentally scolded himself. To dwell on the past served no purpose. The Wraiths were always taught to move forward. There was no sense in brooding on the past as nothing could be done to change it. The only thing left was to learn the lessons here, hopefully preventing them from happening again. To his eyes, this was more than a tomb, it was a warning for future generations. The very reason it still stood was a reminder. He could not forget. He would not.

Glancing up, he saw the first members of his party

walk slowly into what used to be the main entrance of the enclave. Their faces were drawn with pain and anguish. For many of them, this was their first visit to the academy since its destruction. The Master Wraith set his jaw and waited for them to come to him. As they approached, Conrad turned slightly and bowed respectfully. "Chancellor."

Chancellor Alexander paused briefly at the title. He still wasn't used to hearing it, but it pleased him. A soft smile crossed his face. "You don't need to bow, Master Verge. We're all equals here."

Conrad felt the chancellor's words hit his chest and slither onto the ground. Less a Wraith and more a politician, Alexander was especially good at playing the weaknesses of his opponents. This was no doubt the reason he had been elected. In retrospect, the Master Wraith knew Xavier had no chance of defeating him in the election. Xavier was honest and proud—everything a politician was not required to be.

"Did you find what you were looking for, Chancellor?" Conrad asked, still perplexed as to why he was even here.

Alexander smiled with a nod. "Indeed, thank you, Master Verge. This place still has much potential." The chancellor paused. "As do you."

Conrad's expression remained unchanged, despite the shock he felt at the statement.

Alexander dismissed his personal guards and attendants and stepped toward Conrad. "I need a word with you, Master Wraith." He placed his hand gently on Conrad's shoulder in a motion both familiar, yet impersonal. He easily maneuvered the two away from prying ears. "I consider your advice to be among the sagest in the Order," he spoke slowly, "and I need it now."

Conrad tried to take a step away from the chancellor's grasp without looking disrespectful. "I am at your disposal, Chancellor."

"That's exactly what I wanted to hear," Alexander said with a grin. "As you know, the changes to the Order have been rather," he paused and searched for the appropriate word, "sweeping. I need people I can trust at my side to make sure everything goes smoothly. Never let it be said I don't love the Order."

Conrad knew Alexander was playing to his sensibilities as a patriot.

"We need to move forward to survive this war, and ensure that we are here to protect humanity for centuries to come," Alexander continued. "That's why I am reforming the council."

The Master Wraith was unable to hide his shock this time. "I'm afraid I don't understand," Conrad admitted. "Part of your election platform was to dismantle the various councils and centralize the ruling body of the Wraiths."

"That's true." The chancellor nodded. "But I realize in retrospect that the order is far too large and diverse for one man to lead." Alexander stopped and rethought his plan of attack. "I need your help, Master Verge. I would like you to lead the Council of Seven."

Conrad cocked his head slightly. "Me?"

"You are one of the most respected Masters in the Order," Alexander complimented. "To pick anyone else would be foolish on my part."

"What would my responsibilities entail?"

"You would lead the council, handle all disputes, and oversee the assignments of individual Wraiths," Alexander replied. "You would have almost complete autonomy in these matters."

"We would report directly to you?" Conrad asked after a moment.

Alexander nodded. "I have to look at the big picture for the sake of all Wraiths. I can't allow myself to become mired in the day-to-day routine of running the Order. I need good people like you to help me if we are to survive and win this war." The chancellor stopped and waited expectantly.

Conrad took a slow breath and assessed the chancellor. He was wary of this man, but couldn't find fault with his argument. If he were head of the reborn council, Conrad knew he could keep a watchful eye on all the chancellor's dealings. Wiping a bit of rain from his brow, Conrad slowly extended his hand to Alexander.

Alexander smiled broadly. "So you accept my proposal?"

Conrad nodded. "I am honored by this selection, Chancellor."

"Wonderful." Alexander grasped the Master Wraith's hand and shook it firmly. "I think we should begin immediately." He again placed his hand on Conrad's shoulder, "I am leaving it to you to select the remaining six members of the council. Of course, all selections must be approved through my office," Alexander looked Conrad squarely in the eyes, "for security reasons, you understand."

"Of course," Conrad replied quickly.

"With your acceptance, you are also bestowed with another honor," the chancellor spoke slowly and evenly. "I can't allow a Master Wraith to be the head of the Council of Seven. Therefore," a smile flashed on the Chancellor's face, "I am granting you the rank of High Wraith, effective immediately."

Conrad couldn't quell the smile that spread across his face. He had wanted this promotion longer than he could remember. Very few High Wraiths had survived the purge. He would almost be the first of a new line, and as the head of the Council of Seven, he would only have to answer to the chancellor. The opportunity was overwhelming. "Thank you, Chancellor."

A wicked grin spread across Alexander's face but disappeared just as quickly as it appeared. "You deserve it, Master Verge. I can't think of anyone more qualified, or deserving of this honor." He lifted his hand and signaled his guards to return. "We must begin repairs on this great facility at once." He turned and lifted his hands slightly as if addressing a huge crowd. "We will return the academy to its former greatness!"

Conrad watched the new chancellor, his aides, and his guards turn back and walk into the hulking corpse that once was the Wraith Academy. As the party disappeared from sight, his elation abated and a familiar feeling tugged at his senses. Looking up into the sky above, he let the raindrops fall on his face and wash over him. As the air began to chill, he saw the first few flakes of winter plummet from the gray sky. Lifting his hands, he wiped the water from his face and sighed.

He hoped he was wrong. For the sake of the Order and the future, Conrad hoped he was wrong. His thoughts

246

turned to his apprentice. He needed him now more than ever.

*****

Snowflakes fell gently from the heavy gray clouds overhead. Standing silently, he stared into the massive picture window at the holiday scene within. The warm, yellow light spilled out onto the snowy ground and over his body, but provided no warmth. Three mannequins representing a father, mother, and son were arranged around an ersatz Christmas tree frozen in time as they gleefully opened presents he was sure contained nothing. Festive sweaters in the colors of the season wrapped snugly around the mannequins' chests, and caring smiles were painted on their plastic lips. He knew it was all forged but he couldn't help envying them.

Thomas was alone.

Turning away from the department store window, the Wraith started slowly down the empty street. A warm black sweater was wrapped around his chest with a white t-shirt peeking out from beneath. His thick, black boots glistened in the low light as snow hit and melted leaving a watery sheen on the leather. Thomas hiked up his collar and adjusted the long, black scarf wrapped around his throat. He dug his hands into the pockets of his leather trench coat as he disappeared from the brightly lit main street into the darkness.

The last week had brought a particularly cold snap to the area. Too cold for most to be out this time of night, including vampires and Wraiths it seemed. He lost the trail of the vampire he was tracking some time ago. It

247

seemed as if it just vanished. An especially brutal creature, this one had left a string of dead bodies from Sacramento, through Reno, and now in Lake Tahoe. He would find the vampire, but not tonight.

With his head down, he walked along the edge of the rustic road that headed out of town. Dodging the half frozen puddles of slush, he listened to the crunch of snow under his feet. He had traveled this road a dozen times before. He knew where it led. He knew what was there waiting for him:

Nothing.

It had been the same ever since he left Conrad in San Francisco. His vow to track and destroy Bane hadn't produced any results other than whispers and hearsay from vampire clans and other Wraiths of the lord's existence. The trail had gone cold almost a month ago in Canada, but Thomas had neither the heart, nor the desire to return home to England. Feeling like a dog that had been left out in the cold too long, he eyed the warmth and safety of England jealously but knew deep down in his heart, he didn't belong. He knew his choice to track Bane by himself was a bad one in retrospect. He couldn't bring himself to face Conrad.

He felt exiled by his own hand.

As he rounded a bend in the road, he spotted a small log cabin sitting by itself in the distance. Smoke was rolling out of the stone chimney on the roof and a soft yellow light filtered through the windows. It wasn't his, but he called it home. He would live here until the owners returned to claim it. It was peaceful and serene. There were no other souls within miles of this place. He found that he could think and sort through his feelings here. It had become his haven in the wilderness. It was his sanctuary, his refuge from the world.

Turning onto the dirt driveway that led to his front door, he felt his guard come down. His tired muscles relaxed while the darkness washed off him in waves. His posture changed as he slumped forward a bit. His icy blue eyes became dull as the glimmering sheen of intensity melted away.

He was home.

As he stepped onto the wooden deck, he reached for the door handle but something swayed his hand. He stopped as his fingers brushed against the rounded handle and fell away. An odd sensation galloped down his spine sending shivers to the furthest extremities of his body. Taking a slow step back from the door, Thomas melted into the darkness and stared into the cabin's window.

His icy blue eyes hardened as a dark form danced past the pane.

Thomas' hand instinctively slid inside his leather trench coat and wrapped around his scythe. Snapping it off his belt, he held the black metallic cylinder in his right hand, his thumb hovering over the activation stud. He steeled his nerves. He was completely silent as he moved across the wooden deck and spun, pressing his back to the wall.

Closing his eyes for a moment, the Wraith reached out with his enhanced senses. Weaving through the cabin, he found the intruder. As his invisible mental tether slid around the figure, he knew it wasn't human—he paused—at least not entirely. He took a slow breath into his lungs and focused more deeply. There was something about this being that wasn't exactly right. It seemed to shimmer between two realms of existence, both sides fighting for it, yet belonging to neither. He concentrated harder, but felt as if he were being blocked. His mental probes seemed to slide off this being for some reason. Since receiving his gift from Saint, he had never encountered anything like this. His curiosity was piqued.

His fingers loosened slightly from the scythe. Drawing back his mental probes, he stepped away from the wall and turned to face the door. Focusing his mental energy once again, he pushed open the door and stood fast. The dark form within took shape. Thomas felt his mouth fall agape.

His eyes fell upon her for the second time, yet it seemed as though he had known every curve, every detail of her face for an eternity. He had seen her hundreds of times in his mind's eye, but now, she was real. And she was everything he wanted in that moment. Her smile was soft and inviting, while her lush blue eyes spoke volumes about her life experiences. They were intelligent but playful, sultry but restrained. Her blonde hair fell across her porcelain skin and licked her shoulders. She was the woman of his dreams. Desire welled up in his chest and washed over his body in waves.

She was still alive. Thomas knew it. After all this time, she was still alive.

The Wraith found himself unable to speak as he locked gazes with her. Questions welled up in his mind but died as quickly as they tried to pass by his throat. He felt his hands go limp and barely noticed the clatter of the scythe as it fell to the ground. He took a tentative step forward but stopped. His years of training fought to hold him back. His eyes were wide and unblinking as he stared. Forcing his foot forward, Thomas took another step. Swallowing down his fears and doubts, he moved again. Before he knew it, he had crossed the floor and swept the vampiress into his arms.

The two embraced for the first time. His hands pressed firmly against her back while hers ran slowly through his hair. Calm and peace washed over the two as their hearts beat with excitement in their chests. Neither had the desire to break the hold and they were content to spend the rest of their days in each other's arms. There was no pretense, no battle between good and evil—there was only this moment. Everything else was gone.

Thomas slowly pulled back from the woman and pressed his hand tenderly to her face. He had seen it a thousand times in his dreams. He prayed this wasn't another. If it were, he had no intention of ever waking up. He caressed his thumb across the corner of her mouth and her full lips. He smiled softly as he stared into her blue eyes.

"I'm Thomas," he breathed.

She returned the smile and laughed softly. It amused her that they didn't even know each other's names. "Katherine," she replied, "Kat." She stared into his icy blue eyes, slightly confused for a moment. They weren't as she remembered. "I never thanked you," she drew a slow breath, "for saving my life."

Thomas didn't know how to respond. He wasn't sure that a simple, "You're welcome," was the appropriate response. He nodded solemnly instead.

"Your eyes," Kat said, running her porcelain fingers down his cheek, "they weren't always blue."

Thomas shook his head. "No. They were brown."

"I like them," Kat offered. "They're very powerful. It almost feels like you're staring into my soul."

"What..." Thomas let the question fall back, but needed to know. He pressed. "What are you?"

"I wish I knew," Kat answered honestly. Her voice was full of regret. "I don't know what I am anymore." She stared into the Wraith's blue eyes. "Does it really matter?"

Thomas paused. It did not. Reaching out, he pulled her close to his body and wrapped his arms around her again. "No," he said with a breath. "How did you find me?"

"I've been tracking you since San Francisco," Kat answered. "Since I became, well, what I am, you are the only person who showed me any kindness. I had to know..." She stopped and pulled back slightly. "I had to know why."

A flood of emotions washed over the Wraith. He wanted to tell her everything, but didn't want to risk losing her. Talk of prophetic dreams often had that effect on people, yet she was different. Thomas felt that she would understand.

"Kat," he said her name for the first time, rolling it around his mouth. The hard consonants wrapped around the creamy vowel sound creating a unique flavor. It was sweet, but had a distinct bitter bite at the end. It broke too quickly on his tongue and the taste was fleeting.

"It's hard to explain. I've had these dreams," he started slowly, unsure of his own mind, "About you."

Kat's eyes widened. "Me?"

Thomas nodded. "Ever since I can remember, I've dreamed of you. I saw you that night on the roof in San

Francisco, and in every dream, I lost you." He held onto her shoulders, hoping to stop her if she tried to fly. "When that moment actually arrived," his voice wavered. "I couldn't stand the thought of losing you again."

"You dreamed of me?" Kat asked again, trying to wrap her mind around the idea. She felt somehow important now, as if she were part of some grand scheme. Yet at the same time, she found herself doubting his words. It wasn't that she didn't believe him, she just didn't want to. She couldn't deal with it right now. She didn't want to deal with it at all. "Do you trust me, Thomas?"

"Implicitly," he answered without a second thought.

Kat leaned in and kissed the Wraith on the lips. She felt a spark of electricity as they touched. Opening her mouth, she slid her tongue eagerly into his. Thomas quickly reached out with his mind and shut the cabin's door. His hands found their way to the front of Kat's blouse and quickly unbuttoned it. Entwined, the two sank down to the rug below.

Chapter Twenty

Conrad stepped into the council chambers and stopped. The room was mostly intact, except for the massive doors that once guarded the room. The bodies of the Council of Seven, along with several vampires, had already been cleaned out long ago leaving no trace of the battle waged here. The massive columns stood quietly, unwilling to reveal their secrets. At the back of the chamber stood the raised metal platform he had seen the council deliver judgment from many times. A wide row of stairs led up to the platform with half burned candles lining the sides. Aides and acolytes would traditionally keep the candles new and maintained, but they were gone now—as was everything else he knew and valued. The room seemed quiet and lifeless. Once solemn, it now held no dignity and reverence. Its sanctity had been violated and raped by Bane and his army. It was broken.

It was his job to make amends.

Lifting his chin, he walked proudly through the chamber. This was his now. He would restore glory to the council and the Wraith. He knew he was the first in a new generation of council members, a council that would not necessarily have to adhere to the mandates and rules of old. It would be a new age. He would wipe the darkness from the face of the Earth and bring a new era of peace and prosperity to humanity, even if he had to forcefully stop the petty bickering between nations. A second golden age of the Gwyliad Wriaeth would soon be upon them…

He paused for a moment to reflect on his thoughts. They didn't sound like the Wraith he knew. Conrad mentally scolded himself. He was letting his new position corrupt his integrity. It was going to his head too fast. But that didn't feel right either. That wasn't him. Lifting his hand, he held his palm to his forehead realizing for the first time his head was throbbing. Taking a step back, he felt woozy. He balled his fists and pressed them to his temples as he leaned over slightly. The throbbing increased in intensity as sparkling spots appeared in front of his eyes. His world began to spin. Reaching out for one of the columns to steady himself, Conrad missed and spilled to the floor. He tossed his arms out wildly to try and break his fall.

Rolling onto his back, he cradled his right wrist as pain surged up his arm. Conrad bit his lip to stifle it. Lying his head on the cool stone floor, he found a bit of relief.

"Conrad?"

He lifted his head slightly to see a form moving closer in the darkness. As the pounding in his head returned, Conrad immediately abandoned his inquisitiveness and closed his eyes.

"Master Verge?" the voice asked again, this time, with more urgency beneath it.

The High Wraith felt a hand on his shoulder and recognized the soft sound of the voice. "Saint," he breathed.

Saint crouched down next to the fallen Wraith. Sweeping her long, black leather trench coat out of the way, she dropped to her knees. Her black hair spilled over the look of concern on her face. "What happened?"

"I don't know," Conrad answered honestly. "I was just walking through the council chamber, when my head started to throb." He exhaled slowly trying to quell the pain. "I lost my balance and fell." He slowly opened his eyes and looked at the young Wraith. "What are you doing here?"

"Master Xavier told me that you wanted to see me in the council chambers," Saint answered quickly, almost as if in passing. "Are you going to be okay, Conrad?"

"Give me your hand," Conrad instructed.

Saint reached down and grabbed Conrad's right hand.

He quickly jerked it away as if scalded. "Wrong hand," he grunted.

"You didn't say—"

"It's okay," Conrad said, offering his left hand. "I landed wrong in the fall. Help me up."

Saint pulled the High Wraith to his feet and started to dust off his brown leather jacket. "Are you sure you're okay?"

"Yes, thank you, dear." Conrad ran his fingers gently over his forehead and nodded gingerly. Taking a slow, deep breath, he felt the pain begin to pass. "I'll be fine. How's Ben?"

Saint smiled sheepishly. "Playing like a puppy. I swear, that man has more energy."

Conrad could see the signs of love on her face. It made his heart jump. If anyone deserved a little joy and happiness in this world, it was Saint. "Then he's recovering well?"

"Recovered." Saint beamed. "I couldn't get him to stay in bed one more day. I found him down at his auto

256

shop this afternoon pulling an engine from an old Ford truck," she paused, "with his hands."

Conrad laughed. "Very good. I'm glad to hear that." He turned and looked at the platform again. "Walk with me."

Saint, dressed completely in black, turned and walked slowly toward the platform. Reaching up, she adjusted the heavy turtleneck sweater she wore beneath her familiar black leather jacket. She felt slightly apprehensive standing next to the High Wraith. She had known Conrad since she was a small girl, but with his promotion, something seemed different. Perhaps it was just her perception of him that had changed. Or perhaps it was the memory of her last visit to these chambers that made her uneasy. She remembered the slaughter of the original council at Bane's hands, and how she had been too late to stop it.

"You know I have been placed on the Council of Seven," Conrad started slowly, "and I have been tasked with picking six more members to complete it."

"Do you have anyone in mind?" Saint asked without pretense.

"I have a mental list," Conrad smiled. "It's just a matter of asking them now. There is nothing more important than the reformation of this council. We have an obligation to the Wraith, and the chancellor."

"It seems like you want more than that," Saint observed, reading between the lines.

"My motives," Conrad paused, "are just."

Saint nodded. She had no reason not to believe him. He had never lied to her.

Conrad stopped and turned to face Saint. "I would

257

like you to join the Council."

Saint's icy blue eyes widened, but she controlled her shock. "Why?"

"I don't think there's much to explain." Conrad laughed. "You are the Chosen One. To not include you would be a detriment to what I'm trying to accomplish."

Saint smiled awkwardly. She was getting tired of hearing that title. She was no longer a person, rather, the mystical tool of destiny. It was starting to get on her nerves. "Is that the only reason?"

"No." Conrad laughed, sensing Saint's unhappiness. "I value your advice and I trust your instincts." He placed his hand on Saint's shoulder much in the same way Alexander had done to him earlier in the day. He realized this and quickly let his hand slide away. "You are one of the finest Wraiths this academy ever produced, Saint. I would be honored to have you sit next to me on the Council."

"Thanks," Saint said softly. She wasn't sure if she was ready to make a decision. She pushed the question away for a moment. "Who else is on the list?"

"Master Xavier," Conrad answered with a name she would be familiar with. "A few others," he stopped, "and Thomas."

Saint couldn't stop the shock from escaping her this time. "It's not that I don't trust your judgment, but you want Thomas to sit on the council?"

Conrad nodded.

"Do you think he's ready for that much responsibility?" Saint looked warily at Conrad. "We haven't even seen or heard from him in almost six months."

"He is," Conrad exhaled, "the most powerful Wraith in existence." He stopped and played nervously with his fingers. "We owe him a seat on the council."

"You don't trust him," Saint surmised in amazement.

Conrad's gaze fell away from the young Wraith.

"Why?"

The High Wraith returned his attention to Saint. "I can't explain it," he breathed. "There is a seed of darkness in his heart. I can't tell you the future, but the possibility is there."

"The possibility of what?"

Conrad's face fell into a frown. He knew exactly what he wanted to say, but he couldn't push the words out of his throat. His gaze fell away from the Chosen One.

Saint felt her heart sink. The High Wraith's silence confirmed everything she feared. In this time of war and loss, that was the last thing the Wraith needed. And he was her friend. "Then why didn't you force him to come back to England with us? Why did you leave him to his own devices?" She felt a touch of anger creep into her voice. "So now you want to offer him a token seat on the council to get him back to England," Saint said, finally understanding Conrad's logic. "This is just a pain-free way to get him back under control."

"Yes," Conrad replied matter-of-factly.

Saint exhaled and got control over her anger. Reaching down, she took Conrad's hand into hers. "I hope you know what you're doing."

Conrad squeezed her hand and nodded. "I do, too." He took a sharp breath. "I'm leaving for America this afternoon."

"I'm going with you," Saint added quickly.

"No," Conrad dismissed the idea outright. "I need you to stay here and take care of the council in my absence."

Saint laughed. "I haven't even accepted a position yet. Plus, you'll need me." She let her smile fade away. "Just in case."

Conrad smiled softly. "Thank you for your concern, Emily, but I have known Thomas since he was a very young boy. I'll be fine." He placed his hand tenderly on Saint's cheek, then slowly let it fall away. Turning, he started toward the exit.

Saint waited for the High Wraith to disappear from sight. Standing quietly, she felt a devious grin spread across her lips. "Like hell I'm staying here."

***

He awoke still wrapped in her arms. Clothes were scattered haphazardly about the room, while a simple, quilted blanket partially covered their nude bodies. Running his hand down her shoulder, Thomas found the curve of her hips. Her skin was noticeably cool to the touch, as if she had stood out in the elements for too long. He knew it was because she hadn't fed. It was a dangerous sign for an unarmed Wraith. Thomas turned his head and found his scythe in the exact spot he dropped it last night. It was not completely out of his reach where it was located. However, her fanged mouth was only inches from his throat. By the time he called his weapon back to his hand, it would already be too late.

But this was his dream woman...right? What did he

have to worry about?

Thomas slowly pulled a breath into his lungs and returned his attention to Kat. Her blond hair spilled over his shoulder while her slender fingers rested lightly on his chest. A warm beam of morning sun sliced across the floor just to the left of the two and was steadily moving in their direction. He knew she would have to move soon, but he could stay here forever.

Brushing her hair out of her face with a yawn, Kat slid off Thomas and rolled onto her stomach. Moving like her namesake, she lifted her hips into the air and arched her back. Pushing her arms out, she felt the tired muscles in her back slowly begin to relax. As she slid back down to the floor, Kat crossed her arm over Thomas' chest and held her fingers dangerously close to the beam of sunshine. Kat laid her head gently on the Wraith's shoulder, her big blue eyes staring at his face. She allowed a soft smile to cross her lips. He was watching the light creep ever closer to her flesh, a hint of worry on his brow.

Lifting her arm, Kat's fingers hovered just in front of the light. She rolled her hand palm up and casually plunged her hand inside it. To Thomas' amazement, her flesh didn't immediately start to crack and burn. He watched intently as a small wisp of smoke curled up from her palm and dissipated in the air. As she retracted her hand, Kat waited for the inevitable question.

"How did you do that?"

Kat smiled. That didn't take long. "I wish I knew," she offered. "I can't live in direct sunlight, but a little doesn't hurt me."

Thomas lifted her hand and rolled it over, examining

261

it. There was no sign of scorching or burning. It looked as if nothing had happened to it. He slowly lowered her hand back to his chest. "I don't understand. How did you become this way?"

"That night on the rooftop in San Francisco," Kat said slowly, "I changed." She rolled onto her back and slid her arm under her head. "The Troika developed a biological weapon they wanted to use on some visiting Vampire Lord. I was part of the test subjects they used to create it." She stopped, remembering her incarceration. Murky memories of her blood being drained and surgical procedures wafted across her brain. "They offered me freedom in exchange for my services," she added after a moment.

Thomas cocked a single eyebrow. "What services?"

"I was chosen to inject the weapon into the Vampire Lord," she answered. She crossed her arms over her bare breasts, uncomfortable with the subject. "They had no intention of granting me freedom," Kat breathed. "I was merely expendable. The Troika knew the lord would kill me when I injected him."

The Wraith's heart sank in his chest. "I'm sorry." He saw that recounting the story was hurting her, but he needed to know. "What happened that night? When I found you, you were nearly dead."

"Everything went to Hell," she assessed soberly. "The Vampire Lord came to the Troika under the pretense of peace. Perhaps his ultimate intention was peace," Kat surmised, "but only through force. He attacked the Troika without a second thought and easily killed the triad of Vampire Lords. His aide," she felt the phantom pain of bullet holes in her torso, "attacked me without provocation. During our struggle, the syringe containing the bio weapon was cracked and nearly half of it was lost."

"You had no intention of using the weapon on Bane," Thomas said with a wary smile. "You were planning to escape the whole time and become human again."

Kat smiled and nodded. His insight was amazing. She had never told anyone that.

"So you injected yourself with what was left of the weapon," Thomas continued, "but something went wrong."

Kat's eyes narrowed slightly. "The wounds I received during the battle were too great. Perhaps my vampire physiology could've healed them, but the weapon changed me. I wasn't entirely vampire anymore," she looked away, "nor entirely human."

"But I saved you," Thomas interjected. Rolling onto his side, he propped his hand under his face and stared at Kat.

She slowly reached out and ran her fingertips over his face tenderly. "You saved me," she echoed. "I am forever in your debt for that."

Kat reared back and slapped Thomas hard across the face. Her nails created two large cuts in his flesh. Anger flashed across Kat's face. "Nor will I ever forgive you for it."

Thomas jumped back from Kat and eyed her warily and dropped down into a crouching position. A flash of anger rippled across his entire body. Swinging his arm around his back, the Wraith reached out with his mind and pulled his scythe instantly to his hand. He held his

263

thumb on the activation stud, but paused. He set his jaw, unsure of his course of action.

Kat's face slowly softened. She let her gaze fall away from his intense stare. "Forgive me."

Thomas refused to move from his defensive posture. He felt a drip of blood roll down his cheek.

"I didn't mean to snap at you like that," Kat said apologetically.

"Why?" It was the only thought he could muster from beneath the anger.

Kat slowly sat up and pulled the quilt around her naked body. "I…" She felt the words die in her throat. She took a quick breath for strength. "I am grateful to you for saving my life." She paused. "And I hated you, too." She lifted her blue eyes to meet his. They swam with anguish and pain. "I didn't want to live as a vampire. I wanted to die."

Thomas took in her words and tried to digest them. "And now?"

"I am thankful to be alive," she admitted. She searched her mind for a way to explain the irrational feelings she had. "Have you ever read accounts of attempted suicide?"

Thomas felt the word "suicide" slice into his soul. He had been there. He knew the darkness. He knew the emptiness. He knew them all too well, even now.

"These people who try to kill themselves are often very conflicted after an attempt," Kat explained. "There's relief to still be alive, yet anger at the people who cared enough to save them." She found a loose thread on the quilt and began to nervously roll it between her fingertips. "It's difficult to explain," she admitted. "I felt

264

like I had my chance to become human again and failed. You weren't directly responsible for that." Her eyes welled with tears. "But you kept me alive. I should have died that night. Instead," a tear streaked down her porcelain cheek, "I've been forced to live this life. Everything I know is gone. I don't blame you…" She took a breath but let the completed thought die.

"But in a way, you do," Thomas finished. He slowly dropped down to the floor and crossed his legs. "I didn't make you a vampire," he defended himself. "And I didn't ruin your chances at becoming human. I saved your life. Doesn't that count for anything?" He set his scythe behind him and folded his hands neatly in his lap.

Kat's eyes widened. "Yes, yes," she said quickly as she wiped the tear from her face. "Of course it does."

"Then I'm sorry, but I don't understand."

Kat opened her mouth to explain, but no words, no logic could be found to make him understand. She shook her head and let her eyes fall away again. "I'm sorry," she said finally.

Thomas cocked his head slightly. "Why?"

"For unloading my problems on you." Kat swallowed hard. A sly grin erupted on her lips. "You were just trying to save your dream girl."

Thomas returned the smile. "Yeah."

The two sat in silence for a long moment.

An idea exploded into the Wraith's brain. "What if I told you I could save you again?"

"What?"

He smiled broadly. "The Wraith are in possession of the biological weapon you spoke of. We found it in the Troika's building before it was destroyed."

Kat couldn't hide her excitement at the admission. She dropped the quilt and crawled quickly toward Thomas. "Where is it?"

"England," Thomas answered. "But I can get it."

She felt her heart flutter in her chest. "I can be human again?"

Thomas nodded.

Kat looked down at her porcelain hands. "I can be human again," she repeated to herself. Dropping her hands, she looked back at the Wraith. "Why would you do this for me?"

Thomas placed his hand on her cheek. "Because I love you. I've loved you ever since I can remember. I will love you until the stars grow cold. I can't stand you hurting anymore." He paused. "Will you let me help you?"

Kat nodded without hesitation, threw her arms around his neck and hugged him fiercely.

Wrapping his hands around her nude back, Thomas' mind began to whirl. He had no idea what happened to the Troika's biological weapon after it was taken to England, nor was he sure it would be freely given to him.

Darkness swelled from the back of his mind and enveloped his brain. He would attain the weapon for Kat. Of that, he had no doubt.

Chapter Twenty-One

A dark shadow slowly traversed the hellish landscape. Rivers of molten lava spilled down the side of the massive volcano on their suicidal run toward the ocean, while plumes of smoke and soot blackened the sky swallowing the sunlight. Jagged boulders, tossed free of the volcano's mouth during the eruption, littered the geography. Razor-sharp edges reached unseen toward trespassers, ripping and clawing as they went. The temperature soared. No human could survive this toxic place.

Yet he was here.

He watched a wisp of smoke escape from the sole of his boot as the rubber was singed against the superheated soil. The hem of his robe was starting to fray as the threads burned, a disadvantage of wearing actual clothes, rather than using his mental camouflage. This place was nothing to his physiology. The scorching temperatures and toxins held no sway over him. It was only lethal to the living. He was already dead.

Lifting his head, he spied his destination. Nothing more than a dark sliver in the smoke, he knew what it was. And where it led. As he approached, it became more recognizable. An opening had been bored into the skin of the volcano. Slightly over seven feet in height, it was barely four feet at its widest point. A thin lip hung over the opening, but he knew if the lava flow were to change directions, it would offer no protection. Even he could not survive direct exposure to the flow.

Swinging into the opening, the dark figure walked confidently inside. The corridor, carved out of sheer rock, was swallowed by inky blackness. Only a faint red hue from lava deep within lit his way. As the manmade corridor wound deeper inside the volcano, he could feel the heat welling up from beneath. Turning another corner, he stepped into emptiness without hesitation. Falling down the hole, his cloak spread like great raven's wings around him. He neither looked down nor tried to use his hands and feet to slow his descent. He could feel the walls screaming past as he fell deeper and deeper inside. The heat grew more intense, as did the evil glare of the lava.

Hitting bottom with an audible thud, he landed on the balls of his feet. The raven's wings folded around him magnificently. Looking up, he saw another great river of lava just ahead. The molten stone churned and undulated as it tumbled toward some unseen exit. Glowing chunks of rock were tossed free as it lapped against the ever-widening sides of the rut it had created. The orange-red hue glinted off his silver mask nearly hiding his preternatural yellow eyes.

Moving deeper into the volcano, the heat became almost unbearable. Much further, and it would start to cook his body from the inside out, but he was almost there. Turning away from the glowing molten river, the dark figure circled down into a much older passage created by a long inactive lava flow. Walking over the smooth igneous rock, the red glow of the lava began to fade behind him. This part of the volcano was dormant, but not even he knew for how long.

He came upon his destination. Turning inside, he

walked slowly down the manmade stairs painstakingly carved out of the igneous rock. Torches hanging from the walls cast their flickering orange light across the large chamber. A row of three massive columns, made from the same black stone, lined each side of the chamber. The floor was perfectly smooth and polished to a high gloss. His booted feet clicked against the floor and sent echoes into the far, unseen corners.

His golden eyes settled on the elevated platform at the head of the chamber. Thirteen steps led up the front to a rectangular base that was no more than eight feet wide. A single throne occupied the top. The only thing in this place not carved from the stone, it was nonetheless black to match its surroundings. Heavy black cushions lined the seat and back of the iron throne. The back, narrow and slender, was nearly eight feet tall and had a single, hideous, stone gargoyle perched at the top. Looking down over its beaked nose from ruby eyes, the beast's batlike wings were spread proudly looking as if it were ready to pounce and eviscerate anyone who stood too long in front of it.

Walking up seven of the thirteen steps, he dropped to one knee and bowed his head. He waited in silence.

"Lord Bane," came a voice that was scarred and withered yet powerful. "Rise."

The voice resonated as if two distinct sounds were melded into one. The dying, frail intonation of age was underscored by the booming, rumbling sound of distant thunder.

"Thank you, my Lord." Bane slowly stood and let his heavy black cloak fall around his body. His eyes slowly returned to the throne.

Never truly empty, the shadowy form of a figure revealed itself. Draped in a hooded robe as black as the stone this place was carved from, no features were visible, save for the burning yellow eyes. His pure white hands gripped the arms of the throne. Every bone, every vein could be seen as his skin looked thin and stretched. His fingers, slightly longer than a normal humanoid's, wrapped around the edges of the arms like spindly spider legs. "Your campaign is nearing its end," he spoke slowly and deliberately. Every word was carefully chosen before it left the being's mouth. "Our offspring are nearly decimated."

He had never heard the Wraith labeled as the offspring of vampires before. It struck him as odd, yet appropriate. "Yes, my Lord," Bane bowed his head slightly in respect.

Two vampires, similar to the one seated, materialized on either side of the throne. The one to the left leaned over and whispered something inaudible to the Vampire Lord. He nodded once and returned his attention to Bane. "You have served me well, Lord Bane."

"Thank you, Master," Bane said graciously.

The ancient Vampire Lord lifted his skeletal hand and gestured toward the two vampires at his side. "My acolytes tell me that you are eager to attain your new apprentice."

"It is as you have foreseen," Bane admitted. "Everything has come to pass. He is ready to join us."

"He is but a boy," the Vampire Lord grumbled and shook his head slowly. "You are still very impatient, my apprentice. Time is of the essence." He leaned forward on the throne, his face still shadowed by the hood.

"Everything must be precise."

Bane said nothing.

He clenched his fist. "You must draw your armies back, Lord Bane," the Vampire Lord stated as he leaned back again. "The Wraith are about to tear each other apart. We need not sacrifice anymore vampires in this cause."

Anger rumbled in Bane's heart. He was so close to decimating his enemy. He knew pulling back now would be foolish and give the Wraith a chance to regroup and retaliate.

"No," the lord said slowly, "they will not retaliate against me."

Bane scolded himself for leaving his mind unguarded. It had been quite some time since he was in the lord's presence.

The lord leaned forward in his chair again and motioned for Bane to come closer. "No," the lord said as Bane knelt before him on the top step, "I think I am quite safe from any strike the pitiful Wraith could cobble together."

The lord's arm shot out like lightning and snapped around Bane's throat. Standing up from his throne, the lord easily lifted Bane from the ground, even though Bane was almost twice his size. The hood of the lord's robe fell back revealing his horrible visage. Almost no flesh remained on his skull, and what was left was decomposed and rotting away. His bones were bleached white from eons of exposure to the elements, while his golden eyes looked like two unholy orbs sitting in the empty sockets of his skull. He was little more than an animated skeleton.

"Do not question me!" the lord screeched.

Bane struggled against the lord's hand, but it felt like bands of iron wrapped around his neck.

"I made you, Lord Bane. I can just as easily unmake you," the lord warned. Opening his hand, he let Bane fall to the steps.

Bane started to tumble backwards, but caught himself. He quickly returned to his kneeling position before the lord. "Forgive me, my Lord."

Pulling his hood back over his head, the lord sank back into his throne. His hands returned to the exact position they had been in before. "Do not let it happen again, Lord Bane." He paused, letting the scolding sink into his apprentice. "The young Wraith will indeed be your new apprentice. The end is near, but you must be patient."

Bane bowed his head. "Yes, my Lord."

***

Kneeling down in the snow, the young Wraith pulled off one of his leather gloves. Looking over the body, he turned the head slowly to reveal the fang marks on the throat. The blood that clung to the wound was still fresh. He pressed two fingers to the artery just above the bite but couldn't detect a pulse. He was too late. Looking at the victim's face, he knew she couldn't have been more than eighteen or nineteen years old. Lifting his right hand, he carefully closed the girl's eyelids and stood up.

Thomas pulled on his gloves and hiked up his collar. Big flakes of snow were falling softly around him. It felt peaceful and serene, but he knew there was a monster

272

lurking between the flakes. This was the worst snowstorm the region had seen in almost twenty years. The corpse at his feet was quickly disappearing. He knew it would be spring before it would be found again, but that wasn't his concern. He had to find the vampire responsible. Over the past five nights, it had been cutting a swath of death through downtown Reno. Too many had died already.

And it had been almost a week since he had seen Kat. He left her in his cabin on the shore of Lake Tahoe. Alone.

He took a breath in through his nose and slowly exhaled out of his mouth. He watched his breath freeze in the chilled night air. Looking down, he couldn't see many tracks in the snow, and the ones he could were quickly disappearing beneath the white. They would be useless to track this creature. He had to rely on his senses. He had to find this monster quickly. Too many lives had been lost already. He wasn't certain, but he estimated the death toll at around twenty-five in five nights. Not all of the victims were drained of blood. This vampire wasn't merely feeding, it had an insatiable blood lust. It was killing for the sheer thrill of it.

As he started out of the alley, he let his long, black coat fall around his body. He tucked his arms across his chest and let his gaze fall down to his feet. He walked slowly, but with purpose as the snowstorm intensified around him. Nearly a blizzard now, he couldn't trust his eyes. He had to rely on his other senses to guide him. He wiped several strands of his wavy hair out of his face.

Opening his mind, he reached out in all directions. He had come to think of this as his "Mental Web." His tendrils would leapfrog using the inherent mental acuity

273

of the humans he touched, splinter out numerous times and branch out even further. As his web slithered further and further out, he glanced through sleeping minds seeing images that would make even Hugh Heffner blush, bounced off those experimenting with drugs or alcohol for the first time, and past freely through the emptiness that was a television viewer. The invisible tendrils scouted ahead through the darkened corners where vampires liked to hide, but he was having little luck.

He knew some vampires took pleasure in watching humans discover their meals, but this monster wasn't one of them. It fed and fled. Or more probable, it killed and moved purposely onto the next victim. He didn't seem to have motive or pattern. Thomas could detect no connection to the victims or this place. This was the most dangerous breed of vampire: it killed just to kill.

He shook the thought from his head. The vampire would be found. Of that, he had no doubt. No creature was a match for him anymore. He was beyond their meager skills. His advanced Wraith physiology had no equal here anymore.

At least, he didn't think so.

Thomas turned his head skyward but found only the dark gray of the storm. The stars were his companions as he hunted. When he gazed at the blanket of stars, he felt connected somehow. He could almost feel the grand scheme of things as if it were just beyond his comprehension, like a word stuck on the tip of his tongue. When he looked to the sky, he could feel Kat by his side, and Master Verge just behind him. He felt her love caress him, and Verge's confidence support him. No matter where they were, as he stared at the glittering specs of light above, they were right next to him. Frowning, he let his gaze fall back to the snow below.

He was alone. Again.

One of his tendrils slithered past a dead spot. He stopped and pulled back his web save for that single probe. Backing up slowly, he worked tentatively around the area. Cautiously, he explored the emptiness. Humans usually couldn't sense when being probed, but vampires could. He had to be careful.

Leaning his back against the wall of a building, Thomas closed his eyes and focused fully on the spot. Cocking his head slightly, curiosity overwhelmed him. All life had an energy field that surrounded and bound them to each other. This spot was free of that field. It was a hole that didn't reflect or absorb life. He couldn't tell if it was natural or manmade, however it didn't seem to belong on this plane of existence. It felt as if it were a tear in space and time. Completely excluded from this realm, it was a universe unto itself. His probe couldn't penetrate the hole, only glance off it. He worked around the jagged edges carefully. It wasn't expanding, but it wasn't shrinking either. It was neither life, nor death, it simply was.

Opening his eyes, Thomas spied the fire escape above him. Keeping his probe firmly in place, he leapt up and grabbed the bottom rung of the ladder. He swung his legs back then forward and used the momentum to vault onto the lowest landing. Neither pausing nor hesitating, he moved like a shadow up the escape and onto the roof of the building. As his boots hit the flat roof, he accelerated. There was no fear in his heart. He moved unencumbered leaping from one rooftop to the next

275

following the invisible trail of his probe. Springing over an air vent and landing on the balls of his feet, he felt his tendril grow in strength as he shortened it. He was here.

Standing tall, he scanned the rooftop. The usual collection of air vents, antennae, and cooling units were present, but little else. The blanket of snow was pristine and untouched. Sliding his hand into his coat, he rested his palm on the pommel of his scythe. Working across the roof, he listened to the crunch of snow beneath his feet. No other sounds, no smells, no sights other than him and this building. He focused on his target and nothing else existed.

Coming to the edge of the roof, Thomas crouched down and placed his hands on the lip. He peered over the edge finding nothing but a sheer drop to the alley below. He could feel the hole about two floors beneath. Stepping onto the edge, he turned so his back was facing out. He drew his scythe and activated it. Hitting the activation stud again, the top blade sprang open. Making one last sweep with his mind, he hopped backwards and sailed off the roof. Whipping his scythe hard forward, he caught the sill of a window above him. His momentum shifted forward and his scythe acted like a pendulum. He deactivated his weapon. Snapping his booted feet up, he crashed through a lower window, somersaulted on the floor, and rolled into defensive posture while reactivating his weapon.

His gaze swept over the empty room. Trash littered the corners while a single, stained mattress was leaned against the wall. The hard wood floors were stained and warped with age and abuse. Thomas held his double-bladed scythe tightly in his hands as he stood. He waited, holding his breath, for someone to investigate the sound of the broken window. He could feel his heart beating in his chest, but he had control of his fear. He decreased his heart rate as he slowly exhaled.

The smell of death hit his nostrils like a slap. The vampire was near.

His feet moved lightly over the floor as he neared the door. Probing the room on the other side, he felt the edge of the tear…and something more. His eyes widened. His hand slipped off the grip of his scythe and wrapped firmly around the rusty door handle. He twisted it gently until he felt the mechanism disengage. He controlled his fear, even though what stood on the other side of the door was like nothing he had ever faced. Pulling open the door, he flattened himself in the frame. Peering into the room, he felt a lump well up in his throat.

A dark, spinning vortex dominated the center of the room. It churned as if chewing through the fabric of time and space. Purple and white bands swept around the tear and disappeared into the center as more appeared at the edges. Almost perfectly circular, the vortex was just shy of six feet in diameter. A lone altar stood before it. Tall, white candles were melted to the edges of the wooden altar spilling wax down the sides. Thomas watched a drip of wax fall away from the candle and get caught by the vortex. A thick, ancient book occupied the center of the altar. Black diagrams and an ancient text he didn't recognize were scrawled across the open pages. The lettering looked sharp and angry. He suddenly understood. This tear in the universe was created for a purpose.

The creator was standing at the back of the room

working diligently on something the vampire hunter couldn't quite make out. Looking like nothing more than a common gutter vamp, his clothes were tattered and his long, black hair was unkempt. He wore what looked like a green army jacket. The chevrons on the shoulder identified him as a lieutenant, if it even belonged to him. Of course, Thomas realized, it was only his mental projection. But some vampires took on what the Wraith referred to as a Residual Self Image. It was what the creature looked like in life. Yet this was no ordinary vampire. Usually the weak-minded clung to their RSI. This vampire was anything but.

The vampire stopped. Lifting its head like a wild animal, it sniffed the air. Turning quickly on its toes, the vampire's golden eyes narrowed as it snarled at Thomas. Three long scars ran from the center of its forehead, across the bridge of its nose and terminated just below its jaw.

That wasn't the vampire's mental projection…

Thomas wasted no time. Surging into the room and past the vortex, he pressed his attack. Whipping his scythe around his body, he brought it laterally across the vampire's chest slicing open his coat and shirt beneath. Allowing momentum to carry the scythe around his body, he altered the trajectory and brought it slicing down over his head just missing the vampire's face. As the vampire lunged for Thomas with his claws, the young Wraith dropped down and swept the vampire's legs. As the monster toppled, Thomas completed the spin, arced his weapon gracefully around his body, and finally pierced the vampire's chest just to the left of its heart.

Holding the weapon in place, Thomas pulled a

throwing knife from his jacket pocket. Glaring at the vampire, he tossed the knife down hard hitting the creature squarely in the wrist and pinning it to the floor. Drawing another knife from his coat, he repeated the process with the opposite hand. The vampire shrieked in pain as the scythe bore deeper into its chest. Thomas held the weapon firmly.

"Tell me what you are doing," Thomas demanded as the vortex swirled behind him.

The vampire's gaze hardened.

Thomas gritted his teeth. He twisted the scythe deeper into the vampire's chest. "Tell me!"

A bead of blood rolled from the corner of the vampire's mouth, yet he remained silent. His staring eyes were focused on the Wraith.

Thomas held his thumb on the scythe's activation stud. "If I press this button," he twisted the weapon allowing the vampire to clearly see it, "you will die. My second blade will activate and cut your heart in two. Unless you tell me what this is and how to stop it," Thomas paused, "you will die."

The vampire bared his fangs and roared in protest.

Thomas felt the furnace in his heart ignite as anger swelled into his brain. He jammed the button with his thumb. The silver blade leapt forward cleaving the vampire's chest as promised.

Thomas pulled the weapon free with a grunt and started toward the altar. Deactivating his scythe, he slipped it back onto his belt and adjusted his leather trench coat over it. Pulling off his gloves, he deposited them in his pocket and carefully placed his hands on the book. He could feel evil rolling off it in waves. Running his fingers gently over the handwritten text, he tried to make sense of the jagged lines, squiggles, and glyphs that constituted the language. He couldn't understand any of it. Looking across the altar at the vortex, he realized it was slowly growing. One of the candles on the back of the altar teetered and fell backwards only to be sucked in.

It was then he heard the vampire laughing.

Thomas turned and looked at the vampire. The monster's chest was splayed open. It should have been dead. "Should have" was apparently the key phrase in that statement. He leaned his elbow on the corner of the altar and waited. "Well…"

"Just as you can't kill me," the vampire giggled, "you can't close the portal. I am the Vessel, and it is come."

"Portal," Thomas repeated the word slowly. He felt a sense of dread deep in the back of his mind.

The vampire's laughter slowly abated. He looked at the Wraith with a bemused smile. "Your world is about to die. It is coming."

Turning back to the book, he ran his fingers quickly down the page. There, toward the bottom, was the crude sketch of a creature's face. Thomas furrowed his brow as recognition struck him. "You didn't."

The vampire laughed again.

"That's why you've been killing," Thomas said more to himself. "It demanded sacrifices to be born into this realm."

Thomas realized there was nothing he could do now. Pulling his scythe from his belt, he activated the weapon and walked quickly back to the vampire. With one quick swipe, he had severed the head from its body.

The vampire laughed again still alive. He stared at Thomas with his evil golden eyes as the Wraith lifted the decapitated head from the floor. "You can't kill me," the vampire sneered.

Holding the head an arm's length from his body, Thomas walked quickly around the portal to the dirty window on the opposite side of the room. "I think you may have misread the book," Thomas said quickly.

The vampire's laughter ceased. His expression shifted to confusion, then concern.

"You see," he smashed open the window with his elbow, "proximity is the key. The further you are from the portal," he reared back, "the less sway it has on you."

Thomas flung the vampire's head out the window.

He watched the head tumble into the darkness. As it fell further from the portal, it erupted into a blue ball of flame. He could hear the creature screaming as it sailed toward the ground like a falling star. Turning, he watched the vampire's body begin to burn. With no small amount of satisfaction, Thomas returned his scythe to his belt.

Walking around the ashes on the floor, he returned to his position behind the altar. He still couldn't read the writing, but he knew what it referred to. Thomas felt the dread in his mind deepening. There was nothing he could do. He didn't know how to close the portal, or even if there was a way to.

It was coming.

He had two choices. He could either stay and fight—and most likely die—or retreat and seek help. Thomas wasn't comfortable with either idea. He was one of the most powerful Wraiths in existence, yet he still didn't know what his odds were against the coming menace. But if he retreated, he couldn't be sure how much damage the beast would cause before he could gather enough help to hopefully, stop it.

His mind returned back to thoughts of Kat. What would she do if he simply didn't come home? Then Conrad entered his mind. If he could find some way to contact his Master, he was sure enough manpower could be gathered to stop this.

He stared at the swirling vortex before him. Taking a step back from the altar, he paused. Gritting his teeth, he turned away and headed for the door. He wasn't going to die. Not today anyway.

He hoped.

Chapter Twenty-Two

Kat sat quietly in Thomas' cabin reading a paperback. Wearing a pale pink silk robe she had recovered from the master bathroom, and little else, she flipped the pages slowly as she angrily chewed through the prose. She couldn't help but pick apart the novel word by word. The writer in her couldn't be silenced. She wondered for a moment how her novel did, sales-wise. After all, it had been ten years since it was published. It somehow didn't seem as important as it once had.

Her concentration was breaking. Setting the novel face down on her leg, she stared out the large windows into the night. There was a tug at her soul. She could feel a thread pulling on her heart, calling to her, enticing her to come. But to where, and to what end, she didn't know. Standing from the plush couch, she began to pace across the rug that dominated the living room floor. She started to feel like a caged animal. She needed some other view than these four walls. She needed fresh air. She needed... Kat didn't know what she needed.

But she needed out.

Turning from the living room, she headed for the master bedroom. She knew her clothes were still there, heaped on the floor next to the bed. Peeling away her robe, she revealed her perfect porcelain flesh beneath. Disappearing into the bedroom, she didn't see the pair of golden eyes staring in at her from the window.

***

283

Tracking him wasn't easy, but it wasn't impossible. His trail was over a year old. Starting in San Francisco, the High Wraith worked his way inland following vague leads, whispers, and shadows. There were very few Wraiths operating in this area of California since the beginning of the purge. Once a hot spot for vampirism in America, the so-called "Golden State" had gone quiet quick since the Troika was destroyed. No one wanted to incur Bane's wrath as the Russian Triad had. A majority of the Wraiths had been pulled away to other assignments, other battlefronts. This area of the United States was relatively quiet for the first time in a very, very long time.

But he sensed it. His senses were not as finely tuned as Thomas', but he felt the growing darkness from as far away as Sacramento. He knew this void was calling to every being with even a hint of the original darkness in their blood. Wraith, vampires, werewolves, and God knows what else, were all being drawn toward it. As if it were some demonic spotlight, it was pulling all the creatures of the night out of their hiding places.

Conrad frowned. He wouldn't want to be a human in Reno, Nevada right now. He had no choice but to follow the call. But he knew Thomas was here.

He also knew he was being ghosted. He wasn't sure by who—or what—but something had been following him ever since his arrival in San Francisco. His ghost had been careful to stay just far enough behind him to not be detected. It worried Conrad, but not enough to stop. He had to find his wayward apprentice and bring him home. Thomas had been left to his own devices for far too long.

He would deal with the ghost when it decided to reveal itself. There was no immediate threat. Moving ahead was far more important at this point.

He paused as the trail diverged. He could clearly sense the growing darkness further east in Reno, but Thomas' path led toward Lake Tahoe. Conrad drew a deep breath. He was close. He could feel it. Turning, he started down the highway toward Tahoe.

***

Coming around the corner, Thomas felt his heart sink. The stairwell leading down was literally clogged with vampires of every shape and size. As soon as he came into view, all the golden eyes snapped to him. He realized then the vortex was not only bringing something evil into this realm, but was also calling to every monster to protect it. This was worse than he thought—far, far worse.

He glanced over the rail into the spiral stairwell. The bottom was swallowed in darkness. He wasn't sure what floor he was on, but it was a long way down. He couldn't take on all the vampires. There was no hope of winning. They would swarm and rip him to shreds.

They charged.

Jumping onto the handrail, Thomas used his scythe as a balancing pole as he skated down the banister. With a devilish grin, he leapt over a slashing pair of claws. Picking up speed, he missed a second attack, but couldn't avoid the third. He snapped forward as a hand wrapped around his ankle. His chin hit the handrail hard and he felt his scythe break free of his grip. Kicking blindly as pain shot up through his face, he felt his boot connect with soft flesh. A shriek echoed up the stairwell and he was free. As the stars faded in front of his eyes, he pulled himself back to a standing position on the rail. He saw three more hands lunge for him. Flipping backwards, the Wraith sailed into empty space. His leather coat snapped open like bat wings as he fell. Reaching out with his mind, he quickly searched the ground below him only to find more vampires. He blasted all his mental energy down knocking the waiting fangs away just before he hit.

Landing with a solid thud, he felt his knees start to buckle but he fought it. Snapping his head up, he saw his scythe and two vampires charging toward him. Calling his weapon to his hand, he activated it and attacked.

Spinning his scythe up and around, the Wraith easily cleaved the vampire's skull. Ripping it free, Thomas snapped the weapon waist high and reversed his attack. The second blade of his weapon sliced through the vampire's flesh as if it were warm butter. The two halves tumbled free of each other as they were swallowed by unholy blue flame.

Bringing his scythe quickly over his head, he blocked the attack of a second vampire. Knocking the creature back with a kick, Thomas spun and faced his attacker. Armed with a wooden baseball bat, the vampire glared at the young Wraith.

Thomas smiled.

The vampire attacked, but he was no match for the highly trained Wraith. The battle was over before he could even swing the bat a first time. Thomas' scythe was a blur of silver, an impenetrable barrier between him and his attacker. The vampire's bat was almost instantly

286

shredded and reduced to little more than a toothpick. Kicking what was left of the bat free of the vampire's hands, Thomas leapt into the air and kicked the wooden shard straight into the vampire's chest. Stumbling back, the vampire wrapped his hands uselessly around the bat. Tossing his head back, he howled as fire shot from his mouth.

Thomas exhaled quickly and charged outside. Looking up through the falling snow, he saw dozens of pairs of golden eyes glaring at him from the gloom. He was overmatched—by a long shot. He gritted his teeth. Half of his mind wanted to fight until he couldn't, while the other half screamed for retreat. Begrudgingly, Thomas realized that rushing headlong into the vampires would only result in his death. He couldn't afford that right now. He had to get away.

Thomas had a new reason to live.

Without a second thought, he broke left. Two vampires charged out of the darkness following him while the rest kept heading toward the vortex. Thomas hit a dead sprint through the cold and still falling snow. Everything became a dark blur. It was only his preternatural vision and reflexes that kept him running. He ran until his heart threatened to burst free of his chest, it was pumping so hard. His lungs burned and his legs ached. Glancing behind once, he could see the golden eyes fading further and further into the distance. Turning his attention back, he raced home.

Chapter Twenty-Three

Birth was such an annoying process.

From the darkness, there came light and quickly, its body struggled for life.

Its lungs drew their first bitter breath of the oxygen rich mixture the skin tubes of this realm considered air. The oxygen permeated its bronchial membranes, burning as it coursed into its blood stream. It felt as if acid were churning just below its flesh. It coughed trying to break the old air free.

Its skin pulsated with heat from the vortex. Quickly, its flesh began to cool and retain its original structure. Smoke rose around it as the plates that dominated its body began to form. The plates hardened and crystallized under the intense heat. The gray color of the birthing process slowly darkened to a glossy black. The beast's body glittered beneath the lights of the room.

Opening its eyes, it could see little more than a blur of shapes. Slowly, edges began to form and its new world began to take shape. It saw lines, details, and the vibrant colors of what would become its new kingdom.

It was pleased.

Drawing its massive body up, it wobbled as it tried to stand upright for the first time. But it was powerful and quickly, the shakes were gone. It straightened its spine and threw its shoulders back as it stood to its full height. Gnashing its teeth, the beast balled its fists and flexed its powerful frame.

Tossing its horned head back, it roared.

It was less to clear its lungs and more to signal to all that a new era had just begun. This place belonged to it now and all those who dared stand in its way would suffer. A new kingdom had dawned in this realm.

The black vortex disappeared behind it. The birthing was now complete.

The beast turned and saw a pair of golden eyes peering in from the darkness. It motioned with its hand as if calling a stray animal. The vampire slowly and carefully entered the room with the beast. Curious yet cautious, the vampire maintained its distance hugging the walls of the apartment. The beast watched the vampire with its unflinching red eyes. Standing almost eight feet tall, it easily dwarfed the vampire.

"Vampire," the beast said, overenunciating each consonant and vowel sound.

The vampire moved a step closer. "What are you?"

The beast grinned. Lifting its hand, palm up, it slowly made a fist. The vampire paused uncomfortably, yet still curious. He cocked his head slightly and stared at what looked like a thick tube that ran from the beast's elbow and terminated just behind its wrist. A bulbous, bony protrusion spidered out from the end of the vein and wrapped around the beast's wrist.

The vampire took a step closer.

That was his last mistake.

A thin, gray tendril burst from the bony protrusion and coiled around the vampire's throat almost instantly. The speed at which it moved shocked the vampire. He struggled against the tendril, but it was useless. He didn't have the strength to pry the coils open.

The tendril easily lifted the vampire from the floor

and brought him face to face with the beast. "You are a wretched abomination," the beast said calmly, almost as if it were fully assessing the being for the first time. Its voice was deep and dark as though emanating from the very bowels of Hell. "Vampires are nothing more than a disease." The massive creature looked over the puny vampire before him. "You are useless."

The beast tightened the tendril coils around the vampire's throat severing his head. Snapping the tendril back into its wrist, the beast started for the door as blue fire engulfed the room behind him.

***

"You're disgusting."

Kat stopped dead in her tracks, her hands still in the process of pulling on the white t-shirt she had found in the bedroom. She stared into the living room with ever-widening eyes.

Letting her hands fall away from the shirt's hem, she couldn't take her eyes away from the figure standing motionless next to the front door. Her arms were crossed loosely over her chest while her messy purple hair hung down to the small of her back. Black leather pants conformed to every curve of her hips and legs while a black and red corset hugged her midsection and pushed up her already full breasts. A sheer black suede shirt hung off her thin shoulders and terminated just above her hips. She was a punk, probably before and after her death.

"I can smell the Wraith all over you," Punk growled through a thick English accent. Her purple hair covered the left side of her face, revealing a single golden eye.

Three silver hoops pierced her eyebrow, while at least five more hung from her only visible ear. "You're not even a pure vampire."

Kat finally worked up enough saliva in her mouth to speak. She wasn't a fighter. "Who are you?"

Punk pushed herself away from the wall and let her arms fall to her sides. An evil grin spread across her painted black lips. "Death."

Kat cocked her head slightly to the right and allowed herself a half smile. "A little overdramatic, aren't we?"

Punk didn't find it as amusing as Kat did.

Before Kat could even process the movement, Punk was across the room in a black and purple blur. Snatching Kat's throat, Punk threw Kat back smashing the drywall around her. Kat yelped as she crumbled to the floor. Pain radiated in waves from her back. Reaching over her shoulder, she felt a chunk of wood lodged firmly through her now shattered shoulder blade.

Kat felt blood spilling from the wound. She looked up at Punk with tears in her eyes. "Why are you doing this?"

"You're expecting some lavish story of revenge, aren't you? Like you stole my boyfriend senior year, or you were mean to me once," Punk said, feigning sorrow. "That's what you're thinking, right?" She knelt down next to Kat and laughed. "No, it's not that at all. It's 'cause I can, love." She ran her fingers tenderly over Kat's face. "You're a lovely thing, aren't you? All this blond hair and blue eyes," Punk breathed. "I bet you were a cheerleader! Am I right?"

Running her hand behind her back, Kat stared at Punk. Her fingers slowly wrapped tightly around a bit of debris from the wall. She nodded to answer Punk's question.

"I hate cheerleaders." Punk grabbed the wood shard in Kat's back and pushed it deeper inside. "Snobby bitches who think they're better than me."

Kat felt the edge of the wood burst through the skin just below her collarbone. Blood spurted and hit Punk in the face. Punk flinched slightly. Kat screamed in pain and retaliated. Using the debris, she slammed it into the side of Punk's head.

Punk shrieked and fell back, her face filled with shock. Running her hand up the side of her face, she felt the debris. Long and slender, it had pierced her skull just behind her temple.

Kat pushed herself up using the wall for leverage. She started to inch slowly away from Punk. She held her palm over the wound on her chest trying to stop the bleeding as best she could.

Wrapping her fingers around the shiv, Punk grunted and pulled it free. Blood ran freely down her pure white face as she looked at the makeshift weapon. "You bitch." She tossed the shiv aside. "That really hurt."

"You're a psycho," Kat said through gritted teeth. The pain in her chest was almost unbearable.

"Maybe." Punk slowly lifted herself from the floor and popped her neck. "But I'm a vampire, love." She spread her arms wide. "This is what I do."

Kat spun and ran for the front door. Every movement was painful. She could feel her flesh tearing further with each step.

Punk laughed and charged again.

Kat was almost at the front door. Reaching out, she

felt her fingertips hit the handle just as Punk's fingers dug into her hair and yanked her back. Hitting the floor solidly, Kat felt her left lung collapse as the debris slid even further into her chest cavity. She wheezed a bloody bubble as she cried in pain.

"Stop mucking about." Flipping her over, Punk perched on Kat's chest, using her big black boots to pin Kat's arms. "Didn't think I'd let you get away—urk…"

Punk's face became a mixture of pain and confusion as the words died in her throat. Becoming very still, her eyes seemed to focus on something distant. Slowly, her body began to tip sideways. As it did, her head rolled free of her neck and burst into flame.

Kat quickly pushed Punk's body off her chest as it started to burn. Through the ashes and embers flitting into the air, Kat realized what had happened. As Punk's corpse burned, Kat skittered fearfully away from the door, pain shooting throughout her body. Her unblinking eyes stared at the open door. Hitting the back wall of the living room, she tried to take a breath into her lungs. She let her head fall forward as the pain overtook her. Kat finally let her body collapse.

***

He stepped through Punk's ashes still holding his scythe at the ready. He watched the blond vampire skitter away, even though she was badly wounded. A trail of blood crossed the floor behind her. He knew she couldn't bleed to death, but her body was about to shut down. She wasn't going to fight.

Conrad deactivated his weapon and slid it into his

coat pocket.

***

Darkness scratched and tore at him as he tried to fight through it. Lifting his hands, he swung wildly, while at the same time trying to shield his face. It was suffocating as it folded in around him. Spotting a clearing ahead, Thomas charged forward with a speed and fortitude he wasn't aware he possessed. He gritted his teeth as he neared the edge. The darkness was determined to keep him. His feet felt like they were encased in quicksand as his pace slowed. He was so near the edge. His heart pounded in his chest as he focused and pumped his legs even harder.

Breaking into the clearing, he skidded to a stop and took a deep breath into his lungs. Taking a tentative step forward, he saw his small cabin sitting on the edge of a large lake. He felt at ease here, as if the weight of the world just melted from his shoulders. Taking another breath of the clean air, he walked toward the cabin confidently. He belonged here. He belonged with her.

Moving up a well-worn path that led to the front door, he could hear no sounds of the destruction he had left behind. The woods surrounding him were full of animals, chirping crickets, and the soft rustling of foliage. Gone was the darkness that threatened to consume him. This place was warm and inviting.

Reaching for the door handle, he saw a flash of bright blue light in the window. His heart leapt up into his throat. Rage gripped him as the darkness descended again…

***

Thomas' scent was strong in this place—the High Wraith cocked his head slightly in confusion—and on this vampire. He slowly knelt down next to her. "What the bloody hell have you been doing, Thomas?"

"Don't hurt her."

Conrad spun around and had activated his scythe before the last word left her mouth. He furrowed his brow and frowned. "You don't listen very well."

Saint walked quickly into the living room and looked down at the wounded vampire. "Do you know who this is?"

Conrad deactivated his scythe and shook his head. "No. Should I?"

Saint pushed her long leather trench coat out of the way and dropped down to her knees. She pressed two fingers to the vampire's throat, then looked back at Conrad. "This is her."

Conrad waited, still not comprehending.

Saint shook her head in frustration. "Thomas' dream woman."

A sudden shock of understanding hit the High Wraith. He looked from Saint to the blond vampire. "Dear Lord," he breathed.

"I would recognize her anywhere," Saint admitted. "I've heard the story from Thomas enough times to practically dream about her myself. She fits his description," she ran her fingers over the vampire's face softly, "almost perfectly."

Conrad crouched next to Saint. "She actually exists?"

"Apparently." Saint started to inspect her wound. "But not for much longer if we don't get her some medical attention." Saint slid one arm beneath Kat's legs and the other around her back.

Conrad quickly placed his hand firmly on Saint's shoulder. "Stop."

"She'll die," Saint protested.

Conrad shook his head. "Let her."

Saint was too awestruck to speak.

"We can't let this happen," Conrad said barely above a whisper. "A Wraith cannot love a vampire. Especially not Thomas."

"Don't do this, Conrad," Saint warned. "You can't stop destiny. This was meant to happen for a reason. If you do, it will kill Thomas. And…" She drew a long breath and returned her attention to Kat. "She's pregnant."

Conrad felt the words hit him like a hammer. He looked from Saint to the vampire, then back to Saint. "How do you know?"

Saint smiled wryly. "I just know." She lifted her hand and tapped her temple lightly.

"Oh my…" The High Wraith let the statement die in his mouth. Standing up, he took an uneasy step away from both Saint and the vampire. "It's Thomas'?"

Saint shrugged. "That'd be my guess. Vampires can't have children, and neither can Wraiths." She looked back at the vampire. "But Thomas isn't exactly a normal Wraith anymore." She paused. "And this one isn't exactly standard issue vampire either. We can't kill her, Conrad. This baby is a miracle."

"Or the Antichrist," Conrad muttered under his

296

breath. He felt a lump well up in his throat.

"We can't wait any longer." Saint stood with the vampire in her arms. "I have to get her out of here."

Conrad took a deep breath and nodded. "Go get help. Go out the back."

Saint nodded and started to move.

"Be careful," the High Wraith shouted after Saint.

He felt an uneasiness descend on his brain. There was something not right here. Conrad didn't like this at all, but Saint was right. If he killed the vampire, there would be no hope of ever getting Thomas to return to England with him. He had to use any means he could—

"Conrad!" His tone was filled with anger and confusion, and his lack of the use of proper titles spoke volumes about his mind set. "What have you done?"

The High Wraith spun to find Thomas standing in the open doorway. His face was flushed and his eyes wide. A look of sheer horror dominated his countenance. Conrad looked down at the pile of ashes he was standing in and the trail of blood across the floor.

Conrad shook his head and started toward his student. "Thomas, wait. You don't under…"

The young Wraith's scowl hardened with pure rage.

Before he could finish the final syllable of his protest, Thomas was gone.

Conrad rushed to the door and peered into the grayness of the snowstorm. There was no trace of his student. No tracks could be seen in the snow. Thomas was just gone.

The High Wraith stepped fully into the night. Walking off the front porch, he felt the heavy snowflakes hitting the shoulders of his worn brown leather trench coat. He hung his head and let out a long sigh. Looking up into the snow, he closed his eyes and let the flakes fall and melt on his skin. Brushing them away, he started toward the road.

He knew where Thomas was going.

298

Chapter Twenty-Four

The biggest little city in the world was burning. Downtown Reno had descended into the seventh level of Hell as the vortex had pulled all the dark things from their hiding places en masse. Now with a lessened fear of reprisal or death, they pillaged, burned, and killed as they desired. SWAT teams in full riot gear tried to hold their ground and maintain order but their efforts were failing fast. Tear gas against a creature that didn't breathe was somewhat useless. The vampires tore through the police as if they were toy soldiers lined up just to be knocked down.

Their only salvation—the dawn—was still hours away.

Even a full battalion of Wraiths would stand no chance in this chaos. Conrad hated to admit it, but Reno would just have to burn. There was nothing he, or anyone else, could do to stop it. There were more important things to deal with right now.

And he spotted one of them standing about a hundred feet from him. It was mammoth in size and girth. Sheer black, the monster stood in the center of the street below surveying the carnage and destruction. It was only under the pale yellow light of the street lamp that Conrad could even see it. The beast knew it had created this chaos and reveled in it. Its massive horns curved out from the side of its head and forward into sharp points. Laughter roared from its mouth as it snatched a fleeing human with one of its tendrils and squashed it against the side of a nearby building. A vampire that strayed too close was its next victim. Easily torn in two, the beast let the burning halves of the vampire fall at its feet. It seemed as if it didn't care who it killed, as long as it was killing. It was the perfect engine of destruction.

And Conrad had to stop it. He let out a sigh. "Krylbrea demon. Not good."

He pulled away from his vantage point on the roof and rolled onto his back. Trying to stay on the rooftops, the High Wraith had avoided much of the destruction. He had been trying to track his wayward apprentice, but had lost the trail amidst the chaos. It was sheer luck—or a cruel joke by the fates—that led him to this spot. Through the heavy snowflakes, he looked to the sky. Even when dawn came, if it was still snowing this heavily, there would be no reprieve. He had to stop the beast and find Thomas. Little else—

The edge of a blade sliced into the brick of the ledge, barely missing his skull.

Conrad rolled out of the way with a grunt and tumbled into a defensive posture. His scythe was drawn and activated even before he reached his feet. Searching the rooftop, the High Wraith didn't see his attacker, but he knew who it was.

"Thomas," Conrad said slowly, "Don't do this."

Only the sound of distant sirens and the destruction below filled his ears.

"This is a mistake," Conrad slowly started to circle the roof. "She is not dead. I didn't kill her."

"Liar!"

Thomas' accusation echoed over the rooftop, seeming to come from nowhere and everywhere at once.

His hands tightened around the shaft of his scythe. Tremors from the beast's footfalls shook the building. It was close enough now to sense Conrad's presence. If he turned his attention back to the beast, Thomas would certainly take the opportunity to attack. Here was the proverbial rock and a hard place Conrad was always hearing about.

The beast roared below. Conrad had been detected.

He had to move. The High Wraith knew he couldn't take on both Thomas and the beast, so he took a quick step away from the ledge. Feeling the building shake beneath his feet and a deep rumble that filled his heart with dread, he knew his decision had just been made for him.

The building began to topple.

Taking three steps back, Conrad watched the horizon quickly becoming vertical. Conrad glanced across to the next building. It looked too far away. He set his jaw. He didn't have time to worry or analyze, he had to move. Charging ahead, he hit the ledge and jumped with all his strength. A massive cloud of dust swirled up from the crumbling building. Blinded, the High Wraith reached forward hoping to catch the ledge.

He saw it, but it was too late.

He had overshot the edge…just slightly. His knee caught the ledge and snapped his torso forward. Bringing his hands up, he hit hard and skidded forward in the snow.

Pain shot up through his hands and shoulders in protest. His instincts screamed in the back of his mind. Bringing his scythe up without looking, he blocked Thomas' attack. His gaze snapped to his target. Using the

301

blade of his scythe to bring Thomas' weapon down, Conrad kicked up and caught the younger Wraith in the jaw with the heel of his boot. As Thomas stumbled back, Conrad threw his legs into the air and used the momentum to flip to his feet. Dropping into a defensive position, he watched his student wipe a small trickle of blood away from his lip.

Thomas smiled and twirled his scythe playfully.

"Don't do this, Thomas," Conrad warned as he slowly circled. "You're making a grave mistake. I don't want to hurt you."

"You killed her, Conrad." Thomas' voice was low and angry. "I should've known you would. You were always jealous of me."

"Jealous?"

"It must have been hard trying to train a student who was more powerful than you in every way," Thomas arrogantly conceded. "So you took away the one thing I ever loved out of spite. I loved her!" he roared. "She was mine!"

"She isn't dead," Conrad protested. "You have to believe me, Thomas. I don't want to fight you."

An evil sneer grew across Thomas' face. "I don't think you have a choice."

Thomas attacked.

The two Wraiths collided. Their weapons became a blur as they attacked and parried each other's strikes. Each attack was stopped. Each move was perfectly countered. Conrad's head was level. He saw each move, countered, and tried to stop his student. Thomas, however, was fighting with pure anger and rage. He was pulling no punches. Every blow was a kill strike. He

302

meant to strike down his Master.

Thomas saw a hole in Conrad's defense. Striking ahead, he let the High Wraith parry his attack down and kicked his Master solidly in the chest. Conrad hit the roof and skidded into an air vent. Before he had time to react, Thomas was on him again. Slashing laterally, Thomas carved a gash out of the aluminum barely missing Conrad's head. Conrad swept Thomas' legs out from under him, toppling the younger Wraith. Somersaulting back onto his feet, Conrad brought his scythe around his body and over his head. Driving the blade down, he nicked Thomas' arm just as he rolled out of the way. As the blade stuck in the roof, Conrad vaulted forward and hit Thomas in the chest with both feet. The two Wraiths smashed into the air vent destroying it.

Conrad felt a strip of pain down his back. He knew the shredded aluminum had sliced into him. His eyes focused on his weapon, still stuck in the roof.

Thomas sat up next to the High Wraith. There was no trace of his weapon. He followed Conrad's gaze to his scythe.

Amidst the mass of aluminum and snow, the two Wraiths wrestled for control of their weapons. Thomas wrapped his arms around Conrad's chest and delivered several hard punches to the High Wraith's ribcage. Conrad grunted in pain. Balling his fist, he threw his elbow back and connected solidly with the bridge of Thomas' nose. As the young Wraith's head snapped back, Conrad flipped over and slapped his flattened palms against Thomas' ears. Thomas felt his eardrums pop under the pressure followed by a high-pitched whine. He fell back, disoriented for a moment.

Conrad surged forward, his hand reaching for his scythe. As his fingers touched the cool metal of the shaft, he felt it yanked away. He turned to see Thomas standing with his scythe. He nodded and slowly pulled himself to his feet.

"Thomas," Conrad said warily, "think about what you're doing." He watched the young Wraith carefully, all the while searching the debris of the air vent for Thomas' weapon. "If you do this, they will hunt you down. You will never find a moment of peace again." The High Wraith paused. "You will be destroyed."

Thomas spun Conrad's scythe easily in his hands. How many times had he held this weapon for training? Too many to count... It seemed appropriate that this would be the instrument of his Master's death. "You and the Wraith have taken everything away from me: My family, my life, and now Kat." Thomas' blue eyes hardened. A hint of gold appeared at the edge of his irises as his anger increased. "I will see every single one of the Wraiths dead by my hands."

The words shocked Conrad. He didn't understand where this raw hatred was welling up from. "I saved you, Thomas. I saved you from your family's fate. And the Wraith took you in and gave you a new life. You chose to become a Wraith!"

"You could have saved them." Thomas thought back to that night. "You could have saved my family!"

"No," Conrad said slowly. "I was too late to help them. I am so sorry, Thomas. I couldn't help your family." He lowered his gaze slightly. "And I have failed you."

"I will not accept your pity," Thomas hissed. "You

let my family die and now you've taken the only thing I had left. She didn't deserve to die." He felt his voice quiver slightly. "But you do."

Thomas charged.

He swung the scythe down. Just as the blade was about to connect with Conrad, he saw the High Wraith move unnaturally away from the attack. Looking curiously at his master, Thomas saw a thin, gray tendril wrapped around Conrad's midsection. The tendril lifted Conrad into the air and began to constrict as the head of the beast appeared over the ledge. As it climbed onto the roof, Thomas felt a wave of anger grip him.

"That one is mine," Thomas said as he marched toward the beast.

The beast looked at Thomas, then to Conrad. "He is Wraith as you are," he said, slightly confused. "Your petty squabble is not of my concern."

Conrad struggled against the tendril as it squeezed the breath out of him.

"You will both die," the beast concluded. He lifted his wrist toward Thomas.

Thomas' eyes shifted fully to gold as the anger in his heart blossomed into a nuclear furnace.

The beast launched a second tendril at Thomas. Thomas easily sidestepped the tendril and chopped it in twain with Conrad's scythe. The beast roared in pain as its tendril fell to the ground twisting and writhing like a snake with its head cut off.

Thomas marched ahead undaunted.

The beast glared at the Wraith. "What are you?"

Slicing across the beast's chest with the scythe, Thomas didn't bother to answer. The blade sparked as it sliced a groove into the beast's tough hide.

Both Thomas and the beast looked at the groove.

The beast laughed.

Thomas stepped back and reassessed his battle plan. Lowering his shoulder, he charged at the Krylbrea demon. He hit the monster in the thighs with all his strength sending the beast, himself, and Conrad sailing off the edge of the building. The three hit the ground hard. The pavement beneath the beast cracked under its intense weight. The hit knocked Conrad free.

The two Wraiths skittered to their feet as the beast slowly lifted itself from the ground. Standing on opposite sides of the demon, they eyed each other warily. Conrad saw Thomas' golden eyes and felt his heart sink into his chest. In that moment, Conrad knew he had lost Thomas. He returned his attention to the beast as it towered above them. Both Wraiths' weapons weren't close enough to get to before the beast attacked.

Thomas stared angrily at the demon. Nothing would stand in the way of his vengeance. Balling his fists, he summoned all his psychic strength lifting the immense monster from the ground. Bits of wreckage and debris began to float around the Wraith. The ground shook as he beckoned every ounce of his power.

The beast flailed his arms as he twisted into a horizontal position. Thomas strained under the beast's mass. Gritting his teeth, he started the monster in motion. The beast began to spin in place. Faster and faster, the monster gained momentum until he became nothing more than a black blur. With a grunt, Thomas released him.

The beast launched like a rocket. It punched through the side of a nearby building. Its momentum carried the beast through the building as it began to topple out the other side. Hitting the next structure, the beast tore through the outer wall. The building toppled like the one before it in a huge cloud of dust and debris.

As the wreckage settled, all became quiet under the falling flakes of snow.

The beast erupted from the wreckage and stumbled onto the street. Looking down, it found a steel girder piercing its chest. Wrapping its massive hands around the girder, the beast tried to pull it free. It stumbled and fell forward. It looked at the two Wraiths as its eyes glossed over and its final breath escaped its mouth.

Thomas fell to the ground utterly exhausted. Every bit of energy in his body was spent. He looked up and watched Conrad walking slowly toward him. He tried to lift himself off the ground but fell helplessly forward.

Scooping up his discarded scythe, the High Wraith moved slowly through the snow. He didn't activate his weapon. Conrad knelt down next to his former student. "Why did you do this, Thomas?"

Thomas' eyes burned with hatred. "You took everything from me!"

"I gave you everything I could," Conrad breathed. "I never lied to you. I couldn't save your family," he said painfully. "I am so sorry for that. But I didn't kill Kat! She's alive!"

"I hate you!" Thomas tried to push Conrad away but was too weak. He started to pull himself to his feet. Thomas' arms and legs trembled in pain as he pushed himself into a standing position. His arms hung limp at his side. He took an awkward step toward Conrad.

"Don't do it, Thomas," Conrad warned. "Don't make
307

me kill you." The High Wraith activated his scythe.

Thomas' face twisted in anger. Lifting his arm, he called his scythe to his hand. He pressed the activation button and lifted the weapon.

"You were my brother," Conrad said quietly. "I'm sorry."

Conrad's blade flashed once. Deactivating the weapon, he turned and started to walk away. Conrad disappeared into the darkness.

Thomas fell to his knees, his scythe skittering to the ground. He pressed his hands to his chest. Pulling them away, he saw the dark blood spilled on his gloves. He felt weak and unable to catch his breath. There was an odd emptiness in his chest. He slowly realized what it was. His heart wasn't beating. Falling onto his hands, the young Wraith watched his blood spill onto the snow. He finally collapsed, his golden eyes staring into nothingness. His thoughts became distant and hazy. He saw her face one more time, smiling softly as he held her in his arms.

Darkness took him then.

Chapter Twenty-Five

Thomas slowly opened his eyes. He tried to look around, but found only blackness in this place. Lifting his hand to his forehead, he became aware of someone standing over him. He tried to sit up but searing pain shot through his chest.

"Lord Scourge," a deep, dark voice commanded. "Don't move too quickly."

Thomas heard the name and a spark of recognition hit him. He was no longer Thomas Cross. That person had died by Conrad's blade. He was Scourge now. His body felt new and altered as well. He wasn't a Wraith anymore. He was something different. He was even more powerful than before.

Bracing his hands on the floor, Scourge slowly sat up. He ignored the pain in his chest. He looked around. The room was polished black with massive columns running down both sides. He sat at the bottom of a large staircase. At the top, he could clearly see a being seated in a decorative throne flanked by two darkly clad figures. Standing two steps up from him, he saw a form he recognized.

"Bane," Scourge said slowly.

Bane nodded in respect.

Scourge's mortal enemy stood no more than two feet from him, yet he had no inclination to attack. As he stood, he realized he had no reflection in the polished black floor. He knew what he was now…and he was pleased. He had been given a second chance for vengeance. He would not let this one slip away so easily.

Bane turned and headed up the stairs. Scourge followed instinctively. Stopping just shy of the top, Bane knelt down and bowed his head. Scourge did likewise, stopping a step behind Bane out of courtesy, although it would not always be so. It did amaze him, however, that Bane showed such reverence to this being. Then it hit him. Bane was scared.

"Master," Bane breathed, "this is my new apprentice, Scourge."

The Dark Lord sat quietly on his throne, studying Scourge. Only his burning yellow eyes were visible beneath the heavy hood. "Lord Scourge, you may rise." One of his skeletally thin hands beckoned to Scourge. "Please come closer."

The voice hit Thomas like a slap across the face. He knew instantly. It had been there with him since the beginning, whispering in his ear, telling him what to do. The voice was real... It had been the Dark Lord's voice that told him to destroy the vampires who killed his family, to slaughter the servants of the Troika, and to kill Saint while inside Creed's compound. He finally understood. This was his destiny. The Dark Lord had always been with him, taking care of him, watching over him. This was where he truly belonged.

Scourge stood and walked slowly up the stairs. He stood silently in front of the throne. "Yes, my Lord?"

The eyes continued to study Scourge. "What do you want?"

"Vengeance," Scourge answered quickly. "Against the Wraith."

"Why?"

"They took everything from me," Scourge answered. "My family, my life," he breathed, "and the woman I loved."

"Indeed," the Dark Lord replied with a hint of joy in his voice. He turned to Bane. "His motives are very similar to yours."

"They are, Master," Bane answered.

The Dark Lord turned back to Scourge. "How do I know you won't turn on me?"

Scourge smiled devilishly. "You don't."

"Wonderful," the Dark Lord said, while applauding. "You are going to be a powerful addition to my new order, Lord Scourge." The Dark Lord paused. "Lord Bane, I sense your presence is required elsewhere."

"Yes, Master," Bane stood and turned. "Lord Scourge, you will accompany me."

Scourge nodded with a sly smile. "Yes, my Lord."

The Dark Lord watched the two powerful vampire lords walk briskly out of his throne room and disappear into the volcano beyond. He motioned for one of his attendants to lean close.

"I think," the Lord said with no small amount of satisfaction, "Lord Bane's days are numbered."

***

Kat slowly opened her eyes. She tried to look around, but the brightness of the lights blinded to her. Lifting her hand to shield her eyes, she became aware of someone sitting at the foot of her bed. She tried to sit up but pain shot through her shoulder and back.

"Don't try to move," a kind female voice advised.

311

Kat slowly became aware she was in some kind of hospital facility. She could hear the constant beep of the heart monitor to her left. She saw several wires running out from her pale blue gown to machines that surrounded her. "Where am I?"

"You're safe," the feminine voice answered.

Kat watched the figure stand and move to her bedside. "Who are you?"

"Emily, but most people call me Saint." She placed her hand tenderly on Kat's. "How are you feeling?"

"Terrible," Kat replied honestly. She looked at the dark-haired woman standing next to her. She instantly knew what the woman was, yet Kat felt no fear. "Why am I alive?"

"You're a very special woman, Katherine," Saint answered.

"What do you mean?"

Saint slowly rested her hand on Kat's stomach. "We don't know how it's possible," she took a slow breath, "but you're pregnant."

Kat's face flushed. "I'm pregnant?"

Saint nodded.

Only one question came to her mind. "Is it Thomas'?"

"There's no way to be sure without more tests," Saint replied, "but that would seem to be the only reasonable conclusion."

Kat's face was a mixture of fear and joy. She quickly looked around the room. "Where is Thomas?"

Saint frowned, but quickly hid it. "He..." She didn't know if she should tell Katherine the truth. She made a quick decision. "He fell in battle. He and Master Verge

312

were trying to defeat a Krylbrea demon, and we lost him. He died a hero."

Kat's eyes filled with tears.

"I'm so sorry," Saint breathed. She took Kat's hand to try and comfort the woman.

Tears streaked down Kat's face. She covered her mouth to try and fight back the pain.

"I promise," Saint looked Kat in the eye, "that I won't let anything happen to you or your baby. I will protect you." She looked at Kat's sorrowful blue eyes and did her best to remain strong. "This baby is a miracle," she said softly. "And it will always be a part of Thomas. He isn't truly gone as long as we remember that."

Kat nodded. She tried her best to smile as the tears continued to roll down her cheeks. "Can I have a minute alone?"

Saint smiled and nodded. "I'll be right outside if you need me, okay?"

"Thank you," Kat breathed.

Saint slowly let Kat's hand slip from hers. Taking a step back, she turned and headed for the exit. Saint grabbed the handle and slowly pulled it open. Once outside the room, Saint closed the door behind her. Pausing for a moment, she placed her hand on the thick wooden door. She could hear Kat sobbing inside. Her heart sank. Moving to a row of plastic chairs across from the door, she dropped down into the first one.

"How did she take it?"

Saint turned and looked at Conrad with a half-hearted smile. "Not too well."

"I don't think this is a good idea," Conrad protested quietly. "The baby of a vampire and a Wraith—"

"Is a miracle," Saint finished. "We can't terminate this pregnancy."

Conrad shook his head. "The Supreme Chancellor disagrees with you."

"I don't care," Saint answered quickly. "I will not let any harm come to Kat or her baby."

Conrad placed his hand on Saint's shoulder. "I won't be able to help you."

"I know."

Conrad took a breath and stood up. "If word of this baby gets out, both sides will be looking for you. You understand that, right?"

Saint folded her hands and leaned her elbows on her knees. "I know that, too."

Conrad extended his hand to Saint. As she took it, he pulled her up into a tight embrace. "I'll hold the Chancellor and council off for as long as I can. God's speed, Saint."

Saint returned the hug. "Thank you, Conrad."

Letting go, Saint took a step away from the High Wraith. She watched Conrad turn without another look and walk away. He disappeared behind a pair of double doors at the end of the hallway.

Saint walked quickly to Kat's room and pushed open the door. Stepping inside, she opened the small closet door and grabbed a black duffle bag she had placed there earlier. Unzipping it, she grabbed the clothes inside and placed them on Kat's lap. She then started undoing the tubes that held Kat in place.

Kat looked at Saint curiously. "What are you doing?"

Saint worked carefully to undo the tape that held her IV needle in place. "We're leaving. As soon as I get these cords off you, I need you to get dressed. I know it's going to hurt," she added apologetically, "but we don't have a choice."

"I don't understand," Kat said. Her cheeks and nose were still red from crying.

"Not everyone thinks this baby is a blessing," Saint answered honestly. "There are going to be people who try and hurt you to stop the birth." Saint freed the needle from the last bit of tape and pulled it free. Grabbing a cotton ball from the bedside table, Saint used one of the discarded pieces of tape to hold it in place. "I promise I won't let that happen, but we need to get you out of here." She looked at Kat. "And probably out of the country."

Kat nodded. She gritted her teeth and sat up in bed. The pain in her shoulder was excruciating, but she had to protect her baby. Pulling off the hospital gown, she grabbed the shirt Saint provided and slipped it on. As she reached for the pair of pants, she paused and looked at Saint. "Why are you doing this for me?"

Saint smiled. "I owe it to Thomas."

The darkness is patient.

The darkness is all consuming.

Yet, it is its own weakness. One lone, flickering candle can hold it back.

And it can ignite stars.